Lin Carter's

Simrana Cycle

Celaeno Press
2018

Lin Carter's

Simrana Cycle

with contributions by:

Glynn Owen Barrass
Adrian Cole
Lord Dunsany
Charles Garofalo
Henry Kuttner
Gary Myers
Robert M. Price
Darrell Schweitzer

Contents

Introduction

Beautiful is Simrana in the murmurous twilight when great throbbing stars hang flashing in deep skies of mystic purple.

And splendid when dawn breaks golden above the spires of old, barbaric cities wherein dwell haughty kings and wise magicians and stern warriors and dreaming poets and fat priests and cunning thieves and lovely princesses.

A wide world is Simrana, for all that it exists only in my dreams. Many gods it hath: great resplendent gods with noble brows and starry wings; and little humble gods of hearth and field.

Great dragons, coiled and couched on heaped and mounded treasure: and there are dwarves and gnomes deep in the caverned heart of hills; and snowy unicorns tread the dewy fields of morn.

Deep woods hath Simrana, green and shadowy and filled with old silences; and mighty mountains horned with snow; and deserts filled with whirlwinds and with basilisks; and a broad sea well furnished of islands.

Many are the tales they tell in Simrana: of old, proud kings and doomed cities; of jealous gods and crafty sorcerers; very splendid tales they tell.

Here are a few of them. . . .

Happy Magic!

Lin Carter

The Gods of Niom Parma

Lin Carter

The gods of Niom Parma met on a mountaintop near the sea. Tremendous, fierce-eyed, robed in glory, they were come to decide the fate of the alabaster city. And when all were assembled upon the windswept peak under the burning stars, one rose from amongst them, even that Hathrib whom men worship with purple wine poured in ewers of silver, and he spake thus: "Brothers, we are met to unleash our wrath upon Niom Parma, which we builded beside the sea when all Simrana was young. Let us whelm and trample down the alabaster city, for its folk have turned from us and worship newer gods."

Then the great Lord Shu lifted his eleven eyes and three arms in solemn agreement, even that Shu to whom men sing little songs of three notes only. And he spake, saying: "Brother, your words are full of wisdom. Lo! The men of Niom Parma have forgotten us who raised them to greatness over all the coasts of the Nyranian Sea, and behold our temples are neglected and dust gathers upon our altars. Let us, therefore, arise and smite Niom Parma with our wrath that not one stone shall be left upon another."

A mutter of agreement went up among the gods. Their eyes kindled with sparks of wrath, and in their anger they trampled upon the mountaintop until it trembled beneath their tread. And in the cool ways of the alabaster city far below, men cast uneasy eyes aloft and said that storms were brewing in the hills. But it was only the gods in their wrath.

But bright Thaladir, who is the Lord of the Sixteen Arts and Patron of the Nine Sciences, and to whom the priests of men burn the red cinnabar and the white spikenard upon altars of lemon-yellow jade, arose next and spoke against the doom of Niom Parma. "Have patience with our lazy and forgetful children," he said softly. "Observe the heights to which their artisans aspire; consider the nobility of their sculpture, their glowing tapestries, and the exquisite idylls their poets compose. Think, ere you destroy a city famous forever in song and make your memories accursed to all men who love the arts of Niom Parma."

Thunder growled among deep-bellied clouds, and Shadrazur the Lord of Warriors appeared. His one central eye blazed like the crater of the fiery volcano, lava-lit; his black beard bristled with rage; and he clenched in one mighty fist a great ax whose bladed edge glimmered with the small restless blue flames of the thunderbolt.

"Let us hear no more counsels of weakness," he growled, and his voice was like the roar of the bearded lion in its wrath. "For dabbling paints on cloth and stringing pretty words together are toys for childish fools. I say let us grind Niom Parma into the dust, for the people thereof have turned from the red path of war and I love them not."

Thereafter spake each of the gods in his turn, and Phuld and Narabus and Thion the Fair were for sparing the alabaster city, whereas Ladrizel and Gongogar and dark-browed Bal-Sheoth swore that the city should be ground into dust beneath their heel. Thus were they divided, and there was no agreement among the gods of Niom Parma.

At length there stirred a bent form, gray as dust and dark as shadows: It was even Dzelim, the oldest and the wisest of all the gods; aye, Dzelim, who was older than the very moon of Simrana. And the gods fell silent as he arose, for respect of his numberless eons. In a voice slow and rusty he spoke, but his voice echoed with the sound of great winds moving through the mountains.

"It is true the iniquities of Niom Parma are many and great, and likewise it is true that her works are proud and beautiful," he said, "but as we are divided amongst ourselves as to spare the alabaster city or to wither it before the blast of our rage, let us come to our decision by yet another path, else we may bicker on this peak until the very stars of heaven gutter and go out like exhausted candles."

"What, then, do you advise, O Elder Brother?" the gods asked.

"Choose one from amongst your number whose heart is neither melted with admiration for the artistries of Niom Parma nor hardened with rage at the iniquities thereof. Select one both fair and impartial to go down amongst the folk of the city and to decide their fate from the evidence of his own eyes, and swear ye all to bide his returning thence and to abide by his deciding."

And so it came to pass that the gods chose little Uzolba, the Patron of the Fisherfolk. He was a meek and smiling god, kindly and simple, and he cared for nothing more strenuous than drifting lazily on a small fat cloud sniffing the odors of frying fish, which the Priests of the Sea burnt on his small altars in little temples beside the wharves.

And with this choosing, Dzelim was well pleased. When some of the more fierce-hearted of the gods grumbled at the choice of small Uzolba, saying he was a fat and sleepy fool, old Dzelim gently reminded them that while Uzolba had no fondness for the red murk of war, he had likewise little love for the arts of men. So in the end were they decided.

And thus it came to pass that Uzolba took on mortal form for the first time in all the long eternities of his divinity. And he dwindled from his great and shining self down to a small, fat, sleepy little man with bald head and shining face and kindly eyes. He stood there upon the harsh cold stone peak and shivered to the wintry blasts that blew above the world and under the stars. It felt strange to be mortal after bright eons of godhood. Sharp pebbles cut through the thin sandals wherewith his soft feet were now shod, and the cold wind of the summit took small ribald liberties with the skirts of his tunic.

Above him the colossal forms of his mighty brethren towered tremendously. They seemed now to his mortal eyes to be vast and glorious shapes of awe, like sunset clouds, majestic, golden, full of splendor. Once he too had stood thus, no different from them. Now he cowered in the blaze of their terrific glory.

Then the titanic shape that was Dzelim bent down in all his magnificence and touched Uzolba with a dazzling finger. And as Uzolba blinked against the light, Dzelim spake in a voice like distant thunder moving across the heavens: "Go your way, little brother, and make your own decision. We shall bide here, and we promise not to visit our wrath upon the alabaster city until your return thence. Look well, choose wisely. We shall await your coming and this we swear."

"*This we swear,*" the gods echoed.

So Uzolba turned from that windy place where cloudy forms of brilliance towered from the naked rock against the burning stars, and he scurried down the slope. His body was old and fat and rather short of breath, and the cold rocks bruised his tender feet, and he was quite winded and weary by the time he reached the foot of the mountain. And there he paused on the shore of the Nyranian Sea to catch his breath.

He stood there and gazed about him with growing wonder. Never before had he looked upon the sea through mortal eyes, and it was very beautiful. The beach was a curve of soft white sand. Here and there across the sand scuttled small red crabs, hurrying to their little caverns. Tufts and clumps of stiff sea grass rose from the dunes of fine sand, and the tangy salt breeze sang through them like a sighing dirge. The emerald waves rolled in slow and stately, gliding with a whisper over wet, smooth sand to foam in a lacy pattern of creamy bubbles about bright, wet shells. Then, slowly, as if reluctant to leave behind the small treasures they had brought up from the bottom of the deeps, they slid back one by one into the bosom of the sea again.

The water was cold and palest blue-green and deliciously wet as it curled hissing about his toes, beaded with a froth of foam.

Above his head the sky was dim and vast. The purple wings of night withdrew slowly to the edges of the world before the golden birth of day. Tremendous masses of high-piled clouds towered in the east, their upper works and buttresses touched to bright flame and incandescent rose by the first shafts of dawn. One by one, great clouds drifted past over his head, cities and galleons and castles and fantastic dragons of dawn-colored vapor borne on mysterious journeys by the young winds of morning through the upper regions of the sky.

Here and there a white gull swooped and hovered or circled with sharp raucous cries like rusty hinges creaking.

Salt spray stung his lips and struck ruddy color into his cheeks. It was altogether marvelous....

Heretofore he had looked upon the sea through the eyes of a god, and all had seemed quite small and insignificant – for then the supernal glory of his own being had outshone the dawn and his towering height had dwarfed even the very clouds. But now, in the form of a man, and through the dim, small perspective of mortal senses, the wonder of the shore at dawn was breathtaking and humbling to him; he felt small before the glory of the world.

"So *this* is what it's like to be a mortal!" he whispered to himself with delight, as he slowly made his splashy way along the wet beach, stopping to stoop over a glistening shell, to brush wet sand away and admire the clear rich coloring.

Ere long he came upon a fisherman drawing his boat ashore, heavy with his morning catch. Uzolba paused half fearfully to watch the strange figure at his task. He found himself timid. Never had he seen a mortal so close. Yet the man did not seem so terrible and wicked – not at all as sinful and depraved as Hathrib and great Lord Shu had declared men to be.

The fisherman was old and lean and leathery. A stringy gray beard hung to his bare brown chest, and a plain gold ring twinkled in one ear. His patched and baggy pantaloons were stiff with salt and the wind tugged at a huge and ragged turban wound around his brows. He hummed a tune as he dragged his boat up the shore, and Uzolba saw that his sunburnt face was kind and wise and humorous. When he glanced up at Uzolba's hesitant approach, his keen blue eyes twinkled, and when he smiled, it was a good smile.

"Peace and plenty, friend!" the old fisherman hailed him. "'Twill be a pleasant day, I wager – what say you?"

The god made some mumbling reply: Never thereafter could he recall what he said. He stood shyly watching as the lean old man hauled his dripping netful of fish up the sandy shore.

"Aye, a good day, and a warm one, too," the fisherman went on. Then, with a cheerful wink, he added, "Thanks be to good Lord Uzolba, my nets were full at dawn!"

Uzolba flushed crimson and could think of no reply. He was well accustomed to droning ritual solemnities of the priests, but before a simple word of honest thanks he was struck dumb. But he took courage from the obvious harmlessness of the good-natured old fisherman and edged closer. He even essayed a question in a voice that quavered just a little.

"What – ah – what do you think of Niom Parma, fisherman?"

"The city?" The fisherman stopped as if nonplussed. Then: "Well, friend, 'tis a goodly place for them as likes being cooped up behind walls. A bit crowded for such as me. I like to see the land and sky and sea round me. But still, a fair, proud town; aye, fine as anything this side of Yanathloë on the river Thool, so they say. The city folk are good enough. Chorb Zalim, now, the fish merchant, he gives me a fair price for my catch. And there's a snug warm inn by the harborfront where they don't ask your last coin for a drop of ale. The great bazaar is a wondrous fine place, and the harbor is filled with strange ships and foreign sailors with perfumed beards and little gems woven in their hair. 'Tis a fine place to visit when the great ships are in from the isles, and the sailors – why, it's worth your life to hear the tales they tell of the things they've seen, the queer little yellow men, the stone gods, the cities full of blue pagodas, the jungle rivers full of pearls!" He chuckled, shaking his head at his memories.

"But come," he said, "I'm forgetful of my manners. I am Chandar the fisherman. Yourself?"

Uzolba faltered. Then he gave his name as Zabulo, saying the first thing that came into his head, which happened to be his own name, but slightly twisted about.

"Be you a fisherman?"

"No. . . but I have long been associated with the trade," he faltered.

"Well, come along then, friend Zabulo, help me drag my catch up to yonder cottage where I dwell, and you can share the morning meal with me. 'Tis no feast, but I've a flagon of old wine put aside against the winter damps. . . eh?"

So the god and the fisherman went up the dunes to the small snug cottage nestled under the leafy branches of a great zoonabar tree, and all that day they talked and sang songs, and Uzolba was shown the nets spread out to dry in the sun and the small back garden and the bright flowers that grew thick about the door. Chandar demonstrated the art and science of hooks and oars and lines and how to read the currents and the winds and tell tomorrow's weather from tonight's moon. Evening darkened over Simrana: The red sun sank behind the lofty alabaster towers of Niom Parma, and a cold wind came lashing up from the bosom of the dark sea.

But all was warm and cozy within the low-roofed thatched cottage where a fire crackled lustily on the stone hearth, filling the room with cheerful light. They ate the evening meal together, fish and fruit and coarse black bread with the last of the red wine. Before that day, Uzolba had never tasted mortal food. The warm rich glow this simple meal sent coursing through him was curious and comfortable. The drowsy feeling that came from a full middle was vastly more satisfying than was dining on the vaporous viands that had for ages sated his divine appetites.

All that evening, while a young gale shouted about the eaves, they stretched out before the roaring fire and the fisherman spun tales he had caught from the bearded lips of the sailors. In his turn, the god haltingly told some of the wonders of the sea, its marvels and its mysteries.

In bed that night on the brink of sleep, Uzolba determined that on the morrow he must rise early and start out for the city and the fulfillment of the task set upon him by the gods. But somehow, when day came, when they rose and Chandar went forth to fish, there were too many things to be done. He had tasted of the hospitality of Chandar the fisherman, and now he should help with the work by way of recompense. For there were fish to clean, nets to repair, and knives to sharpen. And he could not just walk away and leave the work undone. So he lingered for a time to hoe the garden, water the flowers, pluck ripe fruit from the spreading branches of the zoonabar tree, and gather up driftwood from the shore to feed their fire.

In this fashion, one day drifted into the next, as one wave blends with the waters of another. Uzolba found his new life rich and busy, filled with small homely tasks and brightened with small homely joys. And there were new tastes and sounds and sights to every hand. Everywhere he turned, he looked upon things new and fresh and wonderful. He came to know the sea as he had never known her – he who had been one of the gods of the sea. He saw her in her hundred moods, her thousand faces, her myriad of colors. And then there was the wonder of flowering spring, the marvel of rich autumn sunsets, the miracle of summer rain. The great, slow rhythm of the cycle of the seasons turned like a mighty wheel, and with each turning came a new marvel to be wondered at. The golden moon. Her pearly light upon silken dark waters. The magnificence of stars.

Weeks passed like swift strokes of a gull's wing. Memory of his life among the gods faded, dimmed, and died. There were so many things to see and do and taste and know. Old memories and old purposes were crowded out of mind.

The years passed, and Uzolba, or Zabulo, became a fisherman with Chandar. The two were as brothers, sharing the same boat and roof and fire through cold nights and windy days. Together they enjoyed the pleasures and endured the hardships of this life... and it came to pass that Chandar and Zabulo the fishermen lived together all the days of their lives.

High above the alabaster spires of Niom Parma, the gods waited upon that mountaintop under the burning stars. Yea, long and long they waited, for they could not leave that place and were bound by their vow not to smite the alabaster city until the Lord Uzolba came back to them once more with his decision. For thus went their oath; and they say in Simrana that the oath of the gods cannot be broken.

All this was very long ago, and no man knoweth the ending of the story. Yet Niom Parma riseth yet beside the Nyranian Sea... I know, for I walked her alabaster ways but yestereve within a dream. And as for the lord Uzolba, to whom the Priests of the Sea burn fish on small altars in little temples beside the wharves, why, I cannot but suppose that never did he come again to his brethren on the lonely peak, but lived all his days in the snug small cottage nestled beneath the spreading zoonabar tree.

And as for the gods of Niom Parma, for all I know or care, they may still be waiting upon that windy mountaintop near the sea, tremendous, fierce-eyed, robed in glory.

The Whelming of Oom

Lin Carter

They say that once in Simrana the Dreamworld there dwelt in the Lands About Zuth an idolatrous folk who turned from the Gods, saying: "Let us fashion a God all our own, that we alone of all nations may worship him."

Now there rose near Zuth a mighty mountain all of pure and perdurable emerald, stronger than granite, more lovely than marble. And looking upon it the folk said: "Let us hew our God from this green stone, that he may tower above the works of men lesser than we."

So they set about their labor, to cut and carve the mountain into the likeness of the God they had invented, whom they had named OOM, for that there was no other God with that name known amongst the lands of men. And they did toil for generations in the fashioning of Oom, and little by little he emerged from the glistening emerald as they hacked and hewed, a finger here, there an eyebrow, a nostril, a curve of flank or cheek.

When that their toil was done, this was the likeness of Oom. The peak of the mountain was carven into his head whereon were four faces. The face that looked to the north was grim and foreboding of mien. The face toward the south was benign and smiling. The eastern face howled with a fury of rage. The face turned to the west was closed in sleep.

Eight arms had Oom, folded each two together against his chest.

He sat with his legs thus and so, in the manner of tailors, and in his lap they builded a city magnificent with gems and ivories and glittering marbles; a sacred city that was named On The Knees of Oom. Then they were finished and could rest.

Now the Eight Hundred Gods Who Watch Over Simrana care but little for the doings of men, despite what the priests will say. But that the folk who dwelt about Zuth turned from them to a God of their own devisal was an affront that they could not ignore. And they moved from their accustomed tranquility and were urged to wrath against this new God, Oom, and all they that worshipped him.

And the Highest God said to the least and littlest amongst them: "Go up against Oom and throw him down, yea, and all those that call upon his name. For he is as a stench in Our nostrils and an abomination in Our sight; therefore whelm ye him and cast him down utterly in the dust."

And the Lesser Gods came unto those lands wherein Oom sat smiling upon the south, howling against the east, sternly glowering to the north, and dreaming at the west. And they unleashed against him the forces over which they had the mastering of, and these were the lesser powers of Nature.

SHAMMERING the Sunlight poured upon Oom the fierce blaze of noon, and THUTHOOL the Snow sheathed him in numb whiteness.

UMBALDROOM the Thunder smote him, and SHISH the Rain lashed his emerald flanks.

CHEEL, the God of Morning Dew, pearled him with chilling wetness. KAZANG the Lightning flickered about his crest. HA-SHOOVATH the Wind howled about his folded arms and tore at them with impalpable fingers.

Yet Oom sat unshaken and unchanged.

So it came to pass that the Seven Little Gods withdrew in defeat. But they say in Simrana that the Gods yield not to Necessity, and behold, they who were the Lesser raised a loud cry, beseeching the aid of Gods greater than they.

And the Greater Gods came unto Oom and set their forces up against him as the waves of Ocean go up against the bastions of the great cliffs that front the main.

GLAUN CHELID the Lord of Wintry Cold clasped his bitter cloak of glittering ice about Oom and froze him with that iron grip whereof the rocks are made to cry out and great trees are broke asunder.

RŪZ THANNA the Lord of Summery Heat baked him in blasts of withering flame such as sear the burnt and cindery deserts of the ultimate south in scorching light of molten and fiery suns.

THOOZ LASHLAR the Lord of Mighty Rains hurled against Oom his raging torrents from full-bellied clouds, in roaring floods such as drown kingdoms and wash cities to rubble and feed rivers into gorged and swollen monsters that ravish the earth.

VOSHT THONDAZOOR the Lord of the Tempest set upon Oom his savage servants, the raging Thunderstorm, the ferocious Whirlwind, the screaming Hurricane, and all the legions of the nine and ninety Winds.

But naught availeth against Oom.

In their desperation, the Greater Gods roused even their dread and terrible brother, yea, even SKAGANAK BELBADOOM the Earthquake, from his surly and ominous chambers in the deeps of the clefts of the earth. And he came and shook Oom with all his thunders such as make the very hills to tremble, but he whelmed him not.

Then came forward one whose shadowy face was hidden and whose voice was low and monotonous, who spake softly, saying: "I will whelm Oom, even I, TATOKTA the Lord of Passing Moments."

And they laughed and mocked him, for Time is the least and smallest servant of the Gods.

But he set upon Oom the measureless passing moments, whereof are builded the millions of years. And each small moment, as it went past, bore away from Oom one single grain of dust.

And, lo! Oom crumbled. Before the assault of Time his vast four-featured visage wore smooth until he frowned no longer, neither did he smile, nor howl, nor dream any more.

His limbs fell from him as dust falls, grain by impalpable grain. His massive and perdurable torso eroded and even his knees whereon was builded The City Sacred To Oom, they were no more, and the city itself was but scattering dust. And the people thereof fled by night, saying: "Oom is fallen, Oom is overthrown, let us call no longer upon Oom, for behold the Gods are stronger than he."

And Oom was not. In his place stretched away a barren and desolate desert. And the sands of this desert were green as the powdery dust of emeralds.

And the Eight Hundred Gods rejoiced and trooped in all their glory and gorgeousness past their grey servant Time to their tall thrones amidst the stars. And the eyes of Totokta moved a little sidewise as if measuring their thrones, the splendor and the might thereof, and he said softly to himself: "These, too, I shall whelm with my aeons. But not yet. Not yet..."

So they tell the tale in Simrana.

Zingazar

Lin Carter

They say in Simrana that long had the old sword slept in the great hall, and as it slept it dreamt of War.

Of day and night it knew naught, the old grey sword, nor of months and years. But dimly it knew it had been long and long ago since last the hands of a hero had clasped it by the worn hilt; and long and very long since the arm of a warrior had lifted it gleaming in battle and swung it whistling down to bite through bone and brain and to drink deep of the hot salt blood that was as wine to it.

Sometimes it wondered that the men of Babdalorna rode no more to war; and sometimes it stirred restlessly against its bed of velvet under the glass casing, thinking it heard from afar off the crash of bugles and the ringing of steel and the hoarse shouts of embattled men. But mostly it slept, and dreamt of War, of Red War.

It was not forgotten, the old grey sword, the terrible bright sword, for it was very famous in song: the compilers of sagas knew of its name and the composers of epics remembered it and the little children that played in the streets of the city, they knew it well. In summer when the afternoons were long and hot and their mothers were off to market, they would take long lathes of wood and fix them together with short pieces for hilts, and the leader of the game would say, "Here, you are Al-Gond the Terrible, and this is your sword, Yartha. And I am tall Konary, and here in my hand is Zingazar; now let us battle for the city."

That was its name: Zingazar. And it was a famous name. The savage Athreeb of the forest remembered it; so did the Wild Men of the mountains; it haunted the troubled dreams of kings in Zuth, and in the Lands About Zuth. And among the shadowy tents of the nomads that roamed the cinnabar sands of the deserts, mothers still frightened unruly children with its name; "Be good, or Konary will come, tall Konary, with Zingazar naked in his hand."

The people of the city still spoke of it, the old sword, and on feast days and on the holy days of the God they came to the great stone hall where the trophies of the heroes lay enshrined, and they stood before the glass case and looked upon it with awe.

"That is the great sword Zingazar," the fathers said to their sons. "Young Anarbion bore it against the savage Athreeb of the forest once, and bold Ionax, and Diomardanon, and Belzimer the Bold. And Konary, of course, tall Konary."

And the children would stare at the long bright length of it and at the terrible razor-keen curve of that length, and of the mighty hilt bound about with old dry leather still salty from the battle-sweat of the heroes who had held it long ago, and they would dream wonderful dreams of glittering battle and noble kings and ferocious dark enemies who fled howling from the bright shimmer of Zingazar when it was uplifted against them in war.

The hilt of the old grey sword bore a great gem set deep therein, a gem dim and watery and green, like the eye of an aged man, dimmed and filmed with years. And down the bare, bright, terrible length of the blade ran mighty Runes of Power, magical glyphs of power that held terrific force. These symbols embued the steel sword with something akin to life, a vital force that still burned deep within the substance of the steel, a force that now, alas, burned faint and low.

Thus the old sword slept and dreamed of young Anarbion, and bold Ionax, and Diomardanon, and Belzimer. And of tall Konary...

Beyond the great hall where the trophies of the dead heroes slept lay the towering city of Babdalorna. Very fair was Babdalorna in the centuries of her youth, and strong among cities. But age had come upon her and the glories of war had faded from her tarnished banners and now she slept and dreamed, the ancient city, even as slept and dreamed the long sword of Konary that had slain so terribly for her in her youth.

Once the great city Babdalorna had ruled all the plain between the green sea to the south to the northernmost marches of Zuth; but that was long and very long ago. The old forest had come creeping back, the forest that was her ancient enemy, and now the deep dark woods grew close about the city, almost at her gates. But further than this the wood dared not come, though it too dreamed… dreamed of spreading its oaken arms and of toppling the old walls that stood about Babdalorna… dreamed of scattering acorns down her broad avenues, that they might grow and split the paving stones asunder, and net the foundations of the tall towers with a hundred hairy roots and lurch against the strength of stone till down they came in a thunder of ruin, and all the city should be overwhelmed and trampled down and buried beneath the green woods.

And the fierce Athreeb that dwelt within the wood, they too hungered to see Babdalorna fall, and to see Doom come down on the stone city they had hated long, they and their sires and their sires' sires before them for a thousand years of time.

Sometimes they lurked along the margin of the wood, huddled in the dense shadows, and watched sunset bathe the tall stone towers with red light. And one would say: "Behold how red the sunset burns, and see how red are the towers of Babdalorna," and another would grin, a fierce flash of white fangs in the dark, and he would whisper in reply: "Redder than this shall the streets of Babdalorna run on the day when the forest conquereth and reclaimeth its own!"

But still the forest held back from the gates and still the great marble walls stood unbroken and still the towers lifted their castle-crested heights against the stars: for the woods feared the memory of the great heroes of Babdalorna and the bright terrible memory of the shining steel they bore against their foes. And although a thousand years had passed since greatness had gone from the tall stone city, and a thousand years were past since the bold warriors of Babdalorna rode forth the last time to make Red War, still the ancient memory and the ancient fear remained in the dark hot heart of the Athreeb and the darker heart of the woods wherein they dwelled and whose shadowy and murmurous presence they worshipped as their god.

The years rolled by and greatness came not again to the folk who dwelt within the walls of Babdalorna, neither did they ride forth under bright banners to roll back the old forest once more or to carry shining steel against their foe.

And bit by bit, over the years, fear departed from the dwellers in the forest. "Behold," they would whisper, huddled within the shadow of leaves, "our mighty forest stands before the very gates of accursed Babdalorna, yet they come not forth to hew and hack the stolid oaks; nay, the old heroes come not forth."

And another would say: "Behold, the leaves of the forest drift against the very gates and brush the very walls of doomed Babdalorna, yet the brazen trumpets do not call forth the mailed legions to war against the woods; neither do we see the terrible flash of Zingazar as it is lifted in war; let us then go forth against the hated city and pull down its gates and break the marble walls asunder, and let the forest in."

But the older and wiser among them would say: "Not yet, not yet," and the Athreeb would slink back into the deeps of the whispering woods, remembering ancient fears.

But it came to pass in the fullness of time that the cautions of the Athreeb ebbed and faded, and the hatred in their hearts for the tall stone city waxed hotter and hotter, and the ancient memories and the ancient fears grew feeble, until at last the savage host gathered and murmured for War.

And the old forest woke and stretched its oaken arms and broke the walls asunder. One long jagged crack ran through the ancient marble of the walls from their height to their base, and it was black as death but no wider than a finger's breadth. And the Athreeb held their breath to see if the great horns would call and the mailed heroes would come thundering forth with the terror of naked steel in their hands. But they came not forth.

And again the forest stretched its arms, and a thousand hairy roots clutched at the base of the walls, and the crack widened to a hand's breadth: and still the bright banners flew not on the wind nor the thunder of hooves came, nor the crash of bugles, nor the ring of steel. Heroes dwelt no more within Babdalorna, and bright Zingazar slumbered still among the trophies of forgotten time.

And yet a third time the forest set its strength against the towering walls, and a third time the crack widened, and now it was as wide as is the body of a man. And from the rustling shadows at the margin of the old forest, the Athreeb watched and waited and naught occurred. Then said they, one to the other, "By such a breach we couldst steal by night within the city, and slay and burn and break down thrones!"

And the older and the wiser amongst them no longer said, "Not yet." Now they said: "Soon, soon."

These days the dreams of Zingazar were troubled dreams, and dark shapes with mocking faces moved through them, and it seemed to the old steel sword that it felt the foundations whereon great Babdalorna was built tremble – thrice. So troubled became these dreams, that Zingazar awoke a little from its ancient slumber and the dim green gem set deep within its hilt by the hand of an ancient wizard long since dust – brightened. Restless gleams of light came and went within the enchanted jewel that shone in the hilt of Zingazar like an eye. They went flickering across the arms of the ancient heroes that were set about the hall of stone.

And the shield of Ionax woke and drummed faintly.

The battered helm of young Anarbion rang like the watchman's bell, but thin and far.

The long bronze spear of Diomardanon thrummed against the wall. So also did the arrows of Belzimer the Bold: they rattled in their dusty leathern case, and the great bow of Belzimer thumped against the wall.

A thin singing arose from the old sword, the sword of tall Konary, the sword that each of the bright heroes of Babdalorna had carried in the wars of his youth. Too faint was this singing for mortal ears to hear. It was like the shrill high call of the bat that sings in the stillness of midnight. But the shield, the helm, the spear, the arrows and the bow, they heard the song of Zingazar.

It sang, "Brothers, I hear the step of the foe in the dark of night without the walls, the old beloved walls, of our Babdalorna.

"Enemies gather in the dark of night, O my brothers, yet the people of Babdalorna sleep.

"There is laughter in the wood, O brothers. There is mockery amid the boughs. The leaves whisper of dark things, brothers, and the roots, the dark wet hairy roots, they thirst for blood.

"But greatness and glory are fled from Babdalorna, O my brothers! The heroes, the young heroes, all are gone, all are dead; even the God of Babdalorna slumbers in the dim shrine, O my brothers. And all the people thereof slumber.

"O my brothers, I fear – I, even I, Zingazar the Terrible. Yea, I fear that our ancient enemies are upon us in the night, and there are none to do battle against them, save for us."

And the shield of Ionax drummed against the wall, and in the drumming were words, but too faint for men to hear; only the unsleeping vigor of Zingazar could hear as the shield of Ionax said: "Helpless is the sword, however sharp, to slay of itself; a hand must wield us in war, O my brother."

And the great spear of Diomardanon spake, saying, "I am terrible in war, and sharp and swift to slay, but a hand must cast me forth ere I can kill."

Strange was that converse in the shadow-thronged hall where the trophies of dead heroes lay; but there were none to hear.

The guard that was set to keep clean and polished the trophies of the stone hall was an old man named Ashtok.

He loved the old arms and he kept them well. But on this night he slept, and that deeply, dreaming of Anarbion.

But he had as a son a boy named Amar, and he was twelve years old, and he too slept.

But the dreams of youth are shallow dreams, and the sleep of youth is light and easily broken.

Thus Amar woke in the night: he had heard a sound but he knew not what sound it was. Could any of the folk of all Babdalorna have become so depraved as to thieve the ancient trophies of the heroes? He rose from his bed and stood listening.

The sound he had heard was the bow, the great bow, the bow of Belzimer the Bold, breaking. Naught else could the old bow do to arouse the sleepers, so it broke, which is within the power of a bow.

"Farewell, O brother!" the weapons sang faintly in the darkness of the hall. But the bow of Belzimer made no reply, for the life of a bow lieth within the strength of its wood, and when it be shivered to fragments, that life is gone. Thus had the bow of Belzimer given up its life to arouse the ancient city it had loved and served so long.

"Brothers, I hear no footstep in the hall. I fear me that none cometh, and that the sacrifice of our brother was in vain," sang Zingazar sadly. "Now will I rend myself, for surely that will rouse a slumberer."

"Nay," boomed the white-crested helm of young Anarbion, "for thou alone may save the city yet, therefore will I rend myself, O Zingazar my brother. Farewell: do you remember the battle against the Kings of Zuth, and how we broke the host of Zuth and sent them scattering before us? We three, thou, O my brother, the sword, and I the helm, and young Anarbion. Farewell: we shall fight together no more for Babdalorna."

Then was the boy, Amar, certain he had heard a sound, and that all was not well. And he went to the door of his chamber and opened it, and stepped forth into the hall, listening. And it was in his heart that he should awaken his old father, but he hesitated; he paused; he waited to see whether there should come another sound.

"O brethren," sang Zingazar, "I fear the death-song of our brother the helm hath awakened none! All in Babdalorna lie besotted in sleep and will not rouse themselves."

"I will rouse them," said the deep voice of the shield of Ionax that hung upon the wall. "My bronze is old and eaten with time, but I have one great song left in me. Farewell, O my brothers! Once we stood strong together against the Wild Men of the mountains, the sword, the spear, and I, and Ionax, fair Ionax. How gay and laughing he was, in the springtide of his youth! How strong was I then, that now am thin and brittle and old.

"Farewell," sang the shield, and then it cried, "Babdalorna!" and tore itself from the wall to crash like a great gong against the stone floor and to lie in quivering fragments.

"Farewell, shield," sang the others faintly, "strong wert thou to hold fast the breast of Ionax against the spearmen of the foe."

And the death-song of the shield rang through the hall like a stricken bell. Booming echoes rang and thundered. And the boy knew beyond question that there was danger, and he ran to fetch his old father.

In the hall, the spear and Zingazar waited.

"The boy will come, the boy," sang Zingazar, "hold fast, my brother: thou and I together can break the foemen when they come."

"Nay, O brother, I fear me that none will come," thrummed the spear, the great ashwood spear where it lay propped against the wall.

"A little time, brother," said Zingazar. "The boy will come; often has he stood before my case and stared down at me with love in his eyes, the love of shining steel. He hath a warrior's heart, the boy. He will come: even in his dreams he will rouse him at the song of bronze and steel."

But none came, for the old man had drunk deep of wine that night, and the boy could not rouse him.

And the great spear said: "Farewell, my dear brother: the same hand clasped us once, the strong white hand of Diomardanon, when he went up in war against the wily Athreeb of the wood. Strong were we that day, O brother! Now, farewell."

And with a deafening clatter the great ash-spear fell from the wall to crash against the cold stone floor, where it broke in seven pieces.

But the boy heard, as he came hence from his father's chamber, and he ran on swift and silent feet to the door to the great hall and peered therein, and the sword saw him white in the dark mouth of the door, and the green eye of the gem in its worn old hilt flashed with terrible fires.

The boy curiously examined the wreckage of the hall, and came to stand before the glass case wherein Zingazar lay.

"Now, what has happened in this hall tonight, O Zingazar, I would that thou couldst say!" the boy, Amar murmured, staring down at the shining length of the sword where it lay against red velvet. "Have there been thieves in the night, O Zingazar? O Zingazar, why does that green gem in thy hilt shine so brilliantly, that has gone all these years dull and dim? There is a restlessness about thee, Zingazar; light flickers down thine edge as if thou wouldst be held aloft and busied with man-slaying again, after all these years...."

The boy leaned forward and rested his white brows against the cold glass and stared down sleepily at the bright restless steel.

"I love thee, Zingazar," he whispered softly. "For Konary bore thee once, tall Konary, the noblest of the heroes of Babdalorna: I would be like him; I would fight against Babdalorna's foes; I would bear thee shining and terrible in the forefront of the assault, O Zingazar!"

Then, very softly, he said: "My hand hungers for the feel of thy hilt, Zingazar."

And he said: "I would hold thee once in my hand. I would let my fingers curl about thy grip. I would try the weight of thee against my right arm. Surely I am strong enough to bear up the steel of thee, for I am strong, strong. . . shall I open up thy case, Zingazar? My father slumbereth, and no one shall ever know. How bright burn the fires in thy steel, Zingazar! How brilliant flash the rays from that green gem, thine eye! I shall hold thee aloft once, and brandish thee, as if I were tall Konary come again."

And the boy knelt and opened the lock and drew forth Zingazar. Steel caught the moonlight and flashed, filling the dark hall with blinding rays. The boy's strong fingers closed over the worn hilt of the old grey sword and young thews grew tight across his bare chest as he lifted the old sword with all the strength of his arm till Zingazar was lifted aloft against the darkness.

"Thou art very heavy, Zingazar," the boy whispered, "but I can bear thy weight. There is life in thee yet, Zingazar. I can feel it tingling up my arm. I feel strength pouring into my body from the touch of you: is it the strength of all the foemen thou hast slain?" He brandished the sword in the dark air and heard it sing, whistling as it slashed the air.

"Konary bore thee once, old sword," the boy whispered.

And then he said: "The air is dull and heavy here within. Wouldst thou taste the wind again, O Zingazar? Wouldst thou see the stars and feel the cold white fires of the moon flash in the mirror of thy steel?"

He crept from the hall and out of the building and into the dark street, and there was none to see him in his going.

He said: "The great building hides the moon, O Zingazar. I will take thee out by the wall where the moon can shine in thy deadly mirror, for there are none awake to see!"

And the boy, Amar, crept through the street, the dewy cobbles wet against his bare feet, the wind chill upon his shoulders, until he came to the wall.

"Dost thou remember this wall, O Zingazar?" the boy asked softly. "Yea, surely thou must! For these are the marble walls of Babdalorna and thou hast fought upon them many times, both in blinding noon and in the dark of night. Come, I will bear thee to that black crack, that new breach I saw the other day. We will stand guard together, thou and I, against the dark woods beyond. 'Twill be a great game, O Zingazar; and none will know."

And Amar bore the old sword, clambering over fallen stones, until he stood within the very place where the wall was broken. Beyond lay utter blackness and the murmur of angry leaves and the surly whisper of rustling boughs in the wind.

"Now, Zingazar, we will pretend that we hold the wall against a thousand savage foes!" sad Amar, and he lifted the sword awkwardly, but its point raised: it seemed to lift a little, as the head of an old warhorse lifts when it sniffs the scent of bloodshed on the wind; and a tremor ran down the sword from its eager, trembling point all the way to the boy's arm, and the keen curved blade of the old sword, the savage, thirsty old sword, flashed in the moonfire as it swung whistling down to bury itself in the naked breast of the first Athreeb to creep through the broken wall.

The boy Amar tore the blade loose and turned, lifting it clear, but the blade swung again and the thick-maned head of a second savage jumped from its shoulders and fell to thump like a grisly fruit against the stone while the headless trunk, fountaining black blood, went reeling down to death.

The boy was white with terror and despair flamed in his eyes, but he clasped both small hands about the great hilt of the sword and he lifted it high with all his strength.

Bathed in blood, exulting, the great sword was lifted high against the stars. The moon caught it, blinding, dazzling, in a shower of fiery rays. And from a thousand throats went up one terrible, despairing shriek:

"*Zingazar!*"

The great sword heard and laughed and came down whistling to cleave a third warrior to the breast; and tore clear and swung again to make red ruin of a snarling face; ripped loose and flashed again in the moonfire ere it severed a warrior's arm from his shoulder.

"Zingazar, Zingazar!" the Athreeb moaned in a wailing cry, and the leaves of the dark wood shuddered: "Zingazar."

The sword rose and fell, but now it mirrored the moon no more, for from its keen point to its mighty hilt it was dyed scarlet with hot salt blood. The Athreeb broke and fell before it as wheat falls before the scythe of the harvester. Terror unmanned them, and ancient fears awoke within their hearts and went crawling down their arms, loosening their grasp. They knew the cold bitter kiss of Zingazar from of old: deep in blood and bone and brain were stamped the old, ancestral terrors of that bright length of terrible steel; they fell, and fled, and turned aside in terror from the flashing circle of Zingazar.

The boy panted wearily, his head swam in crimson mists, the breath burned in his lungs, and it seemed that all the muscles of his arms and hands, shoulders and back and chest were afire with torment; but still he wielded the great steel sword against the howling throng of savages before him in the black cleft of the wall.

Mayhap Konary strengthened his arm; perhaps the old heroes awoke within his blood; or it might be that the ghost of a broken helm, a shattered shield, a splintered bow, a shivered spear, lent him somewhat of the strength, the old lean strength, of oak and ash, of steel and bronze. No one can say: but the naked boy fought on.

Ere long, the clamor and the howling and the screams of the dying – that, and the old familiar song of steel ringing in war – aroused the sleeping citizens and they came pouring forth, wild-eyed, in their bedclothes and bare-footed, into the street to see what was untoward. And when they saw the boy alone, holding the narrow cleft against the howling horde, and when they caught the crimson flash of Zingazar as it swept up and down, leaving a spray of crimson droplets hanging on the air, they seized up paving stones and tools, and some of them ran back into the houses and took down the old dusty arms of their ancestors from over the hearth, and they manned the walls, and the gates were flung open and they went shouting forth into the dark to flail and slash and hew at the Athreeb hordes beyond the walls, and all night long they hewed and hacked and trampled down the dark savages until at last when dawn reddened the tower-tops of Babdalorna the ancient prophecy was fulfilled, that which the forest savages had whispered to one another in the gloom of the forest's

edge, and the tower-tops were not so red as were the streets of Babdalorna, which ran crimson from gutter to gutter with blood.

At last they got the boy from his place in the cleft and he was so
exhausted he could no longer stand, but had been leaning against the
side of the cleft as he swung the mighty sword, as still he swung the
mighty sword, and they bore him away and unclasped the red dripping sword from his numb fingers and cried out to all in the streets,
"Behold, here is a marvel and a wonder, for it is the boy Amar who
has saved us!" But Amar, pale as death and the great drops of sweat
standing out all over his white face, shook his head and whispered:
"It is Zingazar, Zingazar, Zingazar, alone has done the deed." And
so it was. And so the day was won.

Long they made feast and festival and the streets were hung
with lanterns and the people drank wine and sang the old songs
again, the songs of War, the anthems of their glory that had gone
by, and all the city rang with victory and triumph so that even the
old sleepy God of the city awoke grumbling within his dusty glooms
and drowsily resolved to sleep no more. And they washed the caked
blood from Zingazar with tender hands and the noblest and greatest smiths of Babdalorna gently beat the new dints and nicks and
scars from the worn and ancient steel, and when all was brightened
anew they laid Zingazar to rest in a new place of honor, aye, and all
the broken weapons that had died in the great stone hall, and thereafter came many men of the city every feast day and every holy day
to celebrate the honor and the vigilance of Zingazar the Terrible.

And for ever thereafter was Babdalorna known for all the
length of Simrana as The City Unconquerable By Stealth.

As for the Athreeb, they fled howling and weeping and blun-
dering back into the uttermost deeps of the wood, those of them
that had perished not before the walls or in the streets of Babdalorna; and in the holy place where they had long been wont to worship
the dark spirit of the wood they cut down their idols and broke the
altars asunder and tore apart their priests and burnt even the mighty
king-oak of the forest, and vowed to war no more against Babdalorna, for lo! the day of its greatness was not yet passed, and Zingazar
still shone bright and terrible as of old.

When all the triumph was done and the city quiet and night had come down and there was silence and gloom of shadows in the great stone hall where the trophies of the ancient heroes lay enshrined, Zingazar lay awake. It remembered the wild drunken glory of the battle, and it thirsted no longer for hot salt blood for it had drunken deep, aye, deeper than ever before, and it was content with its new glorious memories. Yet it sang and restless small glints of light went streaming down its shimmering length, and the green eye in the hilt blazed with joyous fires.

"Eh, brothers," the happy sword sang drowsily, "it was a good fight, the last fight. I would that ye had been there. Farewell, brothers. It was a good fight." And the old sword slept.

Or so they tell the tale in Simrana.

How Sargoth Lay Siege to Zaremm

Lin Carter

They say in Simrana: when Sargoth ruled in Thole there was never such a mighty man of war.

He took Yarz with his spears, and Darbool with his archers, and Naraba he quelled with one bright glimpse of his sword.

As for Aj, that tall-towered city, it fell before the terror of his awful name, whispered once before the gates thereof.

O never was there such a man of war!

Filled with the glory he had won from Yarz and Darbool, and also Naraba, and moreover Aj of the Towers, he rested for a time. The mornings he passed lolling in his tent of tapestries taken in war; the afternoons he sat in a terrible throne fashioned of the skulls of all the warriors and champions he had bested and slain; the evenings he sprawled on many fat cushions stuffed with the beards of conquered kings, listening to harpers sing of his prowess.

He drank very much wine from cups of silver and gold, from goblets of onyx and jade, from ewers of chalcedony.

Once each hour, at the changing of the guard, all his host would strike their swords against their shields like stricken bells, and cry out with one voice: "Hail to Sargoth, that mighty man of war, for never was there such as he!"

One evening as the Moon rose, a globe of palid opal, very fair against the purple sky, he drowsed upon his many cushions, and mayhap he slept a little, and the harpers stilled their song and spake quietly one to the other.

And one harper said: "A mighty man of war is our Lord; there be none greater."

Aye, aye, the harpers nodded, and one said: "He is very great, for he hath taken Yarz; Darzool, too, hath he whelmed with his archers; and Naraba, and even many-towered Aj."

But another said: "He hath not taken Zaremm. Zaremm stands and is unconquered in war. No man hath ever taken Zaremm."

And the harpers shook their heads and sighed, one to the other, and that softly: "Nay, he be mighty in war, our Lord; but of course he hath not taken Zaremm."

And with dawn Sargoth arose and did put on his armor of blazing gold, his great cloak the color of manblood, and his plumed helm the Gnomes had fashioned in the likeness of the visage of Death.

As captive princes knelt in the dust to do on his greaves, he spake in a negligent tone to his captains: "There be a town near about, and its name be Zaremm. Know ye aught of it?"

And the captains nodded, and stroked their great beards, and said: "Aye, dread Lord, the name be known to us. It lies beyond the hills, thus and so."

"Then let us go up against Zaremm," quoth Sargoth, while the widows of emperors did on his spurs.

"Dread Lord," said the captains, hurriedly, and not looking him full in the eye, "mayhap it would be better to wend south away, to Araboul, where there be sapphires, or north to Hurz, where the spikenard tree groweth."

"Mayhap," said he, "and mayhap not. Is the King of Zaremm, then, so mighty a man of war as I?"

"Great Sargoth," said the captains, and very quickly, "there be no king in Zaremm. There, it is told, the Magicians rule."

"Ah! Then let us forth to Zaremm," quoth he, "for I fear no wise men. There is no wisdom hath a sharper edge than this my great sword!" And he mounted his destrier, while the orphaned daughters of extinguished dynasties held the reins.

And greatly daring, one of the older captains knelt, and put his grey beard in the dust before him, saying: "O Sargoth, there is a name for Zaremm."

"What name is that?" he asked carelessly, taking up his great spear.

And the old captain whispered: "Men call it The City That May Not Be Taken In War."

"It is a goodly name," he smiled, and all the trumpets screamed.

As the host drew about the walls of Zaremm, Sargoth, that mighty man of war, looked forth and saw it was a goodly town. The walls they were tall and strong and set about with carven monsters of stone like mighty gargoyles.

He saw also that no warriors manned those walls, and this interested him the more.

He lifted his left hand very slightly, and a thousand men in black mail strode forth under great shields, loudly calling the folk of Zaremm to pray unto their Gods, for their doom was at hand. But no sounds arose from the city, which slumbered beneath the noon, and no bugles cried warning; naught changed in any wise.

He lifted his right hand ever so little, and a thousand men in burnished bronze stepped forth bearing mighty rams and engines wherewith to force the gates and topple the walls. He saw now that a few aged men had strayed forth upon the battlements, and stood, leaning upon their elbows, gazing down at the great glittering host encamped below their walls.

They were lean and old, with snowy beards adown their breasts. Wrapped in voluminous robes of mystic purple were they, scrawled all over with strange signs in gleaming silver. They leaned idly, looking down, and one of them yawned.

And Sargoth reined his restive steed with an iron hand, mailed in gold, and raised his flashing sword to signal the assault, and in that same moment one of the sleepy old men on the battlements above spoke out, lazily, a certain Word.

The hills shuddered at the sound of it, and the earth groaned beneath their feet at the hearing thereof.

And, as the first stone wing unfolded and the first mighty claw of granite scraped and squealed against the battlements, and the first stone dragon launched itself forth from the walls like a titanic juggernaut to crush and kill, then it was that Sargoth knew why they called Zaremm The City That May Not Be Taken In War.

And the Siege of Zaremm was the briefest in all the annals of war. Or so they tell the tale in Simrana.

The Laughter of Han

Lin Carter

In Simrana they speak of Zun.

Very bold and valiant was Zun: there was naught he feared that went on two legs nor on four, and naught that squirmed upon its belly. The heroes of Abzoor had felt, ere now, the strength of his hand and the champions of Polarna the weight of his blade.

The dragons of the swamp knew Zun; so did the wyverns that lurk in deep ravines and the wild mantichores that roam the wintry peaks. All knew Zun and all had cause to fear him.

As for Zun, he feared one thing only and the name of that thing was Laughter. It was as a terror to Zun that he might ever seem ridiculous in the eyes of men; therefore did he make himself very terrible to men.

His eyes burned like fervent rubies through the savage tangle of his locks, and his arms were brown as iron and the thews thereof were like the roots of mighty oaks. From the teeth of the many champions he had conquered he made a necklace about his throat, and the hem of his scarlet cloak was trimmed with the beards of vanquished emperors.

He bore Death naked in his right hand. And even when he slept, the bright blade shared his pillow and never left his side.

Oh, very terrible was Zun! When he strode the streets women went pale as wax and men turned their gaze away, very hastily, and pretended to be looking at something else.

There were kings who had taken to their beds with ills unknown to their physicians, and who could thus grant audience to no one, within the hour that Zun had entered the gates of their cities.

And the physicians said, "Ah!" and nodded wisely, one to the other: for the name of the king's disease was The Fear of Zun.

Everything that a man might do to make himself fearful to other men he had done. It was whispered in the taverns that Zun had rejected wine as fit only for weaklings, and that he had learned to drink the blood of monsters. And it was known in the temples that as Zun had already defeated men and beasts, wizards and entire armies, he would next challenge the very Gods.

And in the heaven of Simrana the Gods conversed idly upon this problem, as they sprawled at their ease on thrones carven from enormous diamonds, sipping the scent of burnt sacrifice as men savor the juice of the vine. Very great was the feasting-hall of the Gods, and very grand to see. The windows thereof were so tall that small clouds came drifting in through the upper casement and floated about the ceiling to and fro, as if confused, having lost their direction. Therein the Gods discussed the problem of Zun, but lazily, for there was no hurry.

There was never any need for the Gods to hurry, as the least of all their servants was Time.

When the matter of a plague in Golzooma and a flood on the river Kish and the falling of certain unstable stars had been disposed of, the question of Zun was raised.

"What shall we do, my brothers, in the matter of Zun?" asked Ahoom Thuabba languidly, he who sees after Whispers and Echoes.

"Zun? Zun? Who is this Zun?" the Gods asked of each other, yawning.

"A mortal is Zun," answered Ahoom Thuabba. "He has whelmed and trampled down all manner of knights and heroes, and has risen victorious over monsters and kings. And, according to our little priests, he will next hurl his challenge at one or another of the Gods. Let us, therefore, destroy him, for what man can challenge the Gods with impunity?"

The Gods were amused at the threats of Zun, and they smiled at the very thought that anything could harm them or imperil their divinity, for, surely, they knew themselves to be invulnerable and immortal and the only thing they feared was that one day their names might be forgotten upon the lips of men. But this was a very little fear, for how can the Gods fall and be forgot?

And all the while their servant Time crouched on his heels in the corner and smiled unto himself a small and secret smile.

Then there spake Thloom Pitrana, who hath charge of the Dawn, saying: "You are wise not to fear Zun, my brothers, for it is true of men and Gods alike that if you fear a thing, that thing shall destroy you. But it is given unto me to see a little ways past tomorrow, and I know that surely as the morning cometh, Zun will challenge the Gods to combat."

"It is unseemly for the Gods to do battle with mortal men," said Ahom Thuabba. "Let us, therefore, ask of Dzelim his counsel, for he is very old and wise."

And oldest and wisest of all the Eight Hundred Gods was this Dzelim. Aye, he was older than the very Moon and half as old as the stars. He slept much, did Dzelim, drowsing on his throne amidst the sunsets, and men worshipped him but little and seldom. This was not because men venerated him not, who had set the Moon in place when he was young, but because of his wisdom. It was the custom in Simrana to sacrifice to Dzelim only men who were truly wise. And in any century there are few such men, and fewer still in our time: but this matter pertaineth not to my tale.

And they roused Dzelim from his doze and put the matter to him squarely. For Hathrib Zwarma had offered to stand forth as their champion, he who was the God of Blood That Is Shed In War. And he was very stark and terrible of aspect, aye, and every bit as dreadful to behold as Zun himself, or very nearly.

And Dzelim spake sleepily, saying: "There is no need for Hathrib Zwarma to take up the challenge of Zun, for it is Han shall defeat Zun."

"Han? Han? Who is this Han?" the Gods asked of each other, but no one knew and Dzelim dozed again on his tall throne amid the sunsets, for Gods tire easily when very seldom is sacrifice made upon their altars, and wise men are as rare in Simrana as they are in the Fields We Know.

And one day there came striding from the Perilous Waste even Zun. He had whelmed and trampled down a behemoth in the Waste, and, before that, he had wrestled to the death a gryphon in the Dubious Wood, and he felt ready to hurl his challenge in the face of the Gods.

So he went up to the city of Zaqqoon that stands amidst the Hills of Nuth, and he went therein. And as always when Zun was in the streets the women paled and men turned their attention to something else. Up the steps of the temple strode Zun and to the very altar of the Gods. And he bore death in his right hand, that thirsty sword, but in his left he held a gauntlet of steel which he thought to throw down before the marble feet of the images of the Gods, which stood ranged and ranked behind their altar.

Now this was a day of festival, and the folk of Zaqqoon had been sacrificing to their Gods, each after the manner of his desire. Some desired opals crushed to powder before them and others preferred the burning of myrrh or saffron; some there were who rejoiced in the loosing of small white birds and others in the slaughter of black oxen with silvered horns, and yet others who fancied the spilling of red wine before their images. And in such a puddle of red wine did the iron-shod feet of Zun slip, so that he fell.

And all the way down the steps of white marble did Zun fall, and the sight of it was ludicrous. But, of course, no man or woman in all that throng dared to laugh at such as Zun the Terrible, no matter how ridiculous he looked, sprawled out on the floor with his cloak wet with wine and his hair in his eyes, rubbing his bruised rump. But there was a lad who laughed, for Zun looked very comical. He was but a child, and much too young to understand that Zun was to be feared.

Now there is a thing about laughter that is very odd, and that is that it is contagious. It is difficult to retain your solemnity in the presence of laughter: soon your lips begin to twitch, and then a chuckle rises unbidden in your throat. Ere long you smile; and thereafter you can hold mirth back no longer.

So it was with the folk of Zaqqoon: first there was only a deathly silence as Zun squatted there, rubbing his rump. Then arose the clear, merry laughter of the child. And before the world was very much older, all the folk of Zaqqoon were shaking with laughter, at which Zun glared about bewilderedly, rolling his eyes and baring his teeth. And at the sight of him, the folk of Zaqqoon laughed even louder. They were soon laughing so hard the tears came into their eyes; thus it was they could not see as Zun slunk, crimson with humiliation, from the temple of the Gods, and crept from the city of Zaqqoon, never to be seen again by mortal men.

Now the Gods were watching from their heaven, where they lay languidly sprawled upon their diamond thrones with the small, lost clouds drifting to and fro over their heads. And Ahoom Thuabba sent a Whisper to speak softly in the ear of the High Priest as he stood before their altar, holding his aching sides, with the tears running down his face. "Who was that child who laughed first of all?" asked the Whisper softly in his ear.

"Han; Han; a boy named Han," answered the High Priest, quickly sobering, for it is not at all amusing to be spoken to by one of the Gods.

Nevermore was Zun the Terrible seen by mortal men, as I have said. But the folk of the land about Zaqqoon had reason to commemorate his passing, which was a relief to their kings and heroes. And thereafter was the city of Zaqqoon made famous because of the vanquishing of Zun, and men called it The City of the Laughter of Han.

Or so, at any rate, they tell the tale in Simrana.

The Benevolence of Yib

Lin Carter

As they tell the tale in Simrana, there was once a beggar called Hish who lived in a leaky hovel near the mud-pits on the outskirts of Abzoor, which riseth by the old grey river Nusk.

He was very poor, was Hish.

Now it is commonly accounted to be the fate of beggars that they be very poor, elsewise they should not have to beg, but this is not true at all. In truth, the beggar fortunate enough to possess an empty eye-socket, a withered limb, or a nice collection of running sores can generally look forward to an annual income of two hundred pieces of silver. And even more, if the crops are good and the land untroubled by War.

But Hish could display none of these advantages. Although he subsisted on dry crusts snatched from between the feet of pigeons and occasional rotting fish cast up on the banks of the old grey river Nusk at high tide, he remained plump and placid and well-fleshed about the face. And as silver clanked and clinked into the bowls of his Brethren in the Trade, it was the lone copper that fell to him, and that but seldom.

Every day Hish squatted in the shade of a flowering himalia in the town square of Abzoor, begging diligently from dawn to dusk, and every night he went home with hardly two coppers to clink together in his purse, hungrier and more woeful than the day before.

Now the beggars of Abzoor have each their customary place in the square, handed down from father to son over many generations of beggary. And seated next to Hish there always sat a beggar named

Thorb. And while Thorb begged no louder nor more piteously than did Hish, nor looked to be any the hungrier, silver fell daily into his bowl and it was known in the Trade that he fed nightly on fat sausages and corncakes, and slept beneath two blankets of red wool.

Thus it was that one day near dusk Hish inquired of his neighbor why it was that Thorb dined comfortably and slept cozily while Hish starved on crusts and nearly froze at night.

"You have not got yourself a God on whose benevolence to rely," answered Thorb. And saying this, he drew from his cummerbund a packet of fine silks wherefrom he abstracted a small God neatly carved out of blue stone.

"This is my God," said Thorb: "His name is Umbool. Nightly I burn before Umbool three grains of incense and smear his heels with mutton-fat, and he, in turn, sees that my bowl is never empty of silver nor my belly of sausages and corncakes. I would advise, friend Hish, that you get yourself a God. Umbool was carved for me by an artisan from Zoodrazai, for the price of nine-and-twenty coppers. He is a very handsome God, is he not?"

"He is indeed," Hish replied politely. "But I do not own nine-and-twenty coppers."

"Then I suggest that you go down to the banks of the Nusk by night and make yourself a God out of river-clay," said Thorb.

And Hish resolved to do so.

That night he went down to the side of the old grey river Nusk and scooped from the shallows amidst the whispering reeds a certain quality of slick yellow clay, the which he shaped into a God and baked it dry over a pan of simmering charcoal.

Since Hish was short and stout and bald, he made his God the same, since men commonly devise their Gods after their own likenesses. Of course, Hish was less skillful than the artisan from Zoodrazai and the God he fashioned less handsome than Umbool: a mere lump he was, in sooth, and crudely-shapen. Nevertheless, he was the God of Hish and Hish loved him. And he called him by the name of Yib: nightly would Hish burn before Yib two shavings of cedarwood, and each dawn would Hish rub into the bald brows of Yib a dab of sour lard.

And the first day after Hish burnt cedar before Yib and rubbed his pate with lard, two pieces of silver clanked into his bowl before noontide. And Thorb grinned and chuckled, saying: "I perceive me, friend, that you have got yourself a God." And Hish proudly acknowledged that it was even so.

Thereafter, silver fell more often into the begging-bowl of Hish and he prospered, after a fashion. When one is accustomed to coppers, one tends to thrive on silver; and, erelong, Hish had set by sufficient funds to purchase a neater hut whose roof did not leak. It stood on higher ground and was happily upwind of the mud-pits. And before the month was out he had also acquired a clay lamp, two red wool blankets, and dined nightly on fat sausages and corncakes.

Thus it was that Hish thrived on the benevolence of Yib, nor was he ever neglectful of the duties he owed unto his little clay God. Never a night passed but that cedar shavings were burnt before Yib, and never a dawn came that the brows of Yib went unrubbed with lard. And there fell ever more silver into the begging-bowl of Hish, and sometimes even a piece of red gold, on feast days.

Now these were riches in sooth for one such as Hish, who had learnt thrift in the days of his poverty, and who now set money by against a time of need or a good business opportunity. And Hish continued to prosper on the benevolence of Yib, and faltered not in his duties to Yib.

And when it was bruited about the town square that the merchant Khibbuth was even then assembling a caravan to trade figs and olives from Abzoor for cinnamon and peppers in the bazaars of Polarna, Hish hastened to buy an hundredth part of the venture with the funds he had put by against just such an opportunity. And for the seven nights and seven days that Khibbuth was absent on the caravan road, Hish devoutly redoubled his devotions to Yib and prayed strenuously that the benevolence of Yib be not now withdrawn.

Nor, it eventuated, did Yib turn a deaf ear to the prayers of Hish, for the merchant Khibbuth prospered handsomely and an hundredth-part of his prospering poured into the bulging purse of Hish. Wherewith did Hish purchase a small house in the suburbs with a little rose garden walled about, and a fig-tree in the midst thereof, and an old woman to cook his roast mutton and to pour his cold beer.

No longer did Hish squat in his usual place in the town square beneath the flowering himalia, for now he went robed in decent blue linen with amber beads clasped about his plump neck, to dine with his new neighbors who were eager to share in the luck of Hish and the favor of his God, and they sought his investment in their own ventures.

Now that he had somewhat risen in the world, it seemed to Hish unseemly that his God should be a poor thing crudely made out of a lump of river-clay; wherefore he hired him a stonecutter to carve him a new God out of sleek jade. And he called his new God by the name of Yeb, and nightly he burnt spices in a brass pan before Yeb and each morning anointed his ears with honey. As for Yib, he was put away in the cellar behind the apple-barrels.

His store of funds and what remained of his profits from the expedition of Khibbuth, Hish quickly invested in the schemes of his new neighbors, who flattered him excessively and introduced him to good red wine instead of beer. But these investments were made unwisely, for the ventures foundered or returned a lesser profit than Hish had assumed likely, despite all of the devotions he made unto Yeb. It may well have been that Yeb, who was handsomely cut out of beautiful and lustrous jade was too proud to view kindly such sordid matters of business, or it may have been that his ears were stopped up by the honey with which they were anointed each morn: whatever the cause thereof, the investments of Hish did not prosper.

However, Hish had by now gained a reputation for being fortunate in the favor of his God, and was rumored to possess riches, hence was his credit in the eyes of men never higher. And since his new neighbors advised him to assume a bold front before the world, Hish bravely borrowed gold from the money-lenders and rented a superb villa in the most affluent suburb of Abzoor, with a staff of servants and a foreign chef to serve succulent gamefowl in rare sauces and delicious pastries at his table, and the finest of wines. And now, when he went forth in his litter to call upon the lords and nobles who were his new neighbors, he went robed in expensive silk with gleaming turquoises clasped about his plump throat.

And, as it was no longer fitting for a gentleman of his social distinction to worship a mere God of jade, and as Yeb had thus far failed significantly to view with benevolence the business ventures of Hish, he soon commissioned (at a lordly fee) King Abirem's own sculptor to cast him a new divinity out of solid bronze, to be heavily gilt, with opals for its eyes. He was very proud of his magnificent new God, was Hish, and he named him Yab. And nightly the servants of Hish burnt costly myrrh on golden plates before Yab, and each dawn they slaughtered a white peacock upon the altars of Yab, and smeared his brazen heels with its blood.

As for Yeb, he was wrapped in burlap and retired to the gardener's shed behind the fruit orchard.

While the new and noble acquaintances of Hish were impressed by his luxury and apparent wealth, the creditors of Hish were less than impressed: in sooth, they grew restive. For the investments and business ventures of Hish prospered not at all, and there came a time not long thereafter when the coffers of Hish were empty and the credit of Hish not worth a copper.

And erelong the creditors of Hish banded together and had him called up before the Magistrates, who dealt sternly with the unhappy Hish. The bailiffs seized all of his property and possessions, not excluding the brazen idol of Yab, which was no particular regret to Hish, as the ears of Yab had been as deaf to his prayings as had been the ears of Yeb, whom the bailiffs also seized, once they had found him in the back of the gardener's shed.

In short, the misfortunate Hish was turned out of his own door with naught more than a clean tunic and the sandals on his feet. That, and the little clay image of Yib, which the bailiffs tossed after him, scorning it as a poor lump of baked river-clay not worth the tenth part of a piece of silver, were all that were left to Hish.

Clutching Yib to his breast and loudly bemoaning his fate, Hish made his way down to the streets of Abzoor to the town square, and having no place left to rest, took up again his old seat beneath the flowering himalia tree next to the place of Thorb. So woeful was his countenance, that more than a few coppers fell into his lap that day — for he had, of course, long since thrown out his old begging-bowl

– and with those coppers that night he rented again his old hovel down by the mud-pits, the one with the leaky roof. It had stood empty since he abandoned it in the first days of his prosperity, and no one had deigned to rent it since. That night he slept huddled on his own pallet, shivering in the thin tunic.

And also that night for old times' sake did Hish burn before the little clay figure of Yib two cedar shavings; nor with dawn did he neglect to rub the bald pate of Yib with a dab of lard borrowed from the neighbors.

That day the new begging-bowl of Hish resounded to the clink of coppers and even to the tinkling of a piece or two of silver. That night he slept again beneath a woolen blanket, having dined heartily but frugally on black bread, and olives, and red cheese.

Daily thereafter Hish was to be seen squatting in his customary place in the town square, nor did he again forget his duties to Yib. And while he did not thrive or prosper, neither did Hish ever again go hungry to his bed, for he continued to rejoice in the benevolence of Yib, whose devotions he never again neglected.

As he himself once put it to his neighbor Thorb: "Beautiful was Yab, whom the King's own sculptor cast for me in rich bronze; and handsomely made was Yeb, whom a stonecutter fashioned for me out of lustrous jade; but the best of them all was Yib, whom I made for myself out of the slick yellow clay of the river."

Or so, at least, they tell the tale in Simrana. . . .

How Ghuth Would Have Hunted the Silth

Lin Carter

Of Ghuth they say in Simrana that never was there a bolder huntsman nor one more wise in his craft. The fierce mantichore of the peaks had fallen to his skills ere now, and the fearsome catobleps of the vales, and even the ferocious senmurvs that dwell in clefts among the cliffs of Yoom.

Few, indeed, were the fabulous beasts of Simrana that had not succumbed to his cunning traps, his subtle nets, his unerring shafts. For it was the vanity of Ghuth to pursue only the beasts of fable, leaving more mundane creatures of field and forest, of wood and wold, to lesser huntsmen of lesser craft and daring to his own.

His hunting-lodge, which was famous in story, rose in the darksome Woods of Wonder below the heights of Yoom: and these Woods were so-called from the number and variety of fabled creatures who dwelt in their glades and groves. Not only were these Woods the lair of the monstrous askar serpent, and the nine-footed horath, and the agouti-bird which feasts only on dew, but also of beasts less reputable and wholesome.

All of these beasts, and many more, had the fearless and crafty Ghuth tracked down and slain, and their horns or heads (suitably stuffed and mounted) adorned the walls of his lodge, where also hung every variety of weapon known to the huntsmen of Abdazour and thirty kingdoms round.

Oh, very famous was the redoubtable Ghuth in these southerly parts of Simrana which fronted upon the shores of the Kylarian

Sea, and he was the favorite of many monarchs. The robes of the Seven Kings of Abdazour were fringed by the beards of lamussa he had slain on the verdant plains of Pirion, and the coronets of their Queens were crested with the gorgeous plumes of goloth-birds he had trapped in the forests of Phathoë.

But never yet had Ghuth slain a silth, and this was a matter that troubled his mind and made fretful his dreams.

Now the shy and elusive silth is the rarest and most secretive of the creatures of Simrana. According to the more reputable and comprehensive bestiaries, whose accounts of the silth are at best scanty and at worst dubious in the extreme, the silth has never been taken in sport. And the reason of this, say the compilers of bestiaries, is that the flesh and form of the silth is as viewless as the ambient air itself, and therefore cannot be seen by the keenest of eyes. Moreover, as the sly and furtive silth perambulates not on two feet nor on four, nor even on six, but glides on its belly like a worm or slug, it leaves no tracks whereby the huntsman might trace it to its lair.

For these reasons, then: its rarity and elusiveness, and from the fact that not even the most famous of the huntsmen of yore were known to ever have slain a silth, was Ghuth determined to perform the feat himself, that his name would go ever remembered in song.

For this expedition he made clever and careful preparation. That he might be as difficult as possible for the silth to see, he donned garments made of the grey and furry skins of bats, which were invisible in the shadows of day as they were in dusk and twilight. Thus clad, he went down the river past the cities of Kalood and Tirioth and Khung, and entered upon that desert waste known as the Desolation of Dhoor which was hinted by rumor to be the haunt of the shy and stealthy silth. It was twilight as he came, curiously armed, past the oasis of Iloon, and dusk when he reached the barren hills of Hoon, and the moon was cool splendor on the horizon as he descended into the deep ravines where some say the silth repose.

As silent of foot as the dreams that drift through the gates of ivory and horn, Ghuth glided through the gloom of chasm and crevasse, and as he slid from shadow to shadow, his furclad form itself but a drifting shadow, was Ghuth alert and wary for the slightest whiff of silth, for the bestiaries all agreed that the worm-slugs leave upon the air a bitter and acrid odor whereby their presence may be presumed. And no huntsman possessed a keener sense of smell than did the renowned and cunning Ghuth.

He had chosen his equipment with care. Bags of fine talcum hung ready at his waist, for at the first scent of silth it was his plan to fling a cloud of the fine powder into the air, reasoning that it would cling to the flesh of the silth, rendering that which could not otherwise be seen clearly visible, even in the dark. For his weaponry, only a short, broad-bladed hunting knife slept in its furry scabbard at his belt, for the flesh of worms and slugs is soft and no keener steel was likely to be required.

Erelong the breeze bore to his nostrils that sharp, acidulous stench he had anticipated, and, noting the direction from which blew the breeze, he flung in that direction the contents of the first bag. As the cloud of fine white dust settled upon the viewless silth, he noted with some unease that the bestiaries had not adequately prepared him for the *prodigious size* of his quarry.

And as the monstrous slug slithered towards him, opening a maw like a sphincter, but lined with row on row of teeth as long and as sharp as needles, he realized another flaw in the bestiaries. For they had not bothered to mention that the silth delights to feed on Man; and the tale is one that lacks a happy ending.

The Thievery of Yish

Lin Carter

In Simrana they speak of Yish, that most misfortunate of all the thieves that dwelt in Abzoor in the land of Yeb.

The tale tells that when Yish connived to burgle the house of Pnash, his colleagues in the Stealthy Science looked dubiously at one another, with little despairing shrugs, and privately deemed him demented. But this was not so; for Yish had for too long endured the worst of luck, and in his extremity of need bethought him of Pnash, and of the many treasures of Pnash.

That Pnash was also an enchanter was a datum he dismissed as trivial and irrelevant, despite the wise adage that it is never wholesome to offend wizards.

No, poverty was his argument, and an eloquent one. As Yish put it: "Why should I starve in tatters, gnawing a savorless crust, when brethren of my craft go clad in luminous silks and speak familiarly of meat?"

Now, the house of Pnash stood at some remove from the city of Abzoor amidst the plains of Nuth. And it was common knowledge to the thieves of Abzoor that every approach to the residence of the enchanter was Peculiarly Guarded. Of this fact Yish took cautious note, and chose for the night of his venturing a moonless and a dark one, trusting to evade discovery in the velvet glooms of midnight.

Forth from the lion-guarded gates of the city he slunk, wrapped in an ebon cloak, and across the plain he glided as silently as do the shadows that the dim stars cast from the scudding clouds. And as he drew nigh unto his goal, he perceived high towers that ringed the house of Pnash about, and his heart sank into his shabby boots when he realized that these were Watchtowers. In the upper works of the nearer of these he could clearly perceive the square and stony, lidless Eye maintaining its stolid and unsleeping vigilance over the plain.

But, for a change, fortune looked favorably on Yish, for at that very moment a wild thing burst from the bushes to lope away, and the Tower turned its granite gaze to follow the thing in its flight, whereby could Yish sidle by its base and pass unseen. And under his breath, Yish thanked the little gods that, however half-heartedly, watch over those of the thievish craft.

The house of Pnash was long and low, with little evil windows like shrewd, sleepy eyes under the lowering brows of the roof. The lock on the door was large and strong; but also it was old and rusty, and Yish tried thirty of the keys on the iron ring he wore on his belt before he found the one that worked.

Within he found thick shadows, and heaps and mounds of ancient books, and piles of pots and jugs and jars, each labeled in queer Eastern characters, and everywhere were cobwebs and dust, enough to make a thief less clever than Yish betray himself with a sneeze.

He ransacked shelves and sacks, boxes, bales, and bureaus, but nowhere were to be found the treasures of Pnash. Now, concerning these treasures the thieves of Abzoor were of several minds. Some said the wizard owned the nine rarest gems beknown to men, each being the only one of its kind, and each prised from a stone fallen from the Moon.

Whereas others claimed him to possess The Song of Sith, that most precious of all poems, each of whose thirty flawless lines is terminated with a rhyme for *orange*, and which is accounted the chiefest treasure of the Kings of Yeb, who kept it in a casket hewn from a single and prodigious emerald. Yet others whispered of a most marvelous Singing Flower, whose entrancing sweetness is coveted by emperors, and which was fetched by wizardry from the orchid-scented jungles of Nasht, wherein dream the forgotten ivory palaces of princes remembered only in song.

The fact was that no one knew! But, of a surety, Pnash guards his treasures jealously and with exceeding craft; hence the treasure must assuredly be one of fabulous rarity and worth.

At length Yish descended into the cellars of the house, discovering them to be gloomy and cluttered and unpleasant. He did not at all like the glass retorts filled with bubbling fluids, wherefrom the weird effulgence of clarified phosphorous glowed with cold and clammy luminance. Neither did he care for the dripping walls of ragged stone where the skeletons of children dangled piteously in rust-gnawed chains. And he little liked the tall black lectern made of gallows-wood and coffin-planks, or the huge, worm-riddled book which lay open thereon, exuding the unsubtle foetor of decay.

He *particularly* did not like the lectern, for the enchanter himself sat behind it, hunched on a high stool, regarding Yish with an unambiguous lack of hospitality in his yellow eyes. . . .

Yish said nothing, for there was, after all, rather little that came to mind to say. And he felt quite uncomfortable in the glare of those yellow eyes. Moreover, it added nothing at all to his peace of mind – such as it was – that those eyes did not ever blink and neither did they possess the iris or the pupil commonly found in the eyes of ordinary men.

Then the enchanter smiled, and poor Yish felt even less comfortable than before: for, in lieu of teeth, the jaws of the magician were lined with rows of pointed diamonds.

"Have you come hither for the Song of Sith," he inquired pleasantly, "or for certain gems downfallen from the Moon, or was it for the Singing Flower?" The tone of his voice, though harsh, was mild, and filled with friendly curiosity.

With some effort, Yish built a smile. It was a shoddy specimen, true, but under the circumstances, we should consider it a commendable effort.

Without waiting for a reply to his query, the enchanter then stepped upon a stone and one portion of the wall sank soundlessly as a falling leaf from sight, exposing a black cavity.

"Herein you will find my treasures," said Pnash softly. "It has taken me many lifetimes to accumulate this collection, and of it I feel an honest pride."

He then snapped bony fingers, creating a sourceless light. Curious despite his precarious position, Yish peered within the opening to marvel at a row of marble statues. These were in the likenesses of men, either lean and crafty or plump and cunning: and all were remarkably lifelike.

"This is my collection of thieves," Pnash said with a nasty and glittering grin. And Yish had barely time enough to commend his spirit to those little gods that, however half-heartedly, watch over those of the thievish craft. . . and to the tale of Yish there is not a happy ending.

Or so, at least, they tell it in Simrana.

How Her Doom Came Down at Last on Adrazoon

Lin Carter

In Simrana they speak of Adrazoon, and of the very great pridefulness of Adrazoon.

Oh, very fair was Adrazoon in her day, with her porticos of pale marble and her peaked rooves of painted tile. Old walls of terra cotta sheltered the green gardens of Adrazoon, and the white petals of lime blossoms spangled the water of the old canals, and plump white pigeons waddled in her sunny courtyards and made their plaintive moan.

O Adrazoon! Adrazoon! Very fair wast thou with thy white lime petals falling, falling, and thy tall towers lifting against the dawn!

I would that thou hadst never fallen, Adrazoon.

Aye, very fair was Adrazoon, and very old, and very wicked, too. Mayhap it was her very age that bred such wickedness in Adrazoon, for hers was the sin of pride. Of her years was she proud, for long ago had Adrazoon attained to an age that was older by far than that age whereunto are the gods of Simrana wont to allow the cities of men to attain.

And for that reason she waxed proud, did Adrazoon; and the Kings of Adrazoon came to look down upon the little kings of cities lesser in age than she, and to exact tribute from them, saying, "Behold, the very gods love Adrazoon that they withhold from her green gardens and tall towers and sunny courtyards that Doom which is, of all cities, the Doom of Adrazoon; and ye do ill, ye little kings, to risk rousing the wrath of Adrazoon upon thy heads, for, behold – is it not as all men know, that the gods love Adrazoon?"

Wherefore since this was indeed true (as all men knew!), did the little kings of the lesser cities in the lands about Adrazoon lay bitter and grudging tribute before the feet of the kings of Adrazoon. Of turquoise and sandalwood was this tribute, of topaz stones and fragrant myrrh, and of the hides of lynxes hunted at dawning on the dewy hills.

But it liked them not, the little kings, and at length they brought their grievance before the gods, and, in the fullness of time (as is ever the way with gods) did the gods hearken thereunto.

And it came to pass, in that place beyond Simrana which shall not be described, but which is the Place the gods have chosen for themselves, that, on their high places and throned between the dawns and sunsets, the matter of Adrazoon, and the Doom of Adrazoon, was raised before the gods, and this was the manner thereof:

Now, it was Suth who was the first to speak, even he that is the lord of shadows and of whispers, and whose other name is Emptiness. And thus spake Suth, saying, "O my brethren, is it not due that we consider Adrazoon, which endures beyond the time of the cities of men, and of the Doom of Adrazoon, which languishes unfallen and which lingers restlessly at the right hand of our servant Time? For the little kings of Thamood and Rorn have made plaint of her by reason of her pride, which is very great, as is her lust for turquoises and sandalwood."

"Very fair is Adrazoon, with her porticos of pale marble and her peaked rooves of painted tile," said Dhuth, even he that is the lord of cobwebs and of rust, and whose other name is Neglect. "Yet still," saith Dhuth, "the little kings of Shamath and of Aad have grievance against her, by reason of her greed for topaz stones and fragrant myrrh."

"Aye, she is fair, ah! Very fair is she, with her green gardens, where the white lime petals bestrew the placid water of her old canals and plump white pigeons paddle in the sun," said Zaard, even he that is the lord of dust and of broken stones, and whose other name is Ruin; "yet still the little kings of Narool and of Zir cry out for us to act against her for her acquisitiveness in the matter of the hides of lynxes hunted at dawning on the dewy hills (for the hides of lynxes are devilish hard to come by in Narool and in Zir): and, besides, she dares claim that the gods love Adrazoon above all the cities of Simrana, and will ever withhold her Doom from her."

"And does this Adrazoon dare claim so much?" demanded Uth Zanderzard, even he that brings down the mighty and lays the prideful in the dust, and whose other name is Change.

"Aye, it is even so, Uth Zanderzard," agreed the gods of Simrana.

O Adrazoon! Adrazoon! Very fair wast thou with thy white lime petals falling, falling, and thy tall towers lifting against the dawn.

I would that thou hadst never fallen, Adrazoon.

Only this morning I found amidst the desert a bit of stone that bore thy name engraven thereupon, O Adrazoon.

I believe only two other such stones have ever been found.

How Jal Set Forth
on His Journeying

Lin Carter

ONE: WHEREIN JAL SETS FORTH TO SEE THE WIDE WORLD

In Simrana the Dreamworld, they say, was once a youth named Jal who dwelt alone with his mother in a simple hut amid the rushes by the marge of a broad, bright river.

Every morning he awoke to look out upon the slow silver floods of this river, Nir, as it went gliding past his window. And Jal longed someday to follow Nir as it flowed through distant realms and fabulous cities on its way to mingle with the waters of the Circumambient Main.

His mother was a hard-working, sensible woman with the remnants of a once-startling beauty. As is the way of mothers, she had little time to listen to his aspirations or answer his questions about the great world and its far and fabulous places. Her usual reply was that he must be content with his lot, nor seek the curious ways of strange peoples. Her remarks would usually conclude with an observation that the radishes needed hoeing.

In time this good woman succumbed to the burthen of her years, and Jal laid her to rest beneath her own hearth-stone, as was custom among the quaint folk of Simrana. No sooner had he done so, and made reverence to her memory with his tears, than it occurred to him that there was no longer any reason why he should not set forth to see for himself the splendid cities of the great world beyond this humble cottage, and to seek therein his fortune.

So it came to pass that one morning Jal closed the door of his cottage and turned his back upon the familiar fields, setting forth on his momentous journey. As for the radishes, they could doubtless fend for themselves, as they had done during the long ages before the Eight Hundred Gods had brought forth Man.

Two: Wherein Jal Cometh To A Dubious Wood

It was a bright, delicious morning. Larks were choiring the dawn, and Jal whistled lustily as he strode forth on the road that lay along the riverbank. Of material possessions he had naught but a good knife thrust through his belt, a wedge of yellow cheese he carried in a leathern wallet slung over his shoulder, and the clothes he wore, which were clean but threadbare.

But although his pockets were empty of gold, his heart beat high and his head was stuffed full of gorgeous dreams. And Jal was happy as only they are happy who leave off futile wishing and set forth to accomplish their dreams. And he whistled cheerfully as he strode along.

For a time he followed the glistening, gliding Nir as it meandered through lush meadows. The velvet greensward was elaborately figured with blossoms of many colors, creamy white, lucent blue, fierce yellow, fervent crimson, and lustrous *nao*, which is a color unique to the Dreamworld and unknown to we who dwell in the Waking World.

So rich and varied were the flowers in their profusion, that the green fields resembled some immense tapestry which lacked only a group of huntsmen and hounds pulling down a milky Unicorn, or perhaps an embattled city of tall towers ringed about with besieging warriors, to lend it a more than ornamental beauty.

Ere long did Nir turn aside from the verdant plain to plunge its foamy floods unexpectedly within the green murk of a dark and unwholesome wood. On the margin of this forest Jal paused, for these woods were of the most dubious and uncertain reputation, wherein, it was told, the unwary traveler might come upon The Unexpected at any turn.

Jal was half-minded to skirt this wood and seek another path, but he had resolved to trace the Nir on its journey, and thus girding, as it were, his courage, he entered into the emerald gloom, though not without one longing backward look at the sun and the open skies.

Three: Wherein Jal Recollects Unwholesome Rumors of the Wood

Jal went a bit uneasily now, wary and watchful, no longer striding boldly along, carelessly whistling as before. And as he moved through the green shadowy silences, he could not restrain his memory from recalling certain decidedly unsettling stories he had heard of these somber woods.

From time to time, wanderers and wayfarers had paused at his mother's cottage for a night's guesting, and from their lips he had gathered grim tales of the Dubious Wood and the wonders that lurk in its depths.

One traveler spake of the Ever-Circling Path, whereon having once set foot you can never leave the trail, which circles about to meet itself again, and thereforth goes round and round forever, until the traveler meets his eventual demise. This path was said to have been constructed by an ill-tempered and inhospitable Magician who found it a more effective and less expensive means of keeping unwelcome visitors from disturbing his thaumaturgical studies than keeping a Dragon.

Jal saw nothing of this magical path, but the further he ventured into the gloomy deeps of the Dubious Wood, the more uncomfortable he felt. All was dark and motionless and silent as a grave. Boughs did not bend to the breeze; leaves did not rustle beneath the padding of unseen feet; nor did aught of birdsong come to his ears, as might be expected in more wholesome woods than these. The only sound he heard, other than the river roaring along at his side, was the occasional and far-off melancholy screams of terror and despair, into whose source he did not pause to conjecture, but hurried his stride, hoping soon to quit the shadows of the haunted forest.

Four: In Which Jal Encounters an Evil Tree, And Strays From The Path

The rather poor reputation enjoyed by the Dubious Wood was in no whit improved in Jal's eyes when a monstrously huge Dedaim Tree arose to block his path beside the rushing torrent.

He paused to regard this unwelcome sight with considerable displeasure. The Dedaim, which is happily unknown to we who inhabit the Waking World, is a species whose unsavory and loathsome fruit bears a repulsive resemblance to human physiognomy. As these grisly growths are attached to their branches in a manner suggestive of tangled and knotted strands of hair, the whole presents the appearance of a gaunt black tree hung about with severed human heads.

Such was the unpleasant reputation of the Dedaim, that Jal was unwilling to pass directly beneath those heavy-laden boughs. Thus did he choose to step from the path and attempt a more circuitous route through the underbrush which was thickly grown. As he skirted the unwholesome vicinity of the monster tree, he was somewhat discomfited to note that, as he crept by, the dangling and loathly fruit turned small hard dry red eyes as if to observe him, and that mouths like withered gashes twisted and writhed in silent shrieks of anger. As Jal had noted no comparable reaction from the placid radishes in his mother's fields, he began to wonder if perhaps her curt counsel that he would be wiser to prefer the fields he knew to strange and far-off places might have some soundness. . . .

This emotion was all the more intensified as he soon discovered he had lost the path and must wander through the dank ways of the grim wood with no notion of his direction. Even the rushing waters of the Nir seemed to have been swallowed up in the green silences.

Five: Wherein Jal Enters Among The Hills of Nuth

Those of the Eight Hundred Gods designated to watch over Jal were performing their sacred functions with admirable efficiency, for ere long the underbrush thinned out and Jal perceived he was approaching the further edge of the Dubious Wood, having traversed its gloomy deeps without mishap. It was with a sense of considerable relief that he emerged from the shadowy dimness of the forest and found a trail that rose steeply underfoot.

At length the trees fell away and Jal observed that he was entering the Hills of Nuth, a region considered by travelers if anything even more ill-omened than the forest wherethrough he had luckily passed withouten scathe. Grey, wrinkled hills rose about him now and the sky seemed overcast with a colorless pall of dull mist. Flickering past above his head went dark winged creatures of the upper air, and, recalling that the dread Tragopan were wont to dwell in eyries atop these Hills, he drew forth from his belt his good knife and trod more warily. The Tragopan are a breed of horned eagles whose voracious appetites, taken in conjunction with their callous and blatant refusal to observe the sacrosanctity of the human person, make them a distinct hazard for the wayfarer.

Whether the dark flying things were in fact Tragopan or no, Jal never did resolve, for he saw no more of them and soon found himself ascending a low sloping rise towards a hill-crest, whereupon, as he drew closer, he perceived Someone to be sitting.

The distance was too great for him to make out the appearance of this man with any distinctness in the uncertain light, and Jal strove to recall whether travelers considered these Hills worthy of avoidance due to fierce robber bandits or to Trolls and hill-goblins of definitely malign intent. Doubtless you or I, not being dreamers, would have taken another path, fearing to meet some ferocious bandit or wicked enchanter in so lonely and ill-reputed a spot. But being young and adventurous, Jal pressed on.

Six: Wherein Jal Makes A Most Unusual Acquaintance

As Jal drew even yet closer, he was astonished to observe that the Person seated by the road was of undoubtedly supernatural origin. For one thing, this Individual was seated some sixteen inches *above* the road, hovering in mid-air; for another thing, he cast a shadow like a glowing pool of rose-pink light, and possessed a complexion of emerald green. And, as Jal drew near, he noted yet other unique peculiarities in the appearance of the curious Entity. He had seven eyes grouped in a semicircular arrangement within his extraordinarily spacious brow, and was adorned with a comparable superfluity of arms and hands.

The first of these clutched a gold serpent, the second clasped a moon-pale and obviously symbolic lily, the third bore an arrow fashioned of blazing rubies, and the fourth held a miniature writhing thunderbolt which somewhat tainted the local atmosphere with the metallic stench of ozone.

The fifth hand grasped a silver crown set with fervent opals and, with the sixth and seventh of his appendages, the Creature supported objects of no known name, purpose, or earthly analogies.

With understandable trepidation, Jal made a modest greeting to the chance-met Stranger, for his mother had instilled a gentlemanly code of good manners in him from an early age. The seven-armed Thing responded with equal civility, acknowledging his presence which revealed, in the place of more common dental equipment, a double row of precious jewels exquisitely cut in the Marquise pattern. Despite the brilliance of his smile, however, the Intelligence seemed somewhat upset at being noticed.

"You do, then, in fact observe me?" inquired the Oddity in a voice whose tones, at least in the lower register, caused the Hills to tremble and dislodged a few pebbles from their crests.

"Most assuredly, Sir," was Jal's polite rejoinder. Whereupon his new Acquaintance seemed considerably non-plussed.

"Since by my very nature I am invisible to mortal eyes, I conjecture you are either a potent Necromancer of considerable attainments, or a semi-mortal of at least partially divine parentage," the Creature remarked.

Seven: Wherein Jal And A Divinity Converse On Matters Of Personal Appearance

As you might well imagine, Jal found this suggestion disconcerting in the extreme.

"A humble traveler, I," he said, "wandering the wide-wayed world to seek my fortune, and, regrettably, I have not aspired to the trade of Necromancy. Then I must indeed be of divine parentage as you suggest, although I have never suspected it. I do marvel that my mother has never acquainted me with this interesting item of genealogical information. Could there be, perchance, some flaw in the structure of your logic, Sir?"

The Personage firmly rejected this. "As I have the honor of being a full-fledged Divinity of the Lower Air, it is therefore impossible for me to be in error," he said. "However, I will agree that it is certainly odd you have remained ignorant thus far of your semi-divine nature and had no cognizance of your elevated station in life. Before our conversation tended in this direction, I was about to observe, purely as one Supernatural Being to another, that I found your quaint choice of personal appearance rather bizarre...."

To this implied criticism, coming, as it did, from a Thing of so remarkable and supra-mundane appearance, Jal replied acerbically that he was considered, among mortals, as a rather handsome lad of sturdy physique and of normal, indeed, of rather attractive, lineaments.

"As for my father, I cannot say, never having had the pleasure of knowing him," he concluded a bit stiffly, "but my mother is said to have been of startling beauty in her youth. Indeed, our neighbors along the margin of Nir have told me she was a ravishing brunette in her time!"

He broke off, seeing that something he had said seemed to have disturbed the Intelligence, whose multiple limbs were a-quiver with agitation and whose numerous eyes were opening and closing in rapid sequence in a most disconcerting manner.

"May one inquire as to your respected mother's name?" the Celestial asked in a quavering voice whose deep timbre dislodged a scattering of pebbles from the precipices about them.

"Certainly, sir," Jal said politely. "Her name was Jala of the River Road."

His reply did not seem to calm the Entity who promptly closed all seven eyes tightly and paled to the hue of thin jade. "Was she not," he inquired faintly, "a lovely young girl, graceful as a lily swaying in the breeze, with a skin like rose-petals, eyes blue as the corn-flower and silken hair the rich hue of ripe wheat?"

Jal nodded. "So I have heard her beauty described, although not with precisely these botanical comparatives," he said. "Of course, you will understand, I was prevented by the condition of my infancy from obtaining a close knowledge of her youthful beauty. But why do you ask?"

The Divinity opened all seven arms wide and said, "My boy, I am your long-lost father!"

The Gods of Neol-Shendis

Lin Carter

The Gods of Neol-Shendis met on a mountain-top near the sea. Tremendous, fierce-eyed, robed in glory, They came to decide the fate of Neol-Shendis. When All were congregated there upon that wind-swept peak, One rose amongst Them, Asador-Niath, Whom men worship with offering of purple wine and young sheep that are without blemish; and He spoke to Them, saying: "Brothers, We gather here to bring Our wrath down upon Neol-Shendis, which We built from the sandy waste-land when Ikranos was young and which now hath forgotten Us, the builders. Let Us then confer amongst Ourselves, and choose the method of doom."

Then arose Lord Duabborath, Who is worshipped by burnt offerings of black bulls and libations of honey and fresh milk, and He spoke, saying: "Thou speakest truth, O Brother! Lo, the people have forgotten Us, Who raised them to kingship over all the coasts of Neol-Shendis even unto the gates of The Eight Cities; for whose victories in battle We lent Our strength. No longer burn they the fragrant sandalwood before Our altars, nor lay wreaths of yellow roses upon Our shrines. And Our priests go hungry in the empty temples. Therefore, let Us smite the city with Our wrath and let Our doom fall upon them, even to the youngest child!"

A rumble of angry agreement came up from the assembled Gods, and Their fierce eyes kindled with wrath. But then spoke the Hieros Tengri, Whose domain is the Twelve Arts and Who is worshipped from altars of onyx: "Nay, Brothers; be Ye not exceeding wroth against Our children. Observe the heights to which they have aspired in the arts. Be mindful of the wondrous statues and the tapestries, which are the marvel of all Ikranos; think upon the golden poetry and the ageless writings of their philosophers, and pause, lest in Your vain rage Ye smite the children and make Your names forever cursed by the lovers and the students of the arts."

Next rose up Sadai-Argyros, Who is a God of the Sword, and Whose name is War. A vast and terrible form was He, clad in armor dazzling as the noonday sun, holding a sword that glittered with restless fires like a lightning-bolt. He spoke contemptuously: "Listen not to these milk-fed words of Our Brother! Dabbling paints on cloth and dreaming over pretty words are the pleasures of weaklings and women. I say let Us smite them with the sword, cleanse them with Our fury, and begin anew!"

An angry muttering surged up after the words of Sadai-Argyros, and the Gods moved restlessly amongst Themselves, as if impatient to visit Their doom upon the helpless city; but then spoke wise and ancient Ghorn Nombo, who was the wisest of Them All. He spoke unto Them, and His voice was like wind moving under hollow mountains, and They fell silent before His words.

"My younger Brothers, let Us pause. The sins of Our children are indeed grievous, yet are their works mighty and admirable. Let Us therefore decide in another manner, for We can argue and debate here amongst Ourselves until Ikranos falls into dust and the million stars of heaven flicker out like candles, ere We come into agreement."

"What advisest Thou, O Ghorn Nombo?" the Gods cried.

Again the ancient form spoke in a voice of thunder: "Choose One amongst You, Who is neither excited to rage by their iniquities, nor blinded with admiration for their accomplishments, One who would be fair and impartial, and by Whose decision Ye will All stand."

"Who? Whom from amongst Us shall We choose?" And so it came to pass that the Gods of Neol-Shendis quarrelled and argued among Themselves there upon the mountain-peak all the night. The heavens shook with storm, for Their voices were thunder, and the flash of rage within Their eyes was the distant lightning. And in the city far below, the people hurried through the streets to flee the storm, and men ran for the shelter of a warm inn before the rain came down.

Finally, as dawn flushed the eastern skies with rose and coral, the Gods of Neol-Shendis came to an agreement. They chose Lord Ischaboath, Who is the Patron God of Fishermen, and Who is worshipped by spikenard burnt upon altars of jade and chalcedony. Smiling, fat, and lazy was old Ischaboath, Who cared for nothing more strenuous than basking on his favorite mountain top and sniffing the pungent odors of cooking fish wafted to Him from the waterfront. Yet He was a wise choice, although Asador-Niath and Sadai-Argyros disapproved of Him, and denounced Him as a fool and an old woman. The Hieros Tengri was well satisfied at the choice, for while the Fishermen's God shared no appreciation of the arts, yet was He mild and gentle and full of peace, and likewise cared nothing for the ways of war.

And thus it happened that Ischaboath took on the form of a mortal for the first time in all the long centuries of His life. He became a small, fat little man with a bald head and pink, smiling face and soft, kindly blue eyes. He stood on the windy peak and shivered in the chill breeze. It felt strange to be human after aeons of Godhood. The pebbles and rough rock cut through his thin sandals and bruised his feet, and he shivered again in the frigid wind.

Above him towered the forms of his Brothers, and suddenly They had become to him tremendous, vast shapes, full of light and splendor, looming in colossal majesty even unto the clouds. Now, he felt different from Them, half-afraid of his gigantic Brethern.

Then the magnificent, blazing shape That was Ghorn Nombo bent down from Its cloudy heights and touched him with a dazzling finger, and spoke to him in a voice that was as the thunder of a hurricane through a forest:

"Go thy way, little brother, and make thy decisions. We shall wait here for thee and promise not to visit Our wrath upon Neol-Shendis until thou returnest unto Us. Look thee well; make thy decisions. We shall abide by them."

Old Ischaboath hurried from that place of tremendous, blinding shapes and eyes that glared down at him like falling stars, and scurried down the mountain slope to the city by the sea. The body he had assumed was old and fat and rather short of breath, so he was quite winded by the time he reached the foot of the mountain, and he had to pause there by the sea-shore to catch his breath.

Ischaboath stood there on the shore and gazed about him with delight. Never had he seen the sea or the sky before through mortal eyes. The beach was a curving stretch of soft white sand, and here and there over it scuttled tiny crabs hurrying to their little caverns. Tufts and clumps of long sea-grass rose from the sand, and the tangy breeze sang through them with a wild and mournful dirge. The emerald waves rolled in slowly, whispering over the wet sand to foam in a lacy pattern of creamy white bubbles around the glistening sea shells and sliding so reluctantly back into the sea again. The water was cold and pale green-blue and deliciously wet as it curled around his toes.

Above him, the sky was vague and lost in tremendous masses of high-piled clouds, tinted coral-pink and peach-yellow by the sunrise, clouds that drifted overhead with slow, awful majesty — cities and islands and castles of richly-colored mist, borne on their mysterious journey by the great, silent winds of morning in the upper regions of the sky.

Here and there, white sea gulls swooped and hovered and arced through the fresh salt breeze with sharp, raucous cries. The salt spray stung his lips and flapped and fluttered his loose garments. It was altogether marvelous.

Heretofore he had seen these things through Godly eyes, and all had seemed small and insignificant, for then the splendor of His Own being had outshone the sunrise, and His towering height had dwarfed the mighty clouds. But now the glory and wonder of this simple scene, through the small perspective of his mortal senses, was dazzling and awesome and breathtaking; and Ischaboath seemed to himself humble and tiny before the magnificence of nature.

"So this is what it's like to be a mortal," he whispered with delight as he slowly made his way along the shore. He stooped often to pick up glistening sea-shells, brushing the wet sand from them and admiring their clear, rich colors. He fingered the stiff, dry sea-grass and let the fine white sand sift through his fingers.

Ere long he came upon a fisherman drawing his boat into shore, heavy with the early morning catch. Ischaboath stopped, half fearful, to watch the man at his task. He found himself timid; never before had he seen a man so close. Yet this one did not seem so terribly wicked and not at all as sinful as Asador-Niath had sworn they all were.

The fisherman was of middle age, tall and spare, with a grey beard that hung to his chest. His skin was burnt by the sun and salt spray to the hue and texture of old leather, and he was garbed in rough woven clothes that were stiff with salt and faded by the sun. His face was kindly and wise. His eyes were keen and bright, set in a net of laughter-wrinkles, and his lips were smiling.

"Peace and plenty, friend!" the fisherman hailed him with a wave of his hand. "'Twill be a pleasant day, eh?"

Ischaboath mumbled a reply and watched as the man hauled a great, dripping net-full of fish on to the shore.

"Aye, a good day, friend, and a pleasant evening 'twill be," the fisherman went on cheerfully, with a jolly wink. "Thanks be to Good Lord Ischaboath, my nets were full this morn!"

The other warmed at this familiar yet reverent remark and took such courage from the fisherman's apparent harmlessness that he edged closer and even essayed a question in a rather quavering voice. He had reminded himself of his task, and so he ventured to ask, "What — ah, what think you of Neol-Shendis, O fisherman?"

"The city? Eh? Well, friend, 'tis a goodly place for them as likes to be cooped within walls. Perhaps a bit crowded for such as me, but still a fine, proud town, as fair as Memnos, I'd wager! Aye, Chorbwa the Merchant gives fair prices for my catch, and the wine-shops don't ask your last coin for a flask. The bazaar is a wondrous exciting place, and the harbour is full of strange sights, with many ships and sailors from the far places, and oh, the tales they tell of the islands they've seen!" He chuckled at the memory.

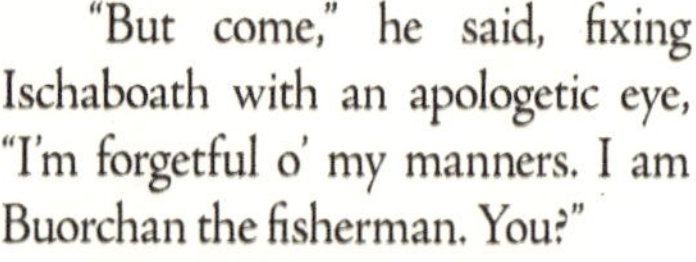

"But come," he said, fixing Ischaboath with an apologetic eye, "I'm forgetful o' my manners. I am Buorchan the fisherman. You?"

The other faltered. "I — I am — Yischa Borat," he said, using the first thing that came into his mind.

"Are you a fisherman?"

"Of — of sorts," he muttered lamely.

"Then we are brothers of the same trade! Come friend Yischa, help me carry my netful of fish up to the cottage, and I'll share my morning meal with you! It's not a feast, but. . ."

And so the two made their way up the sand-dunes to the small cottage nestled by a hill. And all that day they talked together; and Buorchan showed his new friend his nets drying in the sun, his small garden plot, and the flowerbed. He demonstrated to his fascinated guest the skill and art of hooks and oars and how to read the currents and the winds. The day passed swiftly, and before Ischaboath knew it the evening drew nigh and the sun sank redly behind the towers of Neol-Shendis and a cold salt breeze sprang up from the nighted sea.

Within the cottage a warm fire was burning on the grate; and it cast a ruddy, cheery glow around the small room, a room which was comfortable and not ill-furnished. There the fisherman bade the god be seated before the driftwood fire and gave him red wine in a wooden tankard and a goodly meal of fried fish, fresh fruit, and coarse white bread. Ischaboath had never eaten of mortal food before and found the rich glow this simple meal sent coursing through his veins an exciting new experience, vastly more satisfying than the vaporous viands that had previously sated his divine hungers.

All that evening they sat before the cozy fire and sipped ale and wine; and the fisherman told stories he had heard from the sailors, of far-off Shai and Thaijan and Kemis of the Hundred Gates, while the god told haltingly some of the lore of the sea.

Lying in his soft bed that night, relaxed, drowsy, and comfortable, he thought vaguely that next morning he *should* start for the city to finish the task he had been sent here to do; but when morning came, and he rose and broke his fast with the kindly fisherman, there were nets to be repaired and fish to be cleaned; and when Buorchan left for the day's fishing, he could not very well leave the cottage unattended, so he remained to hoe and water the little garden and gather driftwood from the shore for their evening fire.

Ischaboath found this new life rich and rewarding, crowded with a thousand new sights, new sounds, new tastes, smells, and experiences.

Everywhere he looked was some new beauty to be seen, some new wonder to stand in awe before. He came to know the sea as he had never known her, he who had once been a God of the sea — the thousand-faced sea, with her many moods and her million colors. And there was the wonder of flowers to be experienced, the marvel of sunset and the miracle of rain. The great, golden moon. The splendor of her silken, pearly light upon the moving waters. The glory of the stars.

And the days passed like the swift strokes of a gull's wing. His memory of his Brothers and his former life became dimmer and dimmer as the days drifted into weeks and the weeks piled up into months. His thoughts were so brim-full of this new life and all its marvels that his Godly memories were crowded out and faded along the labyrinth of his mind.

The months passed, and "Yischa Borat" became a fisherman with Buorchan. The two men became as brothers, sharing together the same boat and the same roof and the same fire through the cold nights. Together they enjoyed the triumphs and bore the hardships of this life, and Lo! it came to pass that Buorchan and his brother lived together all the days of their life.

And high above the city of Neol-Shendis, the Gods waited upon the mountain top for the Brother who did not come. Yes, They waited long and very long, for They could not leave the mountain top and were bound by Their promise not to strike the city with Their wrath until Ischaboath should return and deliver unto Them a decision. And even though there was no return, yet still They could not visit Their awful doom upon the helpless city, for They had promised; and it was written in the Book of Truth when Ikranos was young, that the promise of a God may not be broken.

All this was very long ago, and no man knows the ending of the story. Yet Neol-Shendis still stands by the sea, and I somehow think that never did the Lord Ischaboath, Who was worshipped by spikenard burnt upon altars of jade and chalcedony, return to His Brothers upon the mountain top. And as for the Gods of Neol-Shendis, for all I know or care, They may still be waiting upon that windy mountain peak near the sea, tremendous, fierce-eyed, robed in glory.

How Shand Became King of Thieves

Lin Carter & Robert M. Price

In Simrana, the Dreamworld, they say, there was once a youth named Shand who had been apprenticed to a brotherhood of Thieves.

The band dwelt in a secret cave amidst the Gray Barrens of Keriash, which lay midway betwixt the three cities of Yathrib, Narglesh, and garden-girt Zaqqoum.

From this hidden lair, the Thieves of Keriash would slip forth by dark of night to slink and steal into the lordly mansions of the wealthy, from whence they returned at dawn with glittering tokens of their skill and boastful tales of their heroic deeds of daring and cunning. You must understand that these were no mere brigands, plying their rough trade with bludgeon and dirk. Far from it, the Thieves thought of themselves as craftsmen, aye, artists who took professional pride in their mastery of the stealthy skills.

Their cavernous home was capacious and comfortable, and afforded them the maximum of security. Nor had they much to fear from the guardians of law and order, since their cave lay beyond the territories dominated by the elites of Yathrib, Narglesh, and bright-roofed Zaqqoum, and hence outside the legal authority of the respective constabularies of the three cities; hence the Thieves lived lives of ease and luxury, admixed with the savory spice of Adventure.

Snug and safe beside a roaring fire on wintry nights, when wine was in the cup and a succulent bullock crisping on the spit, they would swap thrilling tales of swaggering exploits and hazardous deeds. Young Shand would sit at the edge of the fire and drink it all in with the romantic heart of youth, and he dreamt of winning a position of esteem among them.

The opportunity came far sooner than he had dared expect. For you must know that the Thieves were ruled by a King chosen for life from amongst their number by reason of superior daring and ingenuity.

And when the present sovereign, one Babdoul the Shadow, succumbed at length and in the fullness of time to the burthen of his years, and was sorrowfully laid to rest in an adjoining cavern beside his predecessors, it was observed that the position of King of the Thieves of Keriash was once more open.

When they had paid their last respects to the late monarch, the Thieves met in open conclave to determine a suitable goal for which to compete so that one amongst them could demonstrate his pre-eminent mastery of the shadowy arts and, thus, his fitness to fill the highest station.

The deceased Babdoul (it was recounted) had succeeded to the kingship in open contest with his brethren, for of all the seven and seventy only Babdoul the sly, the silent, the stealthy, had stolen the renowned and fabulous Whispering Sword from the very hand of Pna-Soreph the Green Enchanter as he slumbered within his subterranean palace under the Hills of Zoor.

A test demanding comparable ingenuity and resourcefulness must be decided upon.

They discussed the relative merits of this or that oddity or closely guarded treasure. Their disputations became highly technical and tempers ran high and voices became loud and affrontive, and not seldom were dirks drawn and curses hissed betwixt clenched teeth.

It was Red Tasper who proposed that aspirants for the high office attempt to purloin the Holy *Book of Ung Tharba* that was written in the morning of time by the Veiled Prophet, who chose for some recondite purpose of his own to pen the terrific sigils which comprised his sole literary endeavor with a pen dipped in liquescent gold upon twelve hundred tanned aurochs-hides.

The *Book of Ung Tharba*, it was recalled, is sacred to the Masked Priests of Yazoth who worship their deity with certain rituals better left undescribed, lest the squeamish among my readers be offended.

It was also recalled that the Book was concealed from the profane eyes of the curiosity-seeker in this manner: it was sequestered far below the Iron Hills of Harz in the lair of Dzarmungzung, a dragon whose vasty form is clad in seven thousand scales whereof each scale is like unto a shield of hard bronze.

But this proposal the Thieves deemed unworthy of their talents and Red Tasper was voted down.

Zath the Silent was next.

He advocated theft of the many-gemmed Mitre of the Seven Hundred Kings of Yu-Istam, that forgotten and ruinous city long lost amidst the impassable desert to the north which men have rightly named The Crimson Death.

It was the happy custom of the Yu-Istami monarchs that each successor to the ancient throne of his fathers should add to the amazing luster of the crown they had each in turn inherited from their ancestors. To this delightful tradition was added the stricture that each new gem should be of a variety unlike any of the others already set within the sparkling Mitre.

By the time the Gods whelmed utterly and threw down the splendors of Yu-Istam (as in the fullness of time they bring to ruin each and all of the kingdoms of Men), the flashing and gem-encumbered Mitre bore amidst its weight of mineral fires no fewer than two hundred and sixty and three jewels of varieties otherwise unknown among men, including thirty-seven ultra-telluric specimens brought down by wizardry from the cold mountains and bleak plains of the Moon.

Now the Mitre was reputed to lie upon the withered and spice-scented lap of the Last King, Jhalendalir of the Curious Doom, where he sits enthroned among the mummies of ten thousand warriors, each armed with a plumed spear and a mighty scimitar of cold bronze.

The magicians of Yu-Istam, it was told, had set upon the dead soldiery a geas that, should any man lay so much as a single finger on the precious Mitre, the withered King would raise his voice in outrage, whereupon the mummified host of warriors should be upon the moment animate with life wherewith to avenge in blood this insult to the last monarch of the ancient house.

This quest the Thieves passed over as mere play for children, and the voice of Zath was silent again.

Then did Thay the One-Eyed recall to the attention of the brethren the glorious treasure of Pashtakhar amid the odorous jungles of Uzulba, that treasure which men call The Glory of the Jungle. Thus did he advocate the theft of the Song of Kishon-Yeb, that superlative and glittering poem of thirty lines whereof doth each line end on a rhyme for "orange," and which is the chiefest treasure of the Princes of Pashtakhar, who preserve it ever in a casket solid with diamonds.

It is recalled that the Jungle Princes caused the Song to be guarded by an hundred and four automata of burnished iron who ringed about the casket atop a tower of glass.

This task, too, was deemed too simple.

Balimar of the Iron Knuckles proposed the aspirants seek the Flame Pearl which starred the iron crown of Yemshar the Demon of Fire, but that was deemed too simple.

Vasadon of the Garrote suggested the test be the theft of a single tail feather of the Great Simurgh whose nest lay atop the Mountain of Silver, but that was considered mere child's play.

Quetzol the Lean advocated the theft of the Spear of Undoings which the Emperor Hlathla Phome bore ever at his side amidst a thousand plumed warriors, but that was dismissed as unworthy of the high caliber of their talents.

At length, just as insults were beginning to hurtle across the cave and tempers became affrontive, there spoke up from the deep dusty shadows at the rear of the cave the wisest and most ancient of all the Thieves of Keriash, old Drey of the Long Beard, who spake, saying:

"What of the Green Eye of Ning?"

At that name there befell a silence long and deep and ominous.

To all this exchange did young Shand give ear with mounting wonder, and yet with a growing sense of suspicion, for he was already developing a keen ear for the bogus and the dubious from his association with these men. As the convocation broke up with no satisfactory solution, Shand went off to his small, unheated chamber. Once there, he wrapped himself as snugly as he could in his threadbare blankets, promising himself, as he had every night, soon to begin an illustrious career of purloinment with the acquisition of a rich goose-down comforter with matching pillow. And a mattress? Ah, such a goal seemed too much a dream at present, but mayhap some day in the far future when skill and boldness should blossom together.

Sliding his hands into his pockets for a modicum of added warmth, Shand's nimble fingers came into contact with his sole possession, a translucent sea-colored stone, scuffed and about the shape of a smallish coin. Its edges were rounded, its center slightly concave. He had long ago picked it up off a village street, thinking it might bring him luck.

One time, a half-blind crone willing to share a ladel of soup with him refused to take the offered trinket from him in payment for her kindness. But she did give it a good look before she handed it back to the shivering orphan.

"Looks like you've got yourself a peep stone, my boy – you know, a seer stone. In the old days, they said a man might peer into a peep stone to find buried treasure, though I don't believe I ever knew anyone to find any!" A phlegmy cough punctuated her sentence.

Shand had decided the stone could not be worth much since the old woman did not keep it. Not even, evidently, worth a cup of thin, greasy soup! With such unremarkable recollections did the lad sail off to sleep.

The next day, the apprentice of the Thieves found himself alone in the lair of his mentors. Some were probably still abed, others away on errands of larceny. But Shand saw no one about as he methodically took his mundane chores one by one. Some glamorous life of thievery and glory *this* was turning out to be! Amid the stale boredom, his mind wandered again to the stone. He had paused with mop and pail before one of the locked doors to the quarters of the Thieves. It was, um, that of Red Tasper, a man with a reputation to be envied, forsooth! That meant Shand had only two more corridors to mop.

Before resuming his dreary routine, Shand withdrew his stone from his pocket and gave it an idle look, not expecting to see much of anything. But he had expected too little, for a tiny scene was forming on the grainy surface of his luck charm. At first he thought it must be some reflection of something happening further down the hall, though the stone chip had never reflected aught before. Besides, a swift glance up revealed nothing. He stood for some time, obliviously staring into the shallow recess of the stone, unable to decide whether what he saw ever more distinctly was located within the piece of rock or perhaps in his mind, a dream vision triggered by the object.

As the image grew clearer, Shand knew he recognized it! It was the interior of the very apartment at whose door he now stood! Tasper the Red was not there, but something else was: the image began to focus on a particular item, a *book*. Shand knew at once it must be the fabled *Book of Ung Tharba!* It was a great tome of leather pages. It lay open upon a table where Tasper had obviously left it. Shand recalled that the veteran thief could not read, so why had he opened the book at all? Then it was that young Shand noticed what he had not before. There was a jar of unmistakably gold, or gold-hued, *paint* on the same tabletop with a tell-tale brush. Gold-colored blotches were scattered upon the wood, and the open page was but half filled with "sigils"! Shand chuckled. He needed to see no more. It had become clear why old Tasper had been so urgent in proposing that whoever could produce the *Book of Ung Tharba* deserved the Thievish Throne!

His sleepy boredom forgotten, the youngster abandoned his mop and pail and ran along the hall to arrive at the door of Zath the Silent, who had broken his silence to make his case for crowning the new Lord of Larceny with the Mitre of the Seven Hundred Kings of Yu-Istam, provided anyone could procure it. Shand held up his peep stone before the Silent One's door. He was but half- surprised, or maybe three-quarters, to see, again on a work table, a gem-encrusted diadem. And the taciturn Zath sat there, soldering newly painted pieces of glass onto the thing.

On to the chambers of One-Eyed Thay! It was he who had advocated the theft of the *Song of Kishon-Yeb,* an ancient acrostic of sorts, every line concluding with a rhyme for "orange." Now that would be something to see! The seer stone of Shand obligingly zeroed in on another open text, this time a scroll, closely enough to reveal the work of a baffled would-be poet who had at least for the nonce abandoned his efforts. Shand, not particularly adept in the criticism of verse (never even having seen or read a poem), nonetheless knew this one was a dreadful failure, for its creator appeared to have thought that "forage," "storage," "mirage," and "porridge" rhymed with "orange."

Next he spied upon Iron-Knuckled Balimar trying his damnedest to polish a mediocre-caliber pearl, if it even *was* a pearl, to a high gloss. He plainly hoped to pass it off as the legendary Flame Pearl perched in the crest of the Iron Crown of Yemshar. And that explained the rusty old metal band into which crude tools had fashioned a cavity to hold the pearl. Shand shook his blond-tressed head in combined amazement and amusement as he strode off to his next stop.

Vasadon was found at home, pacing about a floor upon which various colorful plumes were laid out. The little-traveled Shand had before seen few of the exotic feathers, with their wide variety of colors, stiffnesses, and lengths. Vasadon carried a pot of glue as he considered which feathers might best be combined to provide a convincing semblance to a tail feather of the Great Simurgh. He must have thought he could pull it off, since no one had ever seen a Simurgh, possibly because none ever existed. Shand was beginning to think that a *lot* of famous things might not exist!

Quetzol the Lean had been adamant that the thief cunning enough to filch the Spear of Undoings should become the next Suzerain of Stealth because of the magical potency of the weapon with its reputed power to nullify curses and abrogate the hexes of one's foes. But from what Shand could see, the object at which the spindle-shanked Quetzol was hard at work would be able to undo only its own reputation.

Once back in his own closet-like room, the apprentice Shand tried to suppress the laughter from the recollections that kept tickling him. This hilarity made it difficult for him to take the nap he hoped would reinvigorate him before the evening's reconvention of the Thieves to negotiate the succession. But it was not to be. When the time came, he made his way unobtrusively to the meeting hall where most of the Thieves had already taken their favorite seats. Shand now saw them in a very different light, not so much as great thieves, but as great liars! If his respect for them went down a notch, his affection for them went up by the same degree. He chuckled at the thought that if the decision was for whom to crown as King of Liars, Shand himself must be the judge!

It was to be a short meeting, but nonetheless one full of surprises. Every one of the Thieves who had proposed seemingly impossible tasks to prove the worth of a new king repeated his appeal, painting the difficulty of the challenge in more dreadful colors than before. But each again was challenged, even mocked by others in favor of their own pet suggestions. Through all this, Shand found himself fairly bursting to tell what he knew. And of this several of the men nearest the lad took notice, unable to ignore the snickering.

'What *is* it, boy?! Would you *mock* these proceedings? Stand *up*, damn you, and tell what you know!"

His mirth vanishing like a purse surreptitiously plucked from a pocket, Shand went white and rose to his feet unsteadily, every eye now fixed upon him.

"Forgive me my lords, but this morning, while doing my assigned chores, I chanced to discover the secret plans of some of you."

He glanced about the chamber to see the reactions of the schemers. Tasper, Vasadon, Quetzol and the rest bore the same scowl, as if all were wearing the very same party mask. He knew this would issue in his expulsion, if not his execution, but there was no turning back now! He told, in halting tones, of the plotting of each Thief, and of the pathetic quality of the deceptions they had planned in order to deceive their colleagues. With each recounted episode, a steadily growing chorus of laughter drowned out the grumblings of a few, and Shand began to feel a modicum of hope again. Perhaps his flayed hide would not become someone else's blanket after all.

But then two or three demanded to know the source of Shand's secrets. Too scared to speak any further, he simply reached into his pocket and held aloft his scuffed and clouded seer stone. All fell silent for a moment, until long-bearded Drey's voice sounded.

"Gods be praised! It is the Green Eye of Ning! Brethren, we have our king!"

And that is how Shand, though but a mere lad, became King of Thieves. At least they say so in Simrana.

Caolin the Conjurer
(Or, Dzimdazoul)

Lin Carter & Glynn Owen Barrass

When they tell the Tale of Caolin the Conjurer, they of Simrana are wont to expostulate on the grim, small ironies of fate. For of all the magicians and enchanters in that Dreamworld, this Caolin was the least ambitious. Where a thousand sorcerers and thaumaturgists sought tirelessly for the Lost Key of Pandellis, the youthful Conjurer was happy enough with his own small magicks and longed for none greater. How ironic, then, that it should be Caolin alone who found the Key and entered into Dzimdazoul, the lost paradisical garden of Pandellis. . . .

It fell out in this wise: Caolin dwelt in the Lands About Zuth, where he had a conjurer's cave in the Yethlerian Hills. There he passed his quiet years studying the few grimoires he possessed, conversing with the shadows of afreets and elementals which he conjured up within the shimmering darkness of his wizard's glass. This glass was the one High Magick he owned amid all his possessions. Once it had been the property of the Lord High Magician of Hathrib, Khond himself, but that was a thousand years ago, and it had long since been handed down from wizard to warlock to witch, and thus passed eventually into the hands of our Caolin.

It was a sheer surface of black crystal, half the height of a man and thrice the stature of a goblin. Within its dark and glimmering mirror one could view at wish whatever scenes of far-off and fabled realms or long-ago deeds one most desired. Or one could call into being the phantom of a long-dead mage, or the likeness of an eternal spirit. From his converse with such as these, Caolin heard many strange tales and gathered a curious harvest of odd and unlikely lore.

Betimes, it was his amusement to permit the magical glass to wander at will, showing what sights it would. Caolin performed this diversion often, for it was a way of viewing phantastical scenes with little or no effort, a philosophy which he pursued methodically throughout his young life. The scenes he observed were many and varied, some mundane in content, others bearing deeds that bade him lean forward, his interest piqued as events from millennia past unfolded thither under his interested gaze. Sometimes the wizard's glass revealed visions of which he could hardly figure the meaning. These appeared like diaphanous dreams, or rugged nightmares, the latter chaotic scenes curling his toes and furrowing his brow as he intently observed.

Caolin bethought long and hard on these strange and spurious visions, for oft they told a tale quite different from those of histories past.

One day, one of the more horrifying phantasms caught his attention so thoroughly he thought to observe it fully. The scene described an eerie, blasted landscape, a blackened plateau of cracked earth and trees burnt to charcoal. This wasted realm was spotted with dancing flames, clouds of flickering orange fire which roved the blighted land with seeming intellect. Other denizens, quite unlike the flame-beings, bore more than a hint of intelligence. These pitiful abominations crawled upon the wasted earth in the forms of men, but men scorched almost to the bone from whatever conflagration had burned their land asunder. Their path was a painful, tortuous one, as on crisped limbs they searched vainly for succour, a release from pain, they could never attain. Their voices, oh how they wailed! Rasping, pleading prayers for death disturbed the scalding air above their crippled, ruined heads.

A blazing sun, hanging bloated in the sky, throbbed with merciless heat upon the victims and their barren world. At random intervals, black spots appeared and disappeared upon its face, putting Caolin in mind of a gigantic eye. Not only that, but on occasion, distant balls of flame dropped like tears from the sun's surface. These flaming orbs, drifting lazily towards the land below, appeared alive also, and if they lived, what of the looming orange sun which birthed them? Such were his suspicions, that when one black surface blot coalesced and turned his way, Caolin abandoned the wizard's glass for less esoteric pursuits.

Some hours later, the young wizard discovered an odd symbol, something like a brown birthmark, had appeared upon his chest. It was a small but curious mark, resembling a stylized picture of a flame. It did not take a wizard of even his meager learning to deduce the comparison between the vision and the mark. The mark itched and perturbed him for days, and Caolin failed to discover any lore related to it from the few tomes he possessed.

So was he moved to utilize other knowledge at his disposal, turning to the wizard's glass to conjure up an afreet from the distant realms of aether.

The venerable entity he thus summoned was tall, incredibly thin, and bore flesh and hair the color of limes. The beard it wore trailed past its knees and feet, to curl upon the flagstones of his floor.

Caolin's first question was to enquire of the fiery vision's meaning.

"Oh young wizardling," the afreet began, "what thou hast observed was the denizens of the once beautiful land of Porpom, which boasted a thousand lakes of the sweetest water, lush towering trees filled with many-colored birds which sang songs to make the angels envious. The sorcerers of Popom, whilst searching for a powerful incantation, brought a curse of fire upon themselves and all those around them. Thou didst witness the outcome, and shouldst take heed that to seek knowledge unprepared can only lead to most dreadful tragedies."

Caolin nodded. He had heard tell of such fiery demons, and of the danger of making pacts with them. "So, mighty afreet," he asked, "I pray you, in your wisdom, explain the meaning of this strange mark upon my chest."

The young wizard unbuttoned his jerkin to reveal his bare chest.

"O cursed Caolin, it is even the mark of the fire sultan, the sign and seal of one men name Cthugha, who reigns o'er all fire, past and future, throughout the cosmos. It is an omen, a portent signifying that thou, poor sorcerer, shalt straightway suffer such immolation as thou hast beheld."

Caolin, quite naturally, balked at such a prospect.

"O compassionate spirit," he replied, fear shaking his voice, "how might one avoid such a terrible, onerous fate?"

The afreet bowed its head, and crossed and uncrossed it eyes. It replied, in a solemn tone, "To thwart the sign of the fiery one, thou must invoke the symbol of the one they call Ithaqua, the demon which walketh on the wind."

The name was unfamiliar to Caolin, yet the description chilled him to the bone.

"Seek the lands of ice and snow," the afreet continued, "where terrors fly upon the lightning and the winds." And at this, the green-skinned afreet bade Caolin farewell, departing in a puff of pink smoke.

"The lands of ice and snow?" Caolin wondered aloud. How was he to find such a place? Nowhere local for certain, for the lands surrounding the Yethlerian Hills were of a permanently sunny disposition. Caolin could barely envision the quest required to discover the fabled realm of which the afreet spoke. Would he even have opportunity to travel thither, with this horrible fiery doom looming over him?

His despairing gaze fell upon his wizard's glass, and Caolin scorned himself for a fool. Why step foot from his cave, when all the lands of past and future, of all possibility, could be brought before him in an instant?

Caolin knelt before the glass and searched his memory for any land similar to the one the afreet had described. Dim images surfaced in his mind's eye, of icy wastes, of tall jagged mountains swathed in snow. Presently the wizard's glass shimmered, and Caolin smiled. His focused imagination had worked on the crystal, invoking the landscape the afreet had spoken of.

A desolate country lay before him, smothered in white and quite forsaken in appearance. The sun above, a dull yellow orb blinded by a film of cataract clouds, sought vainly to warm the icy realm. Thick forests covered the land, their branches bent and sodden from their burdens of snow. The lakes were frozen, as were the rivers, and the waterfalls stood solid, mid-pour. It was a terrible, merciless world, the sterile cold making Caolin shiver where he sat.

Caolin had long since learned that, by force of will, he could scan the conjured scenes, as if moving a telescope. In this fashion did he explore the snowy realm like a bird, flying above and between the white treetops. While he swooped and soared, Caolin searched for something, he knew not what. Perhaps a clue to the afreet's cryptic words, or perhaps, Caolin thought, that by exposing himself to the vision, the mark upon his chest might be cast away.

Some time later, Caolin found himself hovering over a crowd of small trees, stunted and dark within a snowy clearing. Their shapes, twisted as they were, appeared strangely familiar, and looming closer, Caolin finally encountered the denizens of this icy white realm. They were, to a man, woman and child, frozen solid where they stood. Arrayed in a crude circle, they appeared to have perished whilst making obeisance to a tall, gaunt form at the centre of their assembly.

His interest piqued, Caolin drew still closer. What he saw next filled him with horror, for the gaunt figure met his stare from myriad mismatched eyes. It was no effigy! Rather, it was a thing cursed with abominable, ice-coated life. Caolin twisted from the black crystal in terror, dispelling the vision and turning the glass clear again.

Chilled in both body and mind, the young wizard ripped open his jerkin to see if the cursed mark had disappeared. In this he was disappointed, but also surprised, for the flame symbol now had a companion. Directly beneath the first mark stood a pale, intricate design, a shape of six points radiating from a central spoke. Caolin recognized it as an archaic, alchemical symbol for a snowflake.

The mark felt cold to the touch, as cold as the flame above it was hot. In sheer panic, Caolin again sought the help of the wizard's glass, this time summoning up a second afreet from the aether.

"O twice-cursed Caolin," the afreet said, after the mortal had shown it the fresh blemish. "Thou bearest the mark of the ice sultan, the sign and seal of the one called Ithaqua. It is an omen, a portent signifying that one so marked shall perish by freezing."

In truth, these words echoed those the first afreet had spoken; not only so, but this new demon bore a distinct resemblance to it. It was just shorter of beard, its skin tone more pink than green.

Caolin looked from his marred chest to the afreet with a despair which quickly transformed into anger.

"Demon," he said with indignance in his voice, "thy fellow afreet, if not thy brother afreet, prompted a vision which incurred this second curse. How am I to remove two such enchantments?"

The afreet shook its head violently, its greenish-pink jowls wobbling with the movement. It stopped of a sudden, but the eyes continued to whirl. The creature then replied, in a voice wavering and uneven.

"O thou poor Caolin! To thwart thy double fates of fire and ice, thou must invoke the symbol of the lords of water, the deep spawn whose lord and master I dare not name. Seek the watery tombs of R'lyeh, misfortunate Caolin, and there shall thy curses be both doused and melted."

The afreet then departed in a cloud of blue smoke.

The young wizard was not only perturbed but utterly terrified. Forsooth, it did appear that the more he attempted to dodge his fate, the worse it became. Caolin composed himself, no easy task, then took his place before the wizard's glass.

"R'lyeh," he mused aloud. "Watery tombs," he added. Some moments later, sparks of light danced within the black crystal, sparks which coalesced into a blue-tinged, underwater panorama.

Caolin gasped. The immensity of the watery city before him, this realm of gigantic stone monoliths and huge basalt tombs, threatened to turn him dizzy. Spears of light, striking down from a blue-lit ocean ceiling, illuminated the chaotic array of masonry. Much of the city was festooned with seaweed and barnacle, which, rather than concealing the horridness, instilled in every stone surface and weird angle a sort of leprous, cancerous life. The city lay in ruin, and Caolin shuddered at the thought of what geological upheavals could effect something of this scale.

A shoal of fish caught Caolin's eye as the darting, silvery creatures swiftly traversed the broken tombs and sundered domes. On closer inspection, he could see they were not fish, but mermaids, beautiful half-women with long flowing hair and small supple breasts. As curiosity overcame his surprise, Caolin did forget his whole purpose of removing the double curses branded upon his chest.

The young wizard sent his vision forward, trailing the mermaids as they swooped and swam between the monoliths. Soon their route took them, and him, down a titanic staircase, the size of which staggered Caolin with its implications. Strangely enough, the mermaids' descent did not lead him to darkness; rather, the watery depths maintained the blue-tinged light, which instilled in Caolin no little confusion.

The mermaids parted upon reaching the base of the staircase, each fair creature fleeing as if from some sudden disturbance.

Disoriented, Caolin found himself no longer at the foot of the staircase, but rather at the top. Contrary to all common sense, the ocean's blue apex was now above him! The light illuminated a bas-relief almost as immense as the huge door bearing it, the former depicting the tentacled face of some devilfish titan.

Caolin muttered prayers of protection under his breath. More so than any other piece of masonry within the corpse city, the immense door was smothered in leprous white barnacles and swaying, slimy green seaweed. It was both terrible and entrancing, for if this was the door, what blasphemous colossus lurked beyond it?

So spellbound was Caolin, that when the relief's vast, elliptical eyelids flickered open, and the forest of tree-thick tentacles beneath them sprang to life, he was caught completely unawares.

The fright proved too much, sending poor Caolin unconscious to the floor of his cave. He awoke several hours later, with sore body and head. The wizard's glass now lay clear, wholesome and blank. Caolin's memory and fears returned, and, sitting up, Caolin ripped off his jerkin to examine his chest.

He moaned aloud in frustration, for now his chest bore a third disturbing mark! Blue in color, the new blemish was shaped like a simple drop of water.

The young wizard thrust his hands to his face and sobbed, his painful plaints filling the cave with desperation and fear.

"Oh pitiful Caolin, what ails thee such?"

Caolin jumped, and turned. An afreet stood before him, and although short of beard and light of skin, it was, he suspected, the same demon he had encountered twice before.

"YOU!" he cried. "Why, I don't even summon you and yet you

appear to mock me." He stood and faced the afreet boldly. "What great knowledge do you have this time? A land of treacle to smother upon my curses, or a realm of suet to gorge myself free again?"

The afreet smiled, somewhat sadly, and replied. "Curses? Not at all! What thou bearest is a key, the very Lost Key of Pandellis. Some would endure terrible trials to collect the symbols, but thou, O hapless Caolin, hast found what we on the astral plane call a short cut."

"What? WHAT?" To say Caolin was confused, was rather an understatement.

"Thou shalt enter Dzimdazoul," the afreet continued, "the lost paradisical garden of Pandellis, or, at least thy flesh, and the marks upon it, shall."

"My flesh?" Caolin backed away, his fear mounting as he noted the wickedly curved blade clutched in the demon's hand.

"Thy skin, aye. For millennia have I attempted to enter the garden, but my ultratelluric hide, being immune to scoring or injury, cannot take the symbols required. But, clothed in thine, I may pass through without impediment. Forsooth, yon mirror was once mine own wizard's glass, young Caolin, and will be again."

Could this be, Caolin thought in awe, the very Lord High Magician of Hathrib Khond?

As if reading his thoughts, the afreet bowed.

"One more symbol we require, Oh luckless Caolin. For that, thou must visit the realms of the air, or the avatar who representeth such. Men name him Mynarthitep, the Crawling Chaos, and hark, he cometh not as a vision in the glass, but even here, face to face. Hark, his footsteps near!"

Caolin shuddered and yammered in fear. And he looked and saw the thing that stood tall and gaunt and terrible within the door, and he cried out once and once only. And the Tale of Caolin endeth here. And it is not a happy ending.

The Philosopher Thief

Darrell Schweitzer

In Simrana they tell this, although by what authority it is uncertain.

It happened once again, that in the Hall of Thieves they ran out of stories. In the long evenings, the thieves would gather there, having finished counting up their latest acquisitions, and the Head Thief would call for a story of the most fantastic, daring, and elaborately larcenous exploit imaginable – but not imagined; instead, true, for he was not fond of fiction. When such were told the Head Thief would relax, he whose beard spread snowy white and varicolored down past his waist, lumpy with assorted stains, the occasional chicken bone, stolen toothpick, or jewel he had lost in there. He would lie back, content to hear of the glories of his tribe, all of whom he had trained or inspired by the examples of his own youth.

But when there was no story he sighed wearily, as he always did on these occasions, and said, "There must be a deed." Since a deed requires a doer, and the Head Thief was not fond of fiction, that meant someone had to be chosen.

He called upon his ancient and venerable Pole Fetcher, whose function was to fetch the Head Thief's story pole; and when the Pole Fetcher, after considerable delay, returned with the even more ancient and venerable object of his office, the Head Thief took up his story pole – a wand marvelous, made of a branch of the sandrigan tree, infinitely stronger and lighter than bamboo – and reached out to the very farthest corner of the Hall and tapped someone on the head.

"You."

The one who had been selected came forward, an unassuming-looking man of middle years, with a touch of gray in his beard. You might have taken him for a clerk, but for the uncommon depth in his eyes. This, undeniably, was a clever, even prideful man. The Head Thief had chosen well.

"My Lord," said the chosen one, "I propose to burgle Karakuna, the pleasure palace of the gods, which floats through the heavens."

There was a hiss of surprise from the assembled thieves, and muttering, and occasional muted laughter, and whispers of "We know that story" and "Can't you come up with something original?"

But the Head Thief remained unperturbed, for he knew he had chosen well: the man before him was none other than Pharnaces, the Philosopher Thief, whose specialty was the purloining of not mere baubles, but ideas. He was the master plagiarist who had slipped through a door into Yesterday and published the entire works of the poet Zarabiades on the day before the poet was born. More than once he had whispered some enticing secret to send a king off on an impossible quest, thus stealing the royal wits and the kingdom at the same time.

Yes, there had been another, a talented but more conventional thief called Hinyar the Snitcherous, who had burgled Karakuna long ago and come to a bad end thereby. It had made a good story, which filled many an idle hour. But from Pharnaces, more could be expected. This was going to be especially interesting.

"I shall steal," said Pharnaces, "the *secret* of the gods, that which the gods alone know. Thus we of the Thieves' Guild will become the wisest of all men."

It followed, in the minds of the assembled thieves, and to their chief, that the wisest of men would know the most, and therefore be the most successful thieves. They nodded and muttered in assent.

"Just make sure it is a good story," said the Head Thief. "Go, and be rewarded as you deserve."

There was an awkward silence then, for the blessing of the Head Thief also sounded a little like a curse, and the assembled thieves were only relieved by the realization that the command did not apply to them.

So Pharnaces went, and he thought to himself, how does one get into heaven?

In the old tale of his predecessor, it was a matter of traveling through fantastic lands, of defeating or beguiling even more fantastic beasts and men, of climbing on an invisible ladder through the cosmos for forty-seven days to a point beyond the limits of the universe itself, then hitting one's head on the ceiling to which the Chain of Being is attached.

But that seemed like a lot of hard work, and while it had produced a fine tale, the tale was not one which had a happy ending. Pharnaces, being the protagonist of the future tale to be told, resolved to do better. He resolved to be both subtle and original.

He began, most subtly, with a completely unoriginal thought.

He wandered through the marketplace, where prophets sat on stones or logs or old crates and, pointed at the sky, and said, "Give, give, for prayers rise to heaven like smoke."

People would drop coins in the bowls each prophet had placed before himself, and the prophets would rock back and forth in prayer, and the prayers would rise to heaven.

So Pharnaces found a discarded fruit basket, turned it over, sat upon it, pointed his finger upwards and said also "Prayers rise like smoke."

That first day, he earned a few coppers, and a few more the next, and on some days none at all, but he had established himself among the prophets, as unremarkable, bedraggled, and dirt-covered as most of them. Slowly, he began to vary his prophecy, saying not only that prayers rise like smoke, but that the souls of the faithful rise like smoke also, and that the gods themselves, when they choose, similarly drift upward and thus reach the upper heavens where Karakuna, the great pleasure palace, floats among the stars like a fantastic barge, and all things are fulfilled there, all secrets known, all delights experienced when one is gathered at the feasting table of the gods, which is in Karakuna.

He soon began to make a great deal of money. Yet, still he sat in a tattered, filthy robe among the commonplace prophets of the marketplace until they, growing jealous, set upon him with cudgels, stole all his earnings – which he laughingly called "trash" and scattered at their feet. And they drove him, much bloodied, out of the city.

He took up his abode in the far desert, atop a red spire of stone, and there he prophesied to the air, and to the wind, and to the birds, speaking of the wonders of the feasting table of the gods, and of the brilliance of the conversation there, and how the secrets of all things might be let drop in casual remarks in such exalted company. Perhaps he worked a miracle then, for he was fed by ravens, and the whisper of his words traveled on the desert wind, until it reached the city again; and there it entered the dreams of men, and men were soon yearning for that Lost Prophet who had spoken of such marvels, which were far more interesting than the familiar line about prayers and smoke.

Before long there was a sect, the Seekers of the Lost Prophet, and strife in the city as the Seekers were persecuted and slain. But their believers only gained in strength and numbers thereby, until at last the marketplace prophets were themselves overthrown and slain, and a delegation set forth into the desert, carrying with them a sumptuous litter all of silk and silver, to bring back the Lost Prophet into their town to rule over them.

When they found him, he refused the litter, but consented to ride with them upon a camel, and so returned, saying that while it was indeed true that prayers rise to heaven like smoke (even as smoke rises to heaven like prayers), the fuller reality is much more interesting than that, even if one must undergo years of intense meditation to even begin to apprehend it. He, upon his stone spire, had not yet managed to overhear the dinner conversation of the gods, even though he had dreamed mightily and perhaps glimpsed Karakuna drifting against a dark sky on moonless nights.

He ruled in the city for many years, prophesying and preaching, and sending out his sectarians to carry his word, by persuasion or the sword, to the other countries of the world.

In time he came to the attention of that emperor who was the mightiest of Earth's potentates, who demanded of his own prophets to know who this upstart was who dared challenge him. They knew not. So he called his generals to him, and they knew not either, but recommended war; and so the drums of war began to beat, and there was war, and great armies passed over lands like locusts, causing much suffering and the desolation of cities.

In the end the forces of the emperor defeated those of the Lost Prophet, and out of the ruins of his capital the Prophet came in his silken litter (which he did not refuse this time) and bade the conquerors take him to their lord the emperor.

He was carried halfway across the world. He saw many cities builded of fantastic stones and jewels, and he crossed rivers broader and higher mountains than any even he, with all his stolen wisdom, had ever known to exist.

Amid a forest of enormous, carven jade dragons, which occupied but a small side garden in the palace of the emperor, Pharnaces, the Lost Prophet, was unceremoniously dumped out of his litter at the feet of the (enormously fat) enthroned emperor, who saw before him an emaciated, dusty old man in a filthy robe who scrambled unsteadily to his knees, then fell over sideways.

The emperor's guards hauled the prophet up again, and one of them made to strike off his head, but the emperor commanded the guard to hold.

"You?" said the emperor. "You are the one who has caused all this trouble?"

"Your Majesty. It was the smoke."

"Which rises to heaven, so I hear."

"It does, Your Majesty. It rises to the gods."

"But that is ridiculous," said the emperor. "The gods are *here*. I have them."

"I only ask, then, so spend a single night among them, to make their acquaintance and hear their conversation," said Pharnaces craftily, who was the Lost Prophet but had not forgotten that he was also the cleverest of all thieves.

At that the emperor laughed uproariously, and exclaimed that after his torturers were done with Pharnaces, if there was anything left, he would keep that fragment as his court jester.

"First, let me visit the gods," said Pharnaces. "You promised."

"I did?"

The emperor's own philosophers concluded that he had, because an emperor's laughter is not mere noise like that of other men, but is indeed an affirmation, containing ineffable wisdom and numerous legal precedents, which were discussed and dissected – treatises written, whole learned conferences convened on the subject – a thousand voices murmuring like the wind blowing over a stone spire in the middle of a desert night; still discoursing as the emperor and the rest of his court processed away in great state and left them behind.

Pharnaces was mercifully allowed back into his litter. The emperor, whose sacred foot never touched the ground, traveled in his own more grand conveyance, his massive flesh rippling as he chortled softly to himself and muttered, "This is too, too funny. Very amusing. I am grateful to be so entertained. Very funny. Yes, when they're done torturing him, I shall be kind to whatever is left, because it is so funny."

To Pharnaces, it was not funny at all. It was as if the tumblers in a lock were all falling into place now, one by one. He knew exactly what he was doing, as if he had foreseen it, as if he actually were some kind of prophet. *That* notion might be amusing to him someday, when he could look back upon this adventure and smile. But not now.

The imperial party made their way, with musicians playing, with drums beating, through a hundred other gardens. Pharnaces leaned out of his litter to look – even he could not restrain himself – and he was indeed filled with wonder as he saw the other gardens, where the oceans rest when the tides are out, and where the Sun and Moon reside when they are not in the sky. He saw where dragons are born and where they die. He learned many other things, awesome things, but they were not actually the secrets of the gods, so he merely filed them away in the back of his mind for some future hour.

Night fell. He saw the full moon rise *in front* of the emperor's grand temple, and by means that senses could not quite follow (something like smoke rising) he was conveyed to the very threshold of that temple.

He was allowed to climb the almost endless steps by himself. He was admittedly an old man now, and had been through much, and it was a wearisome climb. But he dared not falter and he did not.

Behind him the emperor laughed and laughed.

At the top he waded through vast offerings of gold and jewels and the rarest meats and finest wines, all of which had been left for the gods, but not, apparently, taken by them.

Beyond was a courtyard, which led to many golden palaces, wherein dwelt the priests of the gods, who oversaw the offerings.

It was only beyond the last palace that he came to a massive door, blackened with age, but so cunningly made and skillfully set in its hinges, that even though it weighed many tons, a single, exhausted man of no great stature could push it slowly open.

The inside was dark. Not even a single taper flickered. The only light was moonlight, streaming through a circular hole in the dome, for the risen moon was high in the sky by now.

And Pharnaces saw the gods and goddesses towering above him, all wrought in stone, and covered with dust and stained with rain. Still they were so awesome, so lifelike, that he could almost believe that these were the gods themselves, not just images of them, and that all the divinity ever known to mankind really did reside within the emperor's court, far beyond the reach of prayers or smoke.

It was only then that his pride faltered, that he began to doubt the cleverness of his scheme. Had the chortling emperor been right after all? Was it all ridiculous, to assume that the carven gods would speak, or that he could hear them, or that such things made of stone actually gathered around a feasting table in Karakuna at the top of the universe?

He was afraid then, but he knew that he had come too far to go back. All he could do was wait and listen. First he heard the priests in the courtyard outside, making merry, gorging themselves on the offerings and making surprisingly ribald, decidedly impious jokes as they did so.

The gods themselves were neglected. No one ever came beyond that heavy, black door. Perhaps he was the first person to have opened it in centuries.

He could only wait and listen to the sound of the wind blowing over the hole in the dome, like breath over the mouth of a bottle.

Perhaps that wind was not of Earth, but was the wind that blows between the stars at the top of the universe.

Perhaps he died then, or went mad, or hallucinated what followed, but in light of subsequent events, probably not.

He seemed to hear the gods speaking among themselves. He

thought he heard stone grinding as they relaxed their limbs, or turned their heads as they conversed. Then, like smoke, they rose up out of their massive, carven bodies, and made their way through another black door in the back of the temple, up an enormous flight of stairs, and into the sky. Here Pharnaces had to rely on the tricks of a conventional thief. He put on magic slippers which enabled him to climb stone like a fly, or leap like a frog up steps much too high for any but the gods. With utmost effort he was able to keep up with the receding gods. He was at the top of the stairs before the last of them drifted upward. But he could not climb into the sky, so the best he could do was leap as high as he could, and catch hold of the garment of some god or goddess and so be conveyed like a clinging vermin beyond the spheres of the heavens, beyond the chain that holds all Being in place, and into Karakuna.

So he actually made it to the feasting table of the gods and goddesses. He heard their dinner conversation. He could not forget a word of it, for even the pettiest of divine utterances is indelible and written in the fabric of all things forever; and his mind was bursting, but still he hungered for more, knowing that he had not yet learned the ultimate secret of the gods.

But he was so very, very close.

That was when the foremost of the gods, who is a thunderer, whose beard is like a vast storm cloud, whose hands have parted darkness and light and created worlds, said to the others, "There is an intruder among us."

Then Pharnaces let out a cry, and wept, and crawled down a sleeve and dropped to the tabletop, thinking to confess all, and surrender himself to the wrath of the gods now that he had been discovered; but to his astonishment, no one paid any attention to him, any more than anyone would, at the time of gravest crisis, pay attention to a cockroach scurrying across the dinner table.

For it was the time of gravest crisis, when the true and final secret of the gods was revealed at last, which was that even the gods themselves are not forever; and a skeletal hand in a black sleeve rose from among them, holding an hourglass in which the sands had run out; and Death stood up and swept through the feasting-room with his scythe. The gods did not weep or cry out or beg, for they knew that their time had come and that the end was upon them, and in their demise they maintained a certain dignity.

In an instant it was over.

The ultimate secret of the gods was that there are no gods, at least not any longer.

It was Pharnaces who raved and wept as Death held dominion over all. It was he who presented himself as a final sacrifice to the Lord of the Universe, who never deigned to notice him. It was he who fully understood that the gods themselves were as ephemeral as smoke, like all things imagined by mankind, as the blind cosmos grinds from nothing to something to nothing again and black planets roll at random in the void. He knew that he was dust, that the emperor with his marvelous gardens was dust; that all were the same and equal when they were dust. Smoke and dust. Dust and smoke.

It was he who screamed, "I know! I know!" even as the palace of Karakuna, like a barge with no one at the tiller, drifted down through the sky until it struck a red stone pillar far out in the desert and dissolved like a sand storm that is ending.

Pharnaces found himself stumbling down the mountainside. He crossed the desert, surrounded by swarming ravens. He encountered nomads who took him into a city.

But he did not prophesy. He merely said, "I know! I know!"

In time he came to the ruins of the Hall of Thieves. The Head Thief was long dead. He had disappeared into his beard and no one could find even his bones. A very few old, decrepit thieves still lingered there, not having stolen anything in quite a while, enfeebled and made ridiculous by their age and poverty.

One of them pointed a bony finger and said, "You! I know who you are! You have a story to tell."

But Pharnaces only wept and said again and again, "I know! I know!"

So how his story came to be told in Simrana is still in question. Perhaps it was exhaled into the universe like smoke. Perhaps the night wind carries it, moaning softly, like breath blown over the mouth of a bottle. Perhaps it has entered dreams. Perhaps they dreamed it in Simrana. Perhaps I have.

The Sorcerer's Satchel

Gary Myers

In Simrana they tell the tale of Nilo and the sorcerer's satchel. Nilo met the sorcerer quite by chance by a forest road on a moonlit night. The old man was sitting on the leafy ground with his back to the trunk of a spreading oak tree, warming himself at a little fire he had made between its gnarled roots. No one could have mistaken him for anything but the sorcerer he was. He wore a tall black conical hat without any visor or brim, and a rough brown flowing robe that, had he not been sitting, must have hung all the way to his feet. His head was shaven clean as an egg, and round as an egg were his face and belly. Yet for all the strangeness of his appearance and attire, he had about him a kindly air of wide-eyed innocence and cheery benevolence that few could feel threatened by.

Nilo would not have felt threatened in the daytime. But the night-time was a different thing. In the nighttime it was better to observe from the edge of darkness, and to withdraw behind the darkness before being observed oneself. But the old man had seen him already.

"Greetings, friend," he called to him. "Come and join me by the fire. There is room enough for us both."

So Nilo left the darkness and approached the fire and sat down before it on the side opposite his host.

"My name is Mindorro," his host said then. "There are some who would call me a sorcerer, but I hope you will not hold that against me. There are not so many opportunities for companionship on the road that one can afford to turn them away when they come. The night is dull with no one to talk to, and the comforts of a warm fire and a hot supper are only improved by being shared."

"My name is Nilo," the young man replied. "I am grateful to share your fire, Mindorro. I will be even more grateful to share your supper, for I have had nothing to eat since morning."

There he stopped. For while he plainly saw Mindorro's fire and everything lit by it, he saw nothing resembling a meal. He saw nothing at all but a black leather satchel lying flat and empty on the leafy ground.

"Appearances can be deceptive, Nilo," said Mindorro with a smile. "Perhaps you have noticed my satchel here, though it would be excusable if you had not, flat and empty as it is. You would not think that something as flat as this could contain anything at all. Then what would you say if I were to tell you that the satchel is not empty as it appears, that its flatness holds everything I require to make a hearty meal for us both?"

Nilo did not know what he would say, but Mindorro did not wait for his answer. Instead he turned his attention to the satchel at his side. Drawing back the flap with one hand, he thrust the other up to the elbow in the opening he had made. He felt around in it for a moment before drawing it out again. But the hand was no longer empty. Instead it held a glorious dish, a shining silver platter laden with a pair of perfectly roasted waterfowl.

"What magic is this?" Nilo exclaimed.

"It is magic indeed," Mindorro replied, "magic of the most potent kind. This satchel of mine can supply me with anything I need. Not only with fowl but with flesh and fish, with breads and cakes and biscuits, with soups and salads and fruit and nuts and every variety of beer and wine. All the makings of a veritable feast, and all the plates and vessels and utensils required to serve and enjoy them. For my satchel is not limited to producing items of food and drink. It can also produce gold and silver, wrought and unwrought, and all manner of precious stones. There is really no form of material wealth that it cannot provide me."

Mindorro continued for several minutes in this vein, extolling in the most glowing terms the virtues of his magic satchel. His speech would have been impressive for itself alone, but it was made even more so by the examples he used to point it. For he never ceased to unpack his satchel, to lay out their supper item by item in order as he named them. Every item was presented as beautifully as the first had been. And every item came from a satchel which was not large enough to contain even a tenth of them, and which at no time in the lengthy process ever looked less than completely empty.

"That is enough to start," he said at last. "Now we may eat and drink our fill. And afterward you may confess to me that you have never drunk or eaten better."

The old man had spoken the literal truth. The food and drink were as good as he had said, as good as or better than any that Nilo had ever tasted. Yet enjoyable as they undoubtedly were, Nilo found he could not enjoy them. His pleasure was poisoned by the intolerable thought that the magic satchel belonged to another. His attention was distracted by the nagging problem of how to make it his own.

Is anyone really surprised at this? Who would not wish to possess such a thing, and by its possession be enriched and sustained for the rest of his natural life? And who would hesitate to take such a thing if the right circumstances arose? Nilo was no worse than other men, but he was no better either. He knew perfectly well that theft was wrong. He also knew that it was doubly wrong to practice it upon the host who had treated him so generously. But for every good thought a man may have, there is always a worse one waiting to subvert it. And for Nilo it was this. Mindorro was a sorcerer. If he lost his satchel he could make another as he had doubtless made the first one. But Nilo had only this single chance to obtain one, and if he let it get away it would never come again.

So he made up his mind to steal the satchel at the first opportunity that presented itself. That could not happen while the meal was going on. But when the last of the food had been eaten, and the last of the wine had been drunk, and the plates and vessels had been returned to the satchel they had been taken from, the satchel which even now showed no sign it was not completely empty, then the old man grew dull and heavy, and he sank back onto his couch of leaves and into the lap of sleep. And Nilo knew that his opportunity had come.

He rose from his place and approached the sleeper. Mindorro lay upon his back, his right hand resting over his heart in the shade of his arching belly, his left hand lying protectively on the black leather satchel at his side. Nilo was not happy to see this last. He knew that he could not move the satchel without also moving the hand, but he did not know if he could move the hand without awakening its owner. Yet the prize he desired was much too valuable to be given up without a fight. He tipped the satchel slowly, slowly, until the hand slid gently to the leafy ground. Then he took the satchel under his own arm and carried it away into the forest, to find a place where he could examine it without fear of being disturbed.

For Nilo was not, it must be admitted, entirely sure of his prize. He had been sure while watching Mindorro lay out their supper, because he had watched that laying out with the wonder of a child. But now the reason of a man began to reassert itself, and that reason could never accept the idea of so many bulky objects confined together in so small a space. It did not help that the satchel contained nothing of any detectable size or weight. The longer Nilo carried it the more certain he felt it was empty. He feared that when he opened it he would see it was empty too.

At last he found what he was looking for: a forest clearing low enough to give him cover from anyone seeking him, yet open enough to provide him with a partial view of the moonlit sky. He seated himself on a fallen tree trunk and propped the satchel between his knees. He opened the satchel to the moonlight and looked inside. At first he thought that his worst fears were realized, though perhaps not exactly in the way he had expected. The satchel was deeper for one thing, considerably deeper on the inside than it had appeared on the out. And for another it was not quite as empty as it had seemed. For there in the bottom, in the darkness below the reach of the moonlight, something shifted or stirred.

Nilo could not see what that something was. He could only see that it had a soft and moony sheen, with occasional glints of something brighter. But it was enough to recall to him the gleaming metals and shining gems that had made up the old man's plates and vessels. And so he put a hand inside as he had seen the old man do. He reached in farther than the old man had, so far in fact that his entire arm was buried to the shoulder. But the contents, whatever they were, stayed just beyond his reach. Yet what did that matter? If Nilo's arm was not long enough to reach the bottom, he would find a way to make it longer. He would extend his reach by some simple device like a hook improvised from a broken branch. But first he would have to withdraw his arm.

And that was where the trouble began. For no sooner had Nilo started to raise his arm than something caught it by the wrist and pulled it down again. To say that he was surprised by this does not begin to convey his feelings. Yet was it really so surprising? It had been foolish to suppose that the sorcerer would leave his satchel unguarded. He must have set a trap in it, a noose or manacle to catch and hold any hand that was not his own. It was such a trap as a farmer might set for a rat in a granary. But Nilo was not a helpless rat. He was stronger and more intelligent. For him it should be a simple matter to pull either his hand free of the trap or the trap free of the satchel.

Yet this was easier planned than accomplished. Nilo pulled, but his pulling had no noticeable effect. The two forces, the seen that pulled and the unseen that resisted, were seemingly so closely matched that neither could move in either direction. Nilo did everything he could to tip the balance in his favor. He thrust his free arm into the satchel beside the trapped one so that he could pull with both. He fell from the tree trunk to his knees to reinforce his arms with the power of his back. And at last he saw his efforts rewarded. His trapped arm began to rise again. It rose slowly and painfully, inch by inch, but it rose steadily too. Another few seconds would free it.

Yet hardly had his arm come out of the darkness than Nilo wished it back again. For the unseen force had never relinquished its hold, and when Nilo's wrist rose into the moonlight so did the thing that held it. What he had imagined as a noose or manacle he now saw as part of a living being. It most resembled a human hand, with the same general shape and number of fingers. But it was larger by half than a normal hand. It was also colored a steely blue, and covered in an intricate mesh of silver-edged, diamond-shaped scales.

Suddenly the terrible thing began to pull Nilo down again. This time there was no question of balance. It had only been playing with him before. Now it brought to bear an unbreakable will and a strength that was truly superhuman. It pulled him down from the wrist to the elbow, and from the elbow to the shoulder, and from the shoulder to the chin. The lip of the satchel touched his own lips, as a quicksand touches the lips of a man who is being sucked under it. So far Nilo had struggled in silence, as if he feared that any sound he made would call attention to himself and his theft. He made a sound now though, as he slipped headfirst down the throat of the sorcerer's satchel. It was a loud, prolonged and strangely muffled scream.

The scream, though muffled, was not unheard. Mindorro woke from a pleasant dream with the sound still ringing in his ears. One does not wake in such a fashion without being at least a little alarmed by it, especially when one wakes alone in a forest on a moonlit night. The old man sat up and looked around him to be sure that everything was quiet and safe. And so it seemed it was. He noted the absence of Nilo of course, the nice young man who had shared his supper and his fire. But one could not really count Nilo, for the young man had been free to go at any time he chose. As long as nothing else was missing, and the scream was not repeated, then there was nothing here to give the old man concern.

He smiled, rolled himself over and laid a hand on the smooth black leather of the empty satchel beside him. Then he returned to his pleasant dream. So they tell the tale in Simrana.

An Unfamiliar Familiar

Adrian Cole

Like most gods, those of Simrana are protective of their powers. It is, of course, of little use being divine if one lacks the credibility of being able to enjoy exclusive superhuman powers. Simrana's gods – and who can know the extent of their number? – are thus jealous and, in most cases, arrogant. The very last thing they would wish for would be for a new god, or demigod, to appear among them and begin exercising its supernatural abilities, particularly if they were substantially greater than those of Simrana's incumbents.

For example, the gods of Simrana are not unaware of the terrible, monstrous powers of a certain very dark individual, whose deeds have been secretly recorded elsewhere, and who has various names, none of which are permitted to be voiced in Simrana (and which this humble scribe would rather not mention, for reasons of self-preservation). This being is also known to have a familiar, a devious, self-seeking little creature, and there are more than a few realms in the omniverse and its many dimensions where guardians have been set to forewarn man and god alike of the arrival of this conniving being.

His name has far less power, and although usually spoken softly and guardedly, is nothing as abhorrent as that of his master.

Elfloq has – entirely justifiably – earned a reputation for being mischievous, duplicitous, and untrustworthy, and in many realms would be as welcome as a pestilence and dealt with, with similar direct, terminal action. Those who know of his self-aggrandizement fear his potential ability to summon his master, or more correctly, to trick others into summoning him, for to do so brings with it a dread-ful penalty not to be dwelt on.

The gods of Simrana are fully aware of Elfloq and his diabol-ic dealings. It would be an understatement to say that they would not welcome him into their realm. Consequently, they have made it known to the many priesthoods, oracles and all the multifarious forms of their worshippers that, should this familiar set as much as a toe in Simrana, he must be exorcised with immediate effect. Failure to comply with this edict would result in consequences too painful to contemplate.

Umptus Underbung, known simply as Ump to the few beings that had anything to do with him, was a very minor wizard, although the term does rather stretch credibility when applied to him. He had aspirations and for the most part, sadly for him, his ambitions were not matched by his abilities. Indeed, he had almost reached a point at which he would be forced to admit this unsavory, debilitating fact. He had even given serious consideration to joining the nearby holy retreat up on the Lonely Mountain of Enlightenment, whose Monks of Crepuscular Persuasion were said to welcome new broth-ers. It was possibly only the rumor that these Monks utilized at least a percentage of their new recruits as the principal ingredients in their notorious banquets that gave Umptus pause.

There was, however, another alternative open to him. One that, to Ump, seemed only marginally less attractive than that of a trek to the heights of the holy retreat. Across the dusty plain in which he dwelt was another stone edifice, the home of Zeleshti, whose reputa-tion as a spell-weaver and mistress of nightly powers appeared to be in the ascendancy. Ump had given much thought to the concept of sharing a spell or two with Zeleshti. His own stock of wizardly para-phernalia was limited, and yet there must be something his neighbor might covet. The Spell to Overcome Sleepless Nights, perhaps, or Counteracting the Onset of Dread of Daylight, or the Curse of Un-expected Pungent Aromas?

A difficult decision, he thought, as he mulled it over. Zeleshti would drive a hard bargain, but there must be something he could do that would earn him a suitable reward. Certainly it would not be won in exchange for a bottle of his home-made wine, which, although potent, lacked somewhat in taste. He slumped in an old chair and imbibed half a bottle, soon dozing listlessly.

Elfloq, flitting here and there along the various shadow-paths of the astral realm, realized that, for the moment, his chances of finding somewhere to emerge, some world where he might pry a useful secret or two from unsuspecting inhabitants, were very limited. He knew, however, that there was one world nearby, beyond the tenebrous fabric of the astral realm, a region he had heard of, Simrana.

What he knew of it hardly inspired him and he felt sure it would do nothing to help him further his quest to find his elusive dark master. Nevertheless, mariners flung hither and yon in a storm, however metaphorical, must needs look to any port. Perhaps a brief stay in Simrana would at least enable him to gather his wits for the next stage of his ongoing search. He paused. Simrana's gods were a closely-knit lot and would not tolerate intrusions. The word out on the grapevine shared by his fellow familiars said these testy gods tended to boot visitors out without as much as a by-your-leave.

Even so, Elfloq popped out from the astral and into existence in Simrana. He found himself in a shadowy edifice, obviously not a large one, where the sole occupant was slouched in a low chair, snoring softly, a dark wine bottle slipping from its fingers. This object completed its escape from its owner's grip and hit the floor with a sharp sound, spitting out a last few dregs of wine the consistency of mud.

The sound was enough to bring the sleeping figure back to wakefulness. It stared around it, confused, then its eyes alighted on the squat being that was observing it from across the room.

Elfloq attempted a reassuring grin. Grinning, of any persuasion, was not an art that had been remotely mastered by the familiar, much less the reassuring kind, so he also bowed low. "My abject apologies for disturbing you," he said. "I appear to have somewhat lost my way."

Elfloq studied the little man, if man it was, who was now sitting up stiffly. He was of middling years, though his shabby dress and utter casualness of manner made him look prematurely advanced.

The proliferation of bangles, rings and chains that adorned his neck, limbs and fingers, suggested a man of some magical standing, so Elfloq was wary. He increased the level of flattery.

"It had not been my intention to burst unannounced on such a worthy mage as your good self."

Ump drew himself up, though he was barely taller than his diminutive visitor. "You are not a native of Simrana, I think," he said. He seemed to Elfloq to be mentally searching for something, a name perhaps, or at least a clue to the familiar's identity.

Elfloq knew it was not always in his best interests to disclose his name. "Your assumption is correct. Pardon my intrusion. I'll redirect my energies and move on. . . that is, unless there is any possibility of our doing a little business."

"Business?"

"Well, we could trade a little information. I'm always in search of knowledge. And there must be a trick or two I could exchange. You see, I'm looking for my master. He's a certain shadowy character, necessarily given to treading somewhat dark paths."

Ump widened his eyes in sudden realization. "Gods of the Roaring Clouds – you are Elf—" But he clamped his hand over his mouth before he could complete the name. He also appeared to shrink in size. When he spoke again, his voice emerged as a thin squeak. "Sorry. For a moment I thought. . ." Again his voice trailed off.

Normally Elfloq would have enjoyed exercising terror over any wizard, no matter how minor. For once, however, he felt somewhat frustrated. "No need to speak my name. If you know it, you also know I have, through association, certain powers."

Ump almost squealed. By now his brow was positively gleaming with perspiration. "What do you want?"

"Anything that will give me a clue to the whereabouts of my master. He is always a step or two ahead of me. If not, I'll be on my way. Simrana is somewhat off my usual byways. Probably a nice place to relax and daydream for a year or two, but not exactly a hub of excitement."

"I know nothing about the. . . your master. Not a thing."

Elfloq screwed his batrachian features into an even more grotesque grimace. "I feared as much. Very well, I depart –"

"You can't," blurted Ump.

"Can't?"

"You're my prisoner."

Elfloq gaped. This half-man, this cockroach, this human *fly*, called him prisoner? This was outrageous, laughable. "This is a jest."

"N-no," stammered Ump. "I have set a spell around my abode. No one who enters may leave without my lifting it."

Now that the magician came to mention it, Elfloq admitted to himself that he could feel a kind of disturbance in the atmospherics of the place, a sort of faint humming. He attempted a disarming smile, although he could see Ump was not appeased.

"You surprise me, worthy mage. Why in the Seventeen Hells of the Inconsolable Ones should you wish to detain a nonentity such as myself?"

"You are forbidden entry to Simrana."

"I am? Well, I felt no palpable force attempting to prevent my ingress. Were the terrible guardians asleep? Or drunk? If they shared the contents of that bottle with you, I imagine they may well be incapacitated."

Ump shook his head. "I know nothing of these guardians. That is a matter for the Gods of Simrana. I am merely a good citizen."

"Really? And how do you justify that? Since you have slyly and cruelly trapped me with your wizardry."

"I dare not let you go. If it became known that I had done so, the Gods would exact a terrible revenge upon me. I have no other recourse than to hand you over to them."

Elfloq considered this with no shred of relish. He understood the Gods of Simrana to be somewhat languorous and relaxed, but he had no desire to become a victim of their displeasure. "You are set upon this cold-hearted course?"

"I am," said Ump with a violent nod.

"Nothing could dissuade you from it?"

"Absolutely not."

"That is your last word?"

"Indisputably."

"Even if I were to offer you... a rich reward for freeing me?"

"Nothing you could say would... a reward? What kind of a reward?"

Elfloq recognized that eager look, the desperate need. "I can be very generous. What do you desire?"

Ump looked mildly embarrassed. "There is one thing. I scarcely dare ask."

"Don't be a mouse. Ask, ask."

"Zeleshti, the witch. A sorceress of no small skill."

"Ah, you desire her for your bride."

Ump jumped visibly. "Sky-Gods of Oom-Poobish, no! That would be the last fate I would bestow on anyone! Zeleshti as a bride? Perish the thought. She has the temperament of a demon, the patience of a thunderstorm and the grace of a disturbed scorpion."

"I see. You wish her eradicated. You covet her powers?"

"No, no. I wouldn't have her killed. It's just that, well, she has an extensive library, and her knowledge of certain lore is impressive. If she would only share some of these things with me, I could advance myself, possibly even to the Thirteenth Level of Enlightenment."

"I see you are ambitious," said Elfloq gravely, though he had not the slightest inkling of what this state of being actually meant.

"Then you'll do it? In exchange for your freedom?" Ump again displayed the look of desperation. "You'll win me her alliance?"

"Of course! It is but a small matter." Elfloq hid his concerns. The wretched wizard's description of the witch sounded highly daunting, and Elfloq had no idea whatsoever how he was going to coerce any kind of alliance from her, but such was his life. He would think of something.

The abode of Zeleshti was little more than a heap of stones, disguised perhaps from the prying eyes of the obscure flying things that swooped in and out of the clouds, flashing their notable claws, snapping their long beaks and generally making a nuisance of themselves. Elfloq approached the dwelling with caution, aware that his movements were restricted. The binding spell of Ump, which prevented him from escaping Simrana, was an effective one and held him as powerfully as any chains. He had no other recourse than to fulfill his promise to the wizard if he was to return to the astral realms.

Accordingly he knocked on what passed for a door to the

witch's lair. It swung open with an ominous creak that sounded suspiciously like the twisting of bones. A shadow loomed over Elfloq. This was not a traditional witch as he understood the term. Zeleshti, if indeed it were she, was twice his height and almost three times his width. Her huge, round eyes observed him like moons, her features otherwise twisting in a grimace that would likely have startled any passing wolf pack.

"Name?" she hissed.

"Well, I'm –"

"*Name?*"

"I – I –"

"NAME?"

"I'm from Umptus Underbung."

Her extraordinary mouth widened. "Why didn't you say so, little potato man? Come on, come on, don't stand there. You'll take root. Get inside." She swept him into her abode, where several big fat candles filled the place with sputtering light. Elfloq had never seen the like. Enough gewgaws, trinkets and like bric-a-brac were heaped, shelved and dangled here in a maelstrom of profusion, glittering and scintillating, to make him squint; he almost had to shield his eyes.

"Your business?" said Zeleshti. "Do you want some wine?" she added before he could respond. "It's Bandoolian Red, fit for an emperor." Elfloq made several attempts to speak, but each time she darted another question at him before he could answer the last. He decided they were all rhetorical and contented himself with simply nodding. Once she had him sitting atop a mound of cushions, several feet above the floor, with a tall glass of sparkling purple Bandoolian Red clenched in his fist, she finally stopped bombarding him with questions and flung herself into an even bigger mound of cushions, seemingly exhausted by her efforts at communication.

Elfloq quickly took advantage of the silence before she could break it again. "Ump has asked me to visit you on his behalf. He knows there are certain treasures among his private collection that would interest you." It was, to be honest, a stab in the dark, but Elfloq understood the strange appetites of those who practiced the mystical arts.

Zeleshti tried to lean forward, but the heap of pillows held her fast and threatened to engulf her. She brushed several aside. "What you say is true, little vegetable that walks."

Elfloq decided to ignore what seemed to be an insult, albeit one that seemed relatively innocuous. "He would be only too glad to bestow these things upon you and wonders, humbly, if you might consent to allowing him to dip into your own awesome harvest of magical lore."

"He's a shy one, that Ump. Do I detect a secret meaning to your words, O twisted tuber?"

"Uh, no, I think not, ma'am. Umptus – that is, Ump – merely wishes to ally himself to you, to perform a sharing of certain things."

She giggled. At least, Elfloq thought it was a giggle. Her significant frame shook in such a way as to suggest a giggle, and her face crinkled in a manner that also supported this notion. *Either I've missed something,* he thought, *or she's mad.*

"He would, of course, wish to conduct this alliance in such a way that would be to your complete satisfaction."

There was no mistaking the eruption of giggles that this brought forth from the witch. She produced an enormous spotted handkerchief and dabbed at her eyes. "I do love coded wordplay," she said at last.

"But, ma'am, I spoke openly and honestly."

"Yes, yes, I understand. It's lovely to know that chivalry still exists in this troubled little world of ours."

Elfloq was only too pleased not to have insulted her. The consequences did not bear thinking about. "I take it, great lady, that this proposal meets with your approval?"

She gave him an enormous wink. "Oh, my. Yes, of course. I only wonder why it's taken him so long. We've been neighbors for at least three years. I've so wanted him to woo me. Of his own free will, of course. I could have thrown any number of love-spells over the little darling, but I want the real thing. I want his genuine lust – I mean, love. Well, all right, I admit it, his lust would be very welcome."

"He's the shyest of men, ma'am. And it's taken him a while to find a go-between. He fears that what he has to offer you would not live up to expectations."

"He must let me be the judge of that," she said, licking her lips. "When does he propose – I do so like that word – we meet?"

"His home is open to you. You may visit him at your leisure and sample his wares."

Zeleshti grasped a handful of cushions and crushed them to her bosom, shuddering as she did so. Elfloq at last began to understand that there was more to this than he had initially realized. The witch was indeed interested in Ump. However, amazingly, he thought, she entertained hopes of a more physical alliance. The concept made Elfloq squirm, but such human failings were not for him to comment upon.

"I had no particular plans for the day," said Zeleshti. "And in these matters one should strike while the iron is hot, if you take my meaning."

Elfloq thought better of responding, other than to nod again. He watched as the witch began gathering together the various paraphernalia such creatures like to carry about with them, although he was amazed at the sheer quantity of baggage involved. Umptus lived but a short distance away – the witch appeared to be collecting enough for a protracted interlude away.

"Forward!" she said at last, exiting the house, like an entire camel train on the move. Elfloq hopped along behind her. With any luck Ump would reward him with his freedom promptly. The sooner he quit Simrana, the better.

In a short while they had reached the humble domain of the little mage. Zeleshti, who seemed scarcely out of breath in spite of her immense burden, gazed down at the familiar. "You may announce me," she said in a voice that sent the entire animal and bird population of the area scattering to the four winds.

Elfloq duly rapped on the door, and a moment later it creaked open to reveal the nervous features of the mage. Elfloq bowed low. "Great and illustrious master, I bring you the incomparable Zeleshti, Mistress of the Million Magics, Queen of the Quintessentials, Empress of the Everlasting Excellences."

The witch stared at him for a long moment as if seeing him in a new light, her eyes brimming with an odd kind of hunger.

Elfloq suddenly wanted to slip under the nearest table and remain entirely anonymous. He wondered if he had gone too far in his commendation of the witch.

However, she turned her attention to Ump, barging into his

home, near filling it with her unique presence. "Umptus Underbung," she said. "Such a joy to visit you after all this time. I had no idea you were so eager to usher me into your presence. Your little potato man has told me everything. Your lusty secrets are secrets no more!"

Ump barely managed to drag his eyes away from the towering figure and her enormous collection of bags, trunks and sundry containers, all of which, by some miracle, she had carried across her broad back. Ump looked askance at Elfloq.

"The great sharing of magics you so desired," said the familiar. "She is only too willing to participate."

Zeleshti bent down and planted a wet and noisy kiss on the sweating brow of the little mage, whose jaw dropped open as those exorbitant lips withdrew. "Just let me freshen myself, my delicious bundle of loveliness." She squeezed through the room's clutter, nodding appreciatively at the various grimoires and bottled items of necromancy, disappearing somewhere beyond.

Ump was mouthing her words. "Delicious bundle of... by the Eighty Six Torments of Groggubang, what have you said to her? What promises have you made?"

"It wasn't easy," said Elfloq. "I had to call upon all my deep understanding of the human psyche, the mortal longings and lusts –"

"*Lusts!* What are you talking about?"

"I... er... I have used my magic to bring about this transformation," he lied glibly. "She is as moist clay in your hands. She worships you and desires nothing more than to share everything with you."

"No, no, no, I didn't mean *that!* It's her library I covet. You must undo this at once, before she returns." Ump looked behind him, his face a perfect mask of abject horror and dreadful anticipation.

"But my dear sir, you will have access to her library. You have no idea of the books it contains. Why, when I was in her abode, I saw a sample of them. She had the *Explicit Incantations for the Summoning of Gryphons.* Not to mention Vazzavandix's *Complete Curses* – all nine volumes. Then I saw *Raising the Pestilential Hordes of Zandible the Zombie God–*"

"Really?" said Ump, clearly amazed. "Zandible? Great Gods of the Shadow Regions!"

"Yes, and those, too. Everything you can imagine, and more besides. All yours to peruse, once you've… uh… allied yourself to the indescribable Zeleshti."

Umptus was now visibly torn. He wrung his gnarled hands and scratched his thinning mop of hair. "Well, yes, that's all very desirable, but… the cost."

"Which leaves one more act to perform on my behalf," said Elfloq. "If you could fulfil your part of the bargain and free me from bondage. I will return to the astral forthwith. Simrana will not see me again, I assure you."

Ump eyed him uncomfortably. "But, but… she will devour me, smother me in affection. You've gone too far! You must moderate this affliction upon her."

"Are you saying you will welch on our bargain?"

"Don't leave me alone with her!"

"A pact is a pact! Release me." Elfloq was also looking uneasily at the back of the room, fearing the imminent return of the witch. The prospect of attempting to undo her deep-seated, and to him, inexplicable, desire for the wizard was not one he relished. It would be easier, he surmised, to turn a tornado from its path.

Ump shook his head. Terror infused his every muscle. "But, but, if you should stay, perhaps *you* could distract her. Yes, yes, that would work!"

"Out of the question. If you do not free me," said Elfloq, in a last desperate bid to get the better of the mage, "I will be forced to reveal to the good lady my true identity. If she learns that you have summoned me, one who is expressly banned from Simrana by its Gods –"

"I didn't summon you!"

"You think she'll believe you? You think the *Gods* of Simrana will believe you?"

"You wouldn't dare reveal yourself to them! They'd fry you to a crisp!"

"And risk the wrath of my master? Can you imagine the repercussions if he discovered what had happened? He'd bend every sinew to enter Simrana. I wouldn't give much for its future if he did. He can squeeze a moon into dust on a good day." The former was a gross exaggeration, of course. Unknown to Ump, Elfloq's master had told Elfloq a hundred times that he did not want a familiar and certainly not one who kept deceiving innocent souls into summoning him, given the terrible cost of doing so. He would have been only too happy to have had Elfloq chained to Simrana where he could do least harm. The chances of Elfloq arranging for his master to be summoned to Simrana were very small, given the strong magic exercised by Simrana's Gods to keep him out.

Ump was on the point of gibbering.

"Look on the bright side, Ump. All those books. And as for the lovely Zeleshti, why, you might even begin to enjoy her... ministrations. You're only human."

Umptus sank down, chewing his fingernails. Two terrible fates closed in on him like sharks about to feed. Which had the nastier bite?

"Release me," said Elfloq. "Now!"

Ump jumped as if stung by a large hornet. It was all too much for him. The proximity of the lascivious Zeleshti tilted the wobbling scales of decision. Ump recited certain mystical lines, and as he finished the spell, the form of Elfloq dissolved, leaving a faint smell of burning in the air.

Zeleshti found the wizard sitting alone, shivering as if a sudden cold wind had found a way into the house.

"Oh, has your little servant gone?" she said, peering about the shadows.

"Yes," Ump squeaked. "I dismissed him. He... won't be coming back."

She giggled. It was possibly the most terrifying sound Ump had ever heard. "You mean – we're alone?" She put an entire dictionary of meaning into that one word.

He nodded, his mouth too dry to form further words of his own.

"You little rascal! So eager to begin our liaison. As for your servant, I shall miss him. Quite a character. If it weren't for you, heart of my heart, I would quite possibly have taken him for myself. He was such a sweet potato."

The Summoning Of A Genie
In Error

Adrian Cole

The Gods of Simrana invariably find the behavior of their human subjects laughable, especially when misguided mortals attempt to elevate themselves to higher planes of existence through the use of magic, sorcery and other pseudo-divine practices. Such human misadventures invariably lead to disaster or the unleashing of powers they can't control. Simrana's Gods administer retribution, but generally only after they have indulged themselves in hilarity and having set the world more or less to rights once more. As for the humans, well, they commonly enough express their amusement at the incompetence and embarrassment of others, and yet there are those who seem incapable of learning anything from the disastrous precedents of their fellows.

Take Vendibule Montresang. Wealthy, well-respected, enjoying an eminently comfortable lifestyle in the extremely efficacious atmosphere of the City of Sunlight and Clouds, Bellonimbus. His home was, like many others in the city, palatial, a dizzy complex of beautiful towers and minarets, sculpted in pink stone and set with dazzling mother-of-pearl slates and tiles. His wine cellar was never less than fully stocked with the finest vintages, his library brimming over with wondrous books from all ages, and every comfort lying on either side, room by room, floor by floor. Had the Gods visited him, they would have almost certainly approved and no doubt would have complemented Vendibule on his impeccable taste in all things.

Over the course of his lengthy and productively exciting life,

Vendibule had had several wives, numerous consorts and far too many liaisons to mention. Now, at the ripe old age of eighty eight, he had finally settled into monogamy. His partner, Mirimis Carpetula the Third (though no one seems to have any records of the former two versions) was as much as the octogenarian could handle in his dotage. In fact, apart from pandering to the volatile whims of his beloved Mirimis, Vendibule had for the most part withdrawn from the world, concentrating what little energies he retained on his monumental collection of snails. These he kept in a vivarium designed specifically for the creatures, a place of many huge plants, thick with luscious fronds, leaves and growing things beneath an immense glass dome.

Mirimis never visited the vivarium. She was not well disposed towards snails, nor indeed slugs or anything that slithered, crawled, crept or hopped. She concentrated her own collective instincts on inanimate, glittery things, and had several large chambers piled high with rubies, jewels and all manner of gold pieces from all across Simrana's vast reaches. She also had a predilection for exotic clothing and had several even larger chambers stuffed to the rafters with frocks and gowns and everything between, frequently spending an entire day changing and re-changing into such items.

By way of relaxation, Mirimis had a large collection of exotic alcoholic drinks and liquor, varying from every conceivable blend of spirits to rack after rack of fine wines from the remotest of corners of Simrana (and in some cases far beyond). It would have been unfair to label the fair Mirimis as anything other than an occasional imbiber, as she was, if not temperate, more than cautious about what she drank and in what quantity. It was on the whole enough for her to own these rare, bottled treasures. However, from time to time, she felt an irrational urge to sample one of her favorites, and nothing would turn her aside from her determination to do so, almost to the point where the craving became obsessive.

Sometimes she entered her own private cellar and selected a bottle herself. On other occasions she would send her devout servant, Anderpang, to fetch one. He was a lone soul, haunting the shadowed corridors of the vast Montresang residence, one ear permanently cocked, listening out for the commands of the lady of the house. Although he was stooped, gnarled and lacking in physical beauty (and of indeterminate age) he nevertheless doted on his mistress and was ever at hand to lay down his very soul for her should she desire it. To tread the same ground as she did, to dwell in the same residence, was everything to him.

Anderpang had developed an uncanny ability to become absorbed by the very walls of the palace, as though the stones themselves sucked him in. He would have rivaled any ghost or wandering spirit, often hidden away, close to his mistress, but unseen. In fact, Mirimis called him her 'little spectre,' much to his delight.

So it was that when Anderpang heard his mistress expressing her frustration and annoyance at not being able to find a particularly desirable bottle of sloe gin, he waited attentively to see if there was anything he could do to avert a potential emotional tragedy. He edged closer among the larger urns. Mirimis was stalking up and down, her face slightly flushed, her hands clenching and unclenching in an action that usually presaged an outburst of temper. Such things were to be avoided at all costs.

"This is intolerable!" she muttered. "I know I had at least one bottle left. Thieves! Someone has stolen it! How else could it be missing? My rational self tells me to dismiss the matter and select another bottle for my afternoon's relaxation. However, I refuse to be the victim of circumstance. I am in command here! My wishes are not to be mocked. Why, I'd be the laughing stock of Bellonimbus – nay, beyond our fair city! – should I ignore this matter and go wanting. True, I have the finest wines, excellent blended malts, spirits of unique excellence, but what I desire above all else is a large gin!"

Mallumunce the Merchant stared fretfully out of the dirty windows of his cramped shop, a grubby little edifice squashed in between two much larger buildings, which were both brighter and better visited than his own. The days of thriving business were long gone, he knew. Once he had been the man to go to for most things, particularly the rarities, the magical and mystical. Now everyone was a wizard or a witch, or possessed of enough sorcery and dark arts to get by without the provisions of Mallumunce's trove. In fact, things had reached such a pitch that the old man was seriously thinking of selling the shop – hah! chance would be a fine thing – and retiring.

Movement in the street outside snared the attention of the Merchant. Oh-ho! Could this be a customer? The little figure that peered in through the grime did seem interested. Quick as a flash – remarkably so for one of his age – Mallumunce opened his door, poked his head out and favored the creature at the window with a smile that would have melted a ruby.

"Do come in!" he cawed. "I have things inside to tempt an emperor. Come, come."

Anderpang, for it was indeed he, looked around him cautiously, as though expecting himself to be the subject of scrutiny by at least a score of interested citizens. Seeing that he was not and that the street was populated by no more than a jackdaw and a mangy cat half-heartedly stalking it from an alleyway, he sidled up to Mallumunce and allowed himself to be ushered into the dark grotto of the shop. Its door closed like a sprung trap.

"Well, well, and what can I find for you, little master?" said the unctuous Merchant.

"I am here on behalf of my mistress. I cannot name her, you understand, but she is of high repute, the wife of one of the city's most notable retired traders, probably the most eminent."

"I see, I see. You must be referring to his eminence, Constantinovulos Constantinovulans. Who else?"

"Higher. My lips are sealed."

Mallumunce squawked with surprise. He was practically dealing with the Royal House. "Indeed, indeed. Then I am sure I can provide you with whatever you require. Permit me to suggest a few items that might be ideal for your purposes. I have recently acquired a miniature set of onyx unicorns, each of which will perform a musical dance when placed under a full moon."

"Wonderful, I'm sure," said Anderpang. "Though not for me. My mistress is unmoved by such things."

"Quite, quite. Then how about the unique Splendid Songbird of the Shimmering South? Its feathers are said to exude a rare perfume which, combined with the song, breathes awesome vim and vigor into a listless romance."

"I don't think my mistress wishes to enflame the fading embers of her husband's libido. The shock would probably kill him."

"No, no, that won't do. Perhaps you have something in mind?"

"I do. My mistress desires a strong gin."

Mallumunce screwed up his face. Whether this was in puzzlement, amusement or pain, Anderpang could not say. "Interesting. Interesting. Nevertheless, I can accommodate."

"This would need to be the most puissant example you have. I will not be fobbed off with inferior stock. Try that trick, Merchant, and retribution will be swift and particularly horrible. I'm sorry to be so blunt, but you need to understand the situation."

"Yes, yes. Your mistress expects nothing but the best. A woman of quality, at the pinnacle of the social order."

"Absolutely."

"If you'd like to wait a while, I will peruse my best stocks. I am certain I have the very thing, though of course it is not something I have on display. I ought to say, men have killed for it. Battles have been fought. Kings have fallen."

"Spare me the sales pitch," said Anderpang. "Just get it."

Mallumunce bowed low and retreated into the depths of the shop's rear. Once out of sight he straightened up, though by no more than a few inches. *What has it come to?* he asked himself. Even the humble manservants showed him a lack of respect these days. How rude the little creature had been! And threatening. Preposterous. Ah, well, business was business. There could be a sale here.

Suddenly his eyes lit up. Why, of course, *of course!* The perfect solution, not only to the fulfillment of the little man's needs, but his own as well. *That* bottle! He'd wanted to dispose of it for an age, an age. Now, where was it?

He spent a while ferreting among the rows and rows of dusty bottles of every shape, size and colour, until at last he revealed the one he sought. It was a curious shape, the glass a mottled lizard-green, with a bizarre twist to its neck, and had a thick cork rammed home tight, as if whoever had sealed it intended no one to savor the dubious delights of whatever shifted about within it. The Merchant lifted it from the shelf and handled it as though it would explode at the lightest of touches, the sweat breaking out on his brow as he carried it with extreme caution back to the shop.

Mallumunce recalled all too vividly the circumstances leading to his acquisition of the bottle. Originally it was said to have belonged to one of the higher demiurges of Simrana, a being whose servants scoured the world's darkest, dirtiest places for secrets, power and sorcery to impart to their ambitious overlord, for he desired nothing less than godhood. It transpired that some of the powers he had gathered were too dangerous even for him, and he had been at pains to dispose of them before they could be released, with potentially hellish consequences.

The bottle that Mallumunce now held so delicately was one such object of power. Had anyone known how to destroy it or send it out into the fathomless voids between the remote stars, it would have been dispatched hastily. As it was, the only solution thus far posed was that of burying it in the endless clutter of the Merchant's shop. He had thought to sell it on for a handsome profit, but in the event, no one had been brave – or gullible – enough to take it off his hands. Its reputation, clearly, had gone before it.

As Mallumunce set the bottle down on the shop counter, Anderpang squinted at it. The light in here was poorly filtered and the bottle's contents were hard to define.

"I think you'll find nothing stronger in all of Simrana," said the Merchant.

"You've sampled it?"

"Gods of the Great Deeps Beyond, not I! I suffer from the poorest of health. These days it is all my crumbling form can do to sample anything of even slight power. However, this bottle was once possessed by His Uniqueness the Brazen Champion of Jakarumba, of whose exploits you have no doubt heard. He never conducted a single blistering campaign without recourse to this bottle."

"In which case," said Anderpang, his skepticism giving an edge to his words, "why did he part with it?"

"Why? Why? Well, he. . .retired. Yes, yes. That was it. He swore to purge the Sullen Southlands of all demons and of course, he did just that. Now he sits in private glory somewhere down there in his Sultry Palace of Excellent Pleasures. He no longer had any need for the bottle and its powers."

Anderpang had heard not a word of the wondrous southern conqueror, but history was littered with such beings, many of whom were exaggerations, enhanced for the benefit of a good tale, or in this case, a good sale. "If I purchase this bottle," he said, "my mistress will expect satisfaction. I have already touched on her expectations."

"You have, you have. She will not be disappointed. In fact, I'd go as far as to say, she will be gratified far beyond her highest wishes."

"So what do you want for the bottle?"

Mallumunce had not been a successful Merchant without being a master of guile, deceit and a skill at bargaining second to none, even in this twilight of his career. He named a ridiculously exorbitant price.

"That's a ridiculously exorbitant price," said Anderpang. He named a ridiculously modest price.

"That's. . . that's a ridiculously modest price," countered Mallumunce.

And so they haggled. The truth was that Mallumunce would happily have given his customer the cursed bottle for a song, but he knew to have done so would have sparked the little man's suspicion. For a while the two thrust and parried like swordsmen looking for an opening, until at long last, seemingly beaten back by the determination of the buyer, Mallumunce held up his hands in abject surrender. "My, my. Sir, you drive the hardest of bargains. I am too old for this type of campaign. Besides, I need something to keep me going. I agree your price, although you are little better than a thief."

Anderpang allowed himself a private smile. He would have paid more, had the Merchant fought on. Anderpang handed over a small purse, with a handful of golden coins counted out to fill it.

"Take the bottle," said Mallumunce. "However, you must carry it very carefully. It is volatile. Do you understand? If you rush to your mistress, you may break the seal prematurely. That would be a disas. . . a great loss."

"Thank you." Anderpang produced a voluminous silk scarf and proceeded to wrap the bottle gingerly. Mallumunce stood back, watching nonchalantly, or as nonchalantly as he could appear. His heart was racing, seeing the bottle about to quit his life at last. He mouthed a few polite goodbyes and closed the door behind his customer. Once alone again in the shop, he danced a jig and made for the section of his cellar where he kept his best wine. This sale called for a celebration. And he had money to boot. Excellent, excellent.

Anderpang was well used to stealthy movement, slippery as an eel, light as a butterfly, silent as dust. It was not difficult for him, therefore, to slip back to his mistress's palace, slide within and hide beyond the eyes of the other numerous occupants without mishap. His prize, still trebly wrapped in the silk scarf, he hid away in a forgotten cupboard, to which he alone possessed the key.

Later that evening he found his mistress sitting amid a heaped pile of cushions, silks and blankets, gazing at one of the tinkling fountains as if the jewels of its dancing waters fascinated her. Anderpang knew his mistress's moods too well. He sensed her deep frustration, her coiled fury. Usually this brooding silence ended with one or more items of value, such as a tall urn, or an ornate tea-set, being broken and scattered around the extremities of the chamber.

"Anderpang!" Mirimis called. "Come forward and stop skulking around like a ghoul in a graveyard."

"My apologies, mistress. I sought only to be discreet."

"Yes, well, you get on my nerves when you do that. It may not have occurred to you, but today I am in a very bad mood."

"I am devastated to hear that, mistress. Is there anything a lowly servant such as my humble self can do to alleviate this appalling condition?"

"I doubt if even your talents could bring me respite, my little spectre. I seem to have run out of a particular blend of sloe gin. I could have sworn that I had at least one bottle left. It seems not. This is a catastrophe of the first water. Oh – did I just make a pun? No, you see, even my wit doesn't lift my spirits. Oh, there I go again. How droll of me!"

Anderpang slowly inched the recently purchased bottle from behind him, still wrapped in its scarf.

Mirimis watched it, mesmerized. "What are you hiding, Anderpang? A scarf? Goblins of the Excrescent Mire, why should I be interested in a *scarf*? I have a thousand of them."

"Forgive my impertinence, but I overheard you speaking earlier today, mistress. I believe you expressed a desire for a strong gin."

Mirimis sat up, her attention fully snagged, like a huge fish on a sharp hook. She wriggled among the cushions. "Yes, I did so. A strong gin. Nothing but the absolute best."

Anderpang undid the scarf, and not without a delayed sense of the dramatic. Ultimately the dusty bottle from the shop of Mallumunce the Merchant was revealed. It did not, Anderpang realized, have the look of anything splendid. Indeed, it would easily have passed for something wrapped in a spider's cocoon and suspended in a large web.

Mirimis was, however, fascinated. She stood and approached. "What is that disgusting thing?"

Anderpang held it out to her, careful not to brush any of the dust from it. "It is, mistress, a strong gin. I have it on the best authority that there is none stronger."

"You shouldn't have!" she said, clapping her hands. Meaning, of course, that he absolutely should have.

He proffered it. She hesitated. Yet only for a moment. Then she took it and peered at the deep green glass. She could see something stirring within. She rubbed at the dust, wiping it away to see even more clearly. A little cloud of motes rose up and swirled around the neck of the bottle.

Anderpang stood back, barely masking his delight at seeing the joy on his mistress's face.

Mirimis took the fat cork and twisted it. Again dust eddied. It had an interesting effect, acting like oil on metal parts, for the cork eased loose. In a moment, Mirimis had pulled it free, with a little pop! She tossed it aside, sniffing the contents of the bottle.

"An unusual tang," she said, but undeterred, lifted the bottle to her lips and gently leaned back.

Anderpang's expression froze. He could see the contents of the bottle more clearly. They appeared to be more smoky than liquid. His mistress's expression had changed from one of mild curiosity to one of slight concern. This transformed further, into alarm, as Mirimis realized she could not pull the bottle's mouth from her own. She appeared to be locked in the grotesque parody of a kiss. Something inside the bottle – a dark, writhing gas – was escaping, moving into Mirimis.

Anderpang would have stepped in to interfere, but his limbs had frozen. Mirimis was likewise incapable of resistance. Slowly but inexorably the entire contents of the bottle passed between her lips, teeth, over her tongue, down into her throat – and beyond. As they did so, her already generous body expanded.

Anderpang staggered back as the shape became monstrous, looking him over. The bottle fell from the bloated grasp of his mistress and rolled, empty, across the flagstones. A terrible groan, like the sound of oncoming thunder, rolled from lips that had become the length and thickness of two immense pythons.

In his shop, Mallumunce the Merchant heard the sudden boom of sound high in the upper palaces of the city. It was a frightening roar, to be sure, although of laughter rather than anger. Of course, he knew what it was. Mind you, it was not quite as he might have imagined it. Even at this distance from the palace, there was no mistaking the tone of the laughter. Unexpectedly, it was that of a woman.

"The bottle, the bottle!" he cried. "Already it is open. Well, well, the lady is now possessed of what she desired. She did state categorically that she wanted a strong djinn."

The Sad but Instructive Fable of Mangroth's Tomes

Charles Garofalo

In Simrana, as in every land where wizards lay pen or brush to paper, there are books of magic whose contents or misuse have earned them ill and fearful reputations. Some speak in frightened whispers of the witch Agrina's book *Names of Night*, the tome bound in the skin of her own stillborn child, which contains not only the spells for summoning numerous demons, dark fairies, and other baneful spirits, but the recipes for several lethal poisons all people with enemies fear. Others point shaking fingers (from a safe distance, of course) at the volume by the mad wizard Drezelak, which he never named, but others call *The Gold Book*, due to its rich golden covers inset with many gems. It was with this awful libram that Drezelak raised the horrific storms and ruined and conquered five kingdoms, ruling as the worst tyrant in the history of that part of Simrana until he lost control of a hurricane he'd called up and brought his own palace crashing down about him. And, to be accurate, on top of him. Unfortunately, his book survived.

But the worst of all dangerous books of spells could well be two copies of Burkram's *Easy Spells for the Beginner*.

You may ask, how Burkram's well-known book famed for its harmlessness came to be included with such baneful texts as *The Gold Book?* More magicians than not learned their first cantrips from *Easy Spells for the Beginner;* most still have it in their library. The volume is famous for the simplicity of the spells contained within, and the innocuity of their results. Difficult spells to miscast, but if they should be miscast the result is always a dismal failure rather than a disastrous consequence. Also, the spells are not of the sort that a disgruntled apprentice could use against his teacher, fellow apprentice or shopkeeper who short-changed him. Hardly the sort of books you could call up a dark spirit or set off an earthquake with.

But these two copies of the book were the last copies made by Mangroth, the wizard-scribe.

Deri Mangroth began his career as a wizard in the city of Zardia in the kingdom of Corivor, one of the very nations Drezekak had taken over many centuries before. Although many people who tell the tale represent him as a blunderer who couldn't cast a spell without creating a disaster, research shows he was actually a competent wizard who had mastered many effective spells, such as that cantrip that kept food from spoiling, and how to enchant scarecrows so that they frightened off not only crows and other birds, but also rabbits and hungry insects. The problem was, they were the same effective spells every other wizard had mastered, so Mangroth was hard put to make a living off his magic. Everywhere he turned there was already a wizard or witch with an established reputation offering the same spells for sale he was offering.

Not wanting to end up living in a barrel, the way certain philosophers were rumored to have done, but unwilling to abandon the seven years of study that had earned him his degree in magery, Mangroth thought long and hard on the matter. And he came up with an idea how he could earn a living for himself and still remain in the field of magic. When he'd been an apprentice, Mangroth had paid for his magic lessons by working part time as a scribe, copying other people's letters and manuscripts for them. As might be guessed, a successful scribe must have legible, even beautiful penmanship, and a mastery of spelling and grammar. To make a mistake in the wrong letter could cause a feud, if not a war, and incompetent scribes have been – possibly unfairly – blamed for such unpleasantness in the past.

Mangroth was not only an excellent scribe, and quick at the job, but he had a command and understanding of magic. Therefore it seemed logical to him that he might offer his services to other magicians, copying their magical tomes.

Mangroth soon discovered his idea had been the correct one. Copying down magical workbooks, either to trade with other wizards or to instruct classes of apprentices with, or simply to have a spare book of spells in case of accident, was a long, exacting task for most wizards. No mistakes could be made, or the end results of the spells cast could be wildly at variance with the expected results. To have the tome copied for you, by someone with the skill and attention to detail of a good scribe and the experience and understanding of magic a wizard had, was a service many wizards would happily pay for. To encourage the more suspicious of his colleges who feared he might steal the books or at least copy spells for himself which they preferred to keep for their own, Mangroth would voluntarily cast a geas spell – a magical compulsion – on himself keeping him from doing just that. It quickly got around that Mangroth was the man to see if you wanted a magical volume copied, a wizard you could trust and a fellow you could depend on for quick and excellent service. He did not become rich, but he prospered and became quite comfortable, owning a cottage with roof-tiles of real slate instead of the more usual *floffia* wood, commissioning a tame elemental from another mage to do the cleaning and maintenance, and dining once a week at *Lucides*, a local restaurant famous for its excellent queen crab and Zardian dwarf chicken dishes.

There is no evidence that Mangroth became inflated with pride over his not-insignificant accomplishments. However, even more often than pride, success goes before a fall. The success in this case was a contract with the Zardian Academy of Magery and Allied Arts to make them no less than seven copies of the famous grimoire: *Easy Spells for the Beginner*, by Thaurence Burkram. It was quite a profitable order, and could easily, if filled to satisfaction, gain Mangroth profitable connections to the more influential magicians in the city. I here must digress to explain that the Zardian Academy was not one of those huge, castle-sized wizard schools situated far away from civilization in a secluded valley, with hundreds of pupils and dozens of teachers. No, it was a medium sized red-brick building just a couple of blocks south of the merchant's quarter, which housed at any time four or five wizards and three dozen students or so. However, Mangroth must have enjoyed the fact that it was his *alma mater*, and he could show the teachers who'd all promised he'd make a success of himself if only he'd take the various courses they'd recommended that he'd made good. Of course, taking the courses and spells they'd recommended had been the reason Mangroth had failed in his initial efforts at distinguishing himself as a wizard, since everybody had taken the same instruction, but he was willing to overlook that.

What he shouldn't have overlooked was the fact that, since he'd graduated, the Academy had fallen under the management of one Contuminieas Blout.

Just as the Zardian Academy may not match the reader's mental picture of a wizard's school, Contuminieas Blout fails to resemble the general conception of an evil wizard. Nearly every bad wizard in history and in fiction works his evil through his misuse of his spells and magical knowledge. Blout had never been able to master any spells (for, and perhaps it's a good thing, no magician has ever been able to master every spell) that were not of the most benign or harmless nature. However, he had mastered the art of abusing his power as a businessman, and later as the head of a wizard's school, to squeeze the last penny out of any victims unfortunate enough to cross his path. He leveled unjust fines on numerous students, which they had to pay to graduate. He billed the parents of his students for services that had never been offered, let alone provided. And he always had one excuse or another for holding back some of the wizardly instructors' salaries. All in all, he gave credence to one detractor's (from Thessalopia, where they believe in reincarnation) hypothesis that in his past life Blout must have been a pickpocket. Probably a very successful one who had never gotten caught.

Having seven copies of a very popular magical book at his disposal was more than Blout could resist. On the very day they were delivered to the school, he purloined two copies and sold them to other wizards at a handsome profit. What he'd figured was he could say he was storing the additional two copies against the accidental loss or destruction of the others. He also sold (at a lower rate) the several old battered copies of Burkram's grimoire that the school had in stock.

What Blout had not expected was that eight more potential apprentices than usual would pass the entrance exams that time around. Five copies, no matter how carefully parceled out and shared, would not be enough to serve the (for the Zardian Academy) throng of students he now had coming his way.

Blout remembered the wise old maxim many people resorted to in situations similar to his: "when in trouble, pounce upon the nearest scapegoat quickly." He quickly composed an angry and threatening letter to Deri Mangroth, accusing him of shorting the college and only delivering five copies of Burkram's *Spells*, while collecting the payment for seven. Unless he delivered the remaining two volumes within four days, there would be terrible repercussions, both legal and magical, for him (not to mention a terrible stain on his heretofore spotless reputation). To ensure he made his point, he had one of his subordinate witches magically summon not a pigeon to deliver the message as is usually the case, but the biggest, most ferocious-looking bat she could manage. He wanted to make sure Mangroth took his threats seriously.

Which Mangroth did. The poor wizard-scribe, fearing the dire consequences threatened, undertook the nigh-impossible task of making two copies of Burkram's work in four days (his offer of substituting his own used copy of *Easy Spells* for one of the missing books had been angrily refused). He knew he had produced seven copies, but had no idea how to prove the other two had been stolen or mislaid once they reached the Academy. So rather than face an unjust punishment, he could not think of anything to do but undertake the task.

The task was made even harder by the fact that, after a few days taking care of other tasks, Mangroth had celebrated his successful completion of them with a visit to *Lucides*, where he'd consumed far more than his usual share of good white wine. His hangover was not a major one, as Mangroth had not drunk that much of the wine, but it seemed like an unbearable headache to the wizard, who didn't overindulge too often. Blout's threats did not improve his condition, and by the time the wine had worn off, Mangroth's own frayed nerves no doubt kept the headache going at full speed.

So we have a scribe, bleary from too much drink, with a bad headache, copying two manuscripts in a period of time far too short for the assignment. That he skipped eating and sleeping to get the job finished in time could not have improved his concentration.

Do not forget that any change in a spell's wording can change the spell's effect, turning a potent spell into a worthless jumble of magic words, or a safe cantrip into a bad accident just waiting to happen.

Nobody who was at the Zardian Academy when the books were passed around would soon forget that warning.

The first apprentice to have trouble with one of Mangroth's two flawed books, one Plisicus, got off very lightly. He merely attempted to freeze water into ice, and tried more than a dozen times before one of his masters came up to see what the problem was and discovered that the spell was flawed. It was put down to a one-of-a-kind-mistake and no more was thought of it, especially since Plisicus did finally make the bucket of ice the cook wanted.

Other instances were not quite so minor. Remi Adronicos was attempting the popular wizard's trick of making a pebble temporarily soft and flexible so he could mold it like clay. Nearly every magician uses that one to make figurines, paperweights, and if they get ahold of semi-precious stones, cabochon gems. Instead of becoming clay-like, Remi's piece of quartz melted completely and ran down his hand. Mercifully, the liquid stone was not hot, as the liquid stone from volcanoes is, but it hardened suddenly. Remi had to get his hand chipped loose before he could use it again.

An aspiring necromancer named Tarphon experienced even more serious problems when he tried to use the cruel but useful spell of transforming the brains of frogs and toads into small gems, a common source of pocket money among the magical folk. But instead of the toad he caught becoming a dead toad with a gem in its head, the amphibian changed into a very large, and still-living, snapping turtle. The turtle promptly grabbed Tarphon's ankle in his mouth, and it took the efforts of several other students to persuade the angry animal to let go. Tarphon limped for the rest of his life, although from that day forward he was unfailingly kind to animals.

A female student, Circadia, decided to test to see if the spell was flawed or if Tarphon had just made a mistake somewhere. She twice tried the spell from the same book to metamorphize frog's brains, though under far more controlled circumstances than Tarphon had. It was fortunate that she'd put in the controls. Her first test-subject transformed into a ferocious fanged frog from the Nerian jungles, as large as a squirrel. The second turned into a fearsome water cobra.

It's unknown who attempted the famous spell of planting a seed and making it instantly grow into a small short-lived tree laden with fruit, a popular trick for street performers and a handy source of food and wood. The result had been a nice tree laden with the tempting white apples of Corivor. However, a change had been made in the apples' chemistry, so that everybody who ate one became intoxicated. Half the students and all the teachers at the Academy were reduced to a less than respectable condition. Expulsions and dismissals were only narrowly avoided, due to Blout's subsequent disappearance, and his successor's willingness to forget the whole business.

What couldn't be forgotten was one student's attempts to turn spider webs into wearable silk. Fortunately for all concerned, an attentive wizard recognized the process that was underway and got the students and other wizards to safety before the explosion occurred. Perhaps unfortunately, the perpetrator of that disaster fled, unconsciously still holding *Easy Spells*, so that the dangerous book was not destroyed along with three rooms and part of the hallway.

The cause of all the problems was quickly discovered. Mangroth's last two transcriptions of *Easy Spells for the Beginner* were flawed, so seriously flawed it was amazing that Burkram didn't turn in his grave (a stunt which he actually could have performed). At first, all fingers were pointed at Mangroth for his incompetence and carelessness. However, one of Blout's customers, bothered by conscience, came forward and confessed he had bought a copy of Burkram's book from Blout, blithely unaware that it was not the wizard's to sell, and soon the dishonest mage's part in the disaster was revealed.

Mangroth, fearful of reprisals, fled Corivor and spent the rest of his life hiding behind an assumed name and a long beard in the distant Longian Islands, where he did a thriving business enchanting scarecrows so they actually did scare birds and other pests away. He was notable for being a strict teetotaler and for his unwillingness to put anything in writing.

The fate of Blout is less verifiable. It's true he fled Zardia a little after Mangroth, having been removed from his seat at the Academy.

I can neither confirm nor deny the rumor that one of his enemies caught up with Blout, turned him into a Zardian dwarf chicken, and left him outside a den of foxes.

After some eventful testing, both of Mangroth's too-original takes on Burkram's book are now under heavy guard, lock and key, but their influence is still being felt in Simrana today. A cabal of wicked sorcerers ceased to trouble the world after they tried too successfully to replicate Mangroth's exploding silk spell. Some of the other flawed spells were copied down in their entirety before the books were locked away.

Circadia is now the Dark Witch of the Great Gloom, and is notorious for transforming harmless frogs into dangerous animals. Several towns and cities have instituted laws forbidding the sale or consumption of intoxicating fruit.

Remi Andronicos, on the other hand, now runs a thriving business in Corivor. He makes the rocks melt and pours them into simple molds, where they harden into paperweights, bookends, and similar knick-knacks. Although now a venerable magician, he still visits the shrine of his family's patron goddess at least twice a week and thanks her for letting him not choose the other spell he'd been interested in from Mangroth's book. It seems he knew where a honey-tree was, and the spell was supposed to make the bees ignore him while he took the honey. Considering how the other spells in the book had worked, one can understand his gratitude. The bees would probably have eaten him.

How Frindolf Got His Fill of Revenge

Charles Garofalo

Many stories have been told about folks who tried to bring loved ones back from the dead and merely brought more sorrow on themselves. Yet the tales of those who disturb the dead for less forgivable reasons than love – for wealth, to learn their secrets, or even for hatred – are just as unhappy and far less known. They should be better known, say certain wise folk of Simrana. The tale of Frindolf and what came of the feud he would not let die with the youth Vulg is one such, which some say should be required reading at every school of magic.

Not long ago in the port city of Mordenhem, Frindolf was born a scion of one of their wealthy merchant families. Although not over-indulged by his parents, Frindolf could not help but have an enviable youth growing up amidst the comforts and security of a very rich home. Frindolf never had to go hungry, needless to say, or worry whether something might cost too much, or lack for the best of education. He could look forward to being a respected man in the community and to wearing the bright golden-dyed linsey-woolsey, which only those wealthy enough to afford it might wear in Mordenhem.

Sadly, shortly after young Frindolf had achieved his maturity, his father lost most of the family fortune in some unfortunate investments. The man soon died after these reversals, and Frindolf's mother passed shortly after him. This left Frindolf in uncomfortable circumstances. By most people's standards he was still well off, but compared to where he'd been, he was in desperate straits. He now had to worry about how much his food cost, and had to think twice before purchasing some of the rich delicacies that formerly had graced the family table on a regular basis. He could no longer plan a big, lavish party to celebrate some minor occasion as his parents often had. His clothes, his furniture, now had to be carefully made to last. And instead of the eleven servants that had waited on his family, he now had to make do with merely a cook, a housekeeper, and an unfortunate lad who did odd jobs.

All Frindolf's efforts to reverse his fortunes came to worse than naught. With each attempt more of the family fortune dwindled away. He sold the summer house outside the city to buy shares in a business that had looked very promising. It was burned down by an overzealous competitor. He sold most of his mother's jewelry (and his father's: he liked looking rich, too) to buy a cargo for a merchant ship that had never failed to make a profit. This voyage out they sunk during a hurricane sent by the gods to punish a city they had intended to pass by. It got so Frindolf could have made a handsome profit taking pay *not* to invest in people's enterprises, but he never thought of that.

He tried getting into a trade. He was too old to learn one. He already had the education to become a bookkeeper or a scribe, but the pay was too meager to suit him. Frindolf finally enrolled in a less reputable wizard's academy, since they were not too particular about the age of their students. Even an untalented wizard could generally earn himself a decent living, and Frindolf thought he could rent out his huge city-house as a meeting hall for wizards. After more than a year of passing grades, good performance, and even blameless behavior, Frindolf got expelled on the word of a seeress (admittedly one with a good track record of accurate predictions) who foresaw he'd become an evil necromancer who'd disturb the rest of the dead, something even witches and wizards shrank back from in fear.

Those plans dashed, he began to look around for wealthy families he could marry into. He found neither the eligible young brides nor their parents were interested in him, not even shabby genteel people like himself. There was a reason for this. As each scheme to improve his fortune fell flat, Frindolf had become more angry, more bitter, and more hostile to the world in general and to those around him in particular. His savage temper had become legendary throughout Mordenhem. Had he been wealthier, there might have been families inclined to push their daughters at him, foul disposition or no, but, as it was, parents who knew him always weighed their daughters' safety against the benefits of having him as a son-in-law.

Besides, Frindolf had taken to drinking heavily after the wizard school debacle. This improved neither his finances nor his temper, and, like many irascible people, Frindolf always retained a cold-blooded assessment of which people he could (and could not) insult or strike, should his frequent intoxication so incline him. It was always humble tradesmen or his distant and poorer cousins who received the brunt of his abuse and violence, never some high-placed personage who could have him brought before Mordenhem's judges, much less some violent barbarian who might take after him with an axe. His servants, as is often the case, became his favorite targets. To his cook, maid, and the others he was the sternest of judges, and an overseer requiring prompt service and unquestioning loyalty from everyone working for him. The errand boy, Vulg, was the main sufferer from his master's disposition, since he could not leave. Early on, Frindolf had made him sign a contract of indenture, something he could not force on the other, older servants. The cook and housekeeper could, at least, flee Frindolf's house if he became too much for them, but Vulg could have been cast into prison for leaving before the six years were up. Considering how Frindolf treated Vulg, prison might've been the better situation.

And considering how Frindolf regarded Vulg, one would've thought he'd be happy to get rid of the ill-favored and dull-faced youth. Somehow Vulg was responsible for every social misstep, every bad business decision, his master made. Vulg could never do the simplest chore, even if he followed Frindolf's instructions to the letter. Vulg had the worst timing in the world, bursting in on his master when the man was drunk and in a mean disposition, simply because Frindolf had called his name. Vulg became all too familiar with his master's cane and belt, and the back of his hand, and, when Frindolf was drunk enough, his attacks with the handiest object available. Only the constant reminders from his master of the fate of indentured servants who deserted their masters kept Vulg in the struggling merchant's house. It will scarcely surprise you to learn that Frindolf finally did fulfill his oft-repeated threat to kill the "useless, disrespectful" Vulg. Already well in his cups following a disappointing dinner of crab stew, a sea cabbage salad, and fresh bread and butter, accompanied by a fiery white wine from the midlands, Frindolf suddenly developed a desire for mead... which was not in his stock of wines, beers and spirits. In fact, mead is usually available in Mordenhem only during the summer and autumn festivals, neither of which were currently being celebrated. However, nothing would do for Frindolf but to summon Vulg and send him out for some of the beverage, with the promise of terrible consequences should he fail to procure it.

Vulg hurried away, running from wine-merchant to inn to what few grocers were still open that time of night. Five times he was turned away empty handed, for while Frindolf had given him money to buy the mead, none of the merchants had any mead to sell him. On the sixth try, Vulg found a merchant who did have some old mead that was close to turning. He paid the man's higher-than-reasonable price for it to have something to bring his irascible master.

Of course, Frindolf's usual hot temper had heated to absolute vileness while waiting for his desired tipple. Nor was it cooled when Vulg returned with inferior product, and less coins in change than the hard-pressed businessman expected. "I send you out for mead and you bring me this sour piss that a confirmed drunkard wouldn't touch!" he roared at the unfortunate Vulg. "And you try to cheat me by holding back some of my change!"

"Please, sir," the boy begged. "I counted the change carefully and made sure it was correct. And that's the only mead I could find...."

The rest of his argument turned to screams as Frindolf grabbed a heavy stick and began beating the unfortunate boy with it. Howling, Vulg turned and ran into the street, only for Frindolf to follow him out and catch him before he could make his getaway.

Frindolf swung the cane for a long time, and with all his strength. Before he was finished Vulg had stopped begging and crying... not to mention moving and breathing.

Frindolf returned to his mansion, thinking that was the end of it. Of course, he still expected Vulg to get up and follow him, whimpering and sniveling as he had after past chastisements, into the house. He was quite put out the next day to wake up and find he no longer had an errand boy.

He was more put out when the law took a hand. Frindolf did not expect to have to answer for Vulg's death, of course. The lad *was* just a bond-servant, and he *had* been trying to run away. Surely they did not expect surly old Frindolf to answer for behavior so eminently justifiable.

Unfortunately for him, the justices of Mordenhem were not without worldly wisdom, and they knew where allowing a master to wantonly kill a servant could lead. Other cruel or foul-tempered people would hear of it and think it all right to slay a bond-servant when the whim took them. Other indentured servants with real or imagined grievances against their owners would take fright and run away to avoid a fate similar to Vulg's. And then who would see to the needs of the nobility? A crime indeed! Better to make an example of Frindolf to avoid future trouble.

They could not execute Frindolf for killing a servant, or even imprison him, but they could fine him. The fine for slaying somebody in the streets was far from small. Nor was the blood price they ordered him to pay Vulg's still-living parents, and made sure he did so. Frindolf saw much of his dwindling funds go into the grasping hands of bailiffs and those worthless slum-dwellers who had brought the less-than-worthless Vulg into the world. Nor was that his only loss. Vulg's fate had frightened his other servants, who, not being indentured, were allowed to leave – and quickly did so. Nor were any willing to apply for the jobs and replace them, save for a few desperate and totally unsuitable paupers Frindolf angrily sent from his door. Frindolf found he now had to clean his own house, make his own bed, and cook his own meals, despite the fact that he could still afford a couple servants if he were careful with his funds. Nor did Frindolf appreciate the fact that he was now shunned by the circles he had been used to traveling in. Few wanted to share the unsuccessful merchant's disgrace, and even fewer wanted to be around Frindolf when he lost his temper again.

A wiser man than Frindolf might have reviewed his past deeds at this point, might have realized that he'd caused much of his own troubles, and perhaps attempted repentance and reformation. A more practical man than Frindolf might've realized he'd sunk his own ship in Mordenhem, sold his house and whatever he couldn't carry with him, and started somewhere else afresh. But Frindolf being Frindolf, he fumed against Vulg, and continued to blame him for every ill circumstance in his life. Vulg had done it all to him, bringing him bad mead, trying to short-change him, and tricking his poor, undeserving master into killing him just so Frindolf would suffer.

The more Frindolf thought about it, the more he became convinced Vulg, and Vulg alone, had brought him to this sorry state. Finally it became clear to him that Vulg, despite being dead, had not been adequately punished for his sins and the betrayal of his blameless and benevolent master.

But how to punish the dead? Many priests had many theories, but nobody knew for certain where the spirit went after death, except when the spirit didn't go anywhere and haunted the place of its death, which got everybody nervous. If Frindolf could have been sure that Vulg had gone to some place where they punish disloyal, dishonest servants, he could've been contented. The wretched boy dancing on hot coals or pushing a stone of back-breaking weight uphill for eternity would have partially contented the brooding, vindictive merchant. But he dreaded that perhaps the judges in the afterlife might be as imprudent as the ones in this world, showing the brat undeserved mercy. The thought of Vulg sleeping peacefully for eternity or even enjoying the benefits of some paradise was more than Frindolf could bear. Suddenly Frindolf remembered his year's training in the arts of magic, and how he'd been cast out despite the great progress he was making, all because of the mumbled prophecies of that old idiot who called herself a seer. Hadn't he shown potential back then, and hadn't she predicted he'd become a wicked necromancer that would disturb the dead? At the time, he'd thought her just a crazy old woman. Now, however, Frindolf had a dead person he desperately wanted to disturb.

Frindolf ransacked his attic and soon discovered the textbooks from his wizarding days. It did not take him long to relearn what he'd forgotten over the intervening years. Caution was sadly lacking in his nature, and now his righteous wrath drove him on.

Of course his school books held nothing of the kind he sought; none such would be vouchsafed to mere apprentices. Once up to speed again, Frindolf managed to obtain, through devious means, and at a price one dislikes to contemplate, several more powerful, darker books of magic. After he found the correct spells for reviving a corpse, some more money changed hands. A roustabout desperate for wine money unearthed a coffin in the graveyard one night and salvaged the grisly contents (for Vulg's body had lain in the grave nearly three years at that point), depositing them in a rough cloth sack upon Frindolf's doorstep late one night. Clouds covered the moon and stars over Mordenhem, and a cold, chill wind blew through the city. These are the nights where black magic is worked, mainly because the bad weather discourages potential witness from being abroad.

In his basement, far away from his collection of rare wines, Frindolf prepared the dark ritual. Incense and camphor covered the stench of the long-dead corpse, and a sheet over Vulg's mortal remains kept Frindolf from having to look on the hideous relic. Magic circles with many details were drawn around the cadaver and where Frindolf was going to stand. Great care had been made to get every word and name of power in the circles right, and as he entered the circle Frindolf made sure his feet didn't break or smudge any of the chalk. In his hand he held a list of the names of several gods and caretakers of the dead, not evil beings, but still grim, dangerous powers that most people thought best left alone. Plus Frindolf had acquired the most important thing for summoning a dead one's spirit, Vulg's full name, the one his parents had given the boy, not just what everyone had called him. That had been absurdly easy for the merchant to procure: he'd simply remembered it from all the times it had been spoken at his trial. He'd even managed to struggle the great and ornate pendulum-clock from the master dining room all the way downstairs without breaking it, so that he would know for certain when the correct hour of casting the spell would be. For the first time, Frindolf was grateful everybody had thought the clock too big and ugly to buy when he'd tried to sell it. Soon Vulg would pay for bringing so much trouble down upon his master's head. Soon he'd be a living boy again, facing a Frindolf who was acting on cold, premeditated rage rather than sudden anger. Several clubs and whips had been placed on a table in the basement where Frindolf could easily grab one. A short sword and a battle axe that had hung on the wall for years were also available for the merchant's use.

Frindolf had long decided a single death, or even two of them, were in no way suitable punishments for the likes of Vulg. Although the dark grimoires never mentioned the idea, he saw no reason the ritual for reviving the dead couldn't be used more than once on the same victim. He intended to kill Vulg again many times, each time using a different weapon. If he were not satisfied with that, he'd figure out how to get a rack, or hot irons, without tipping off the neighbors what was going on. Vulg would pay for what he'd done to his master over and over again, during however many years Frindolf himself would remain above the earth. At the appointed hour (which, against general belief, was not midnight) Frindolf intoned the long spell summoning Vulg's spirit back from the other world and into his moldering corpse. As he did so, the night's peace was disturbed by a thunderstorm, whose roars and rumbles Frindolf could hear even down in his cellar. Were the gods and powers angered by Frindolf's blasphemous disturbing of the dead, and voicing their displeasure? Or were the forces he was invoking causing the storm to show their power? The vindictive merchant neither knew nor cared, as revenge crawled closer and closer to his eager grasp.

Then there was one final crash of thunder, the loudest yet, and for a moment all the ritual candles Frindolf had lit flared up brighter, as if stirred by a light wind. And the bones and long-decayed flesh of Vulg reknit before his killer's eyes. Recomposition washed over the body, and then the long-dead boy was struggling to his feet. Vulg stood naked before his master, pale, shaking, and looking less like somebody just brought back to the land of the living than someone who'd suffered from some grave disease for a long time and was ready to start on his way *to* the land of the dead. Vulg spoke not a word, but the sheer terror in his eyes as he beheld Frindolf again was pitiful to behold.

"Hah, you young knave!" gloated Frindolf. "You thought you'd escaped your deserved punishment, didn't you? But I'm still your master, and even dying hasn't taken you from my grasp, or from the treatment you so well deserve!" With that, Frindolf seized a horse-whip from the table and ripped into the emaciated figure standing before him. Vulg did not scream and struggle like the last time, he merely fell down and groaned. The boy's hold on the life he'd been wrongfully dragged back to was not strong, and he soon expired a second time under Frindolf's blows.

Frindolf grimly pushed Vulg's corpse, which had quickly become the decayed thing it had been before the summoning, with a long-handled shovel to the closet he'd prepared to keep the boy in between resurrections. He was in no way pleased—the boy had not suffered anywhere near enough, and the second punishment had been neither as enjoyable nor as satisfying as he'd expected it to be. He resolved the next time he brought back Vulg he'd allow him a few days or weeks to regain his strength and what little wit the youth had had before destroying him again. That way he could make the brat's death more drawn-out and lingering, and the time Vulg waited for his well-earned execution and dreaded it would be a terrible punishment in itself. However, the next time Frindolf summoned the spirit of Vulg, nothing happened. No spirit came, no god complained, and the corpse remained the malodorous clay it had been. There was a reason.

In his eagerness to execute Vulg again (for Frindolf would never consider what he was doing as murder), and then to get rid of the unsightly and stenchful corpse, Frindolf had forgotten to recite the second ritual he'd copied down, the one that would dismiss the spirit back to the otherworld. That meant that when he summoned Vulg from the otherworld again, Vulg wasn't there to come. Instead Vulg's spirit walked the streets of Mordenhem, invisible and intangible to nearly all, and the few who could see ghosts were not around to notice him. Vulg was less than happy. Three years ago, he'd passed on to neither paradise nor punishment, but only to the gray realm where those who were not good enough for one place or bad enough for the other go. Many say it's a dreary and uninviting place, but Vulg, measuring it against the poverty and want of his earlier years and the pain and abuse of his later ones, hadn't found it a bad place at all, and would've been happy to spend the rest of eternity there. Nor was he pleased with Frindolf. He'd died believing his final punishment had been a great injustice, as had many of the earlier punishments the merchant had inflicted on him. Since the last beating had left him in improved circumstances, he'd been willing to forgive the treatment. However, hauling him back for further abuse changed the entire deal. Vulg might have been from a lowly neighborhood, but he knew his former master had broken many laws both human and divine dragging him back from the afterworld. It was far worse than anything Frindolf had done to him in his previous existence, and this time Vulg was ready finally to hit back at his former master. He could not become a ghost. Angry ghosts come back to the land of the living through their own will and rage for revenge or justice. Vulg had been dragged back to this world against his will. Supposedly a spirit who cannot cross over to the otherworld will, in time, be reborn, often as a lowlier animal than a man. Usually those so reincarnated show more intelligence and awareness than the regular beasts, and even than some men. One day, when Frindolf was out walking, a large dog, who had shown no sign of savagery before, got angry and went for him. Frindolf was severely bitten on both his arm and his leg before he managed to bash the dog over the head with his stick. A couple of years later a horse, that had up to now carried Frindolf dutifully, suddenly kicked the merchant so hard he limped for the rest of his life. The horse was destroyed, but that didn't help the merchant's aching leg. From then on, every stray beast in the city seemed to have it in for Frindolf. Bees stung him. Mosquitoes bit him. An alley cat took to singing outside his bedroom window and proved amazingly hard to catch. For several months a pigeon seemed to lie in wait for Frindolf, especially if he was wearing a new suit. How a mere bird could recognize when he was wearing his good clothes was something no one was able to answer. One time, even a parrot took it upon himself to go for Frindolf. The businessman had been passing a pet shop with many unusual creatures in cages when the gaudy jungle bird suddenly rounded on Frindolf and started calling him names everybody swore the fowl had never learned from them. Frindolf's angrily striking at the bird made things far worse, for his blows broke the wooden cage that had separated man and bird. Before he was stopped, the parrot, a big yellow-and-green one from the jungles of Arbatuque, had managed to remove most of Frindolf's right little finger and half his left ear with his beak. In time, people came to comment on Frindolf's terrible luck with animals. Some thought it might be a curse placed on the merchant by the gods for killing his servant so casually. Others thought that Frindolf, with his arrogant temper and abrasive personality, might just be provoking all the creatures.

Strangely, no one, not even Frindolf himself, suspected it might be the angry spirit of the murdered boy, who'd not only had his life taken from him, but even his peace in the afterworld and finally his humanness. Why Frindolf never suspected is a mystery, for the knowledge was right there in the books that lay forgotten on his table. Perhaps the vengeful gods had covered his eyes, so to speak, so he couldn't see where his punishment was coming from and deal with the problem. Or perhaps he denied it and tricked himself into thinking he had nothing to do with the hostile creatures, that this bad luck had nothing to do with his own evil actions. As might be expected, between the problems oppressing him and the repeated "accidents" courtesy of Vulg, Frindolf lived to no great age. After he'd died, battered, bitter, bitten and old before his time, Vulg's corpse was discovered in Frindolf's basement by his heirs. It was quietly reburied and a priest paid to lay the ghost to rest. So Vulg returned to the afterworld he so preferred to the land of the living. Some say the powers that rule the dead punished Frindolf further by making it impossible for him to get at Vulg ever again, but how can they know?

What is known is that the poor relatives Frindolf had so disdained inherited his house and money. Not ever being wealthy like Frindolf's side of the family, they found their new life comfortable and luxurious and felt no great urge to curse the fates they weren't richer. The books on magic were given to a retired witch, who could be trusted to make no unsavory use of them as she had long ago gone blind. They never indentured a servant, however, and were loud voices in the movement to ban the custom of indenture from Mordenhem.

Or so they tell the tale in Simrana.

The Good Simranatan

Robert M. Price

One wintry afternoon a certain man was journeying down the long road to his village after a successful trading journey when a group of bandits set upon him like a pack of jackals. They took everything he had, even his furs. As was their custom, they choked him to within an inch of his life and left him to die of the cold in the high mountain pass. Already as they disappeared from his sight, he began to lose feeling in his hands and feet. He despaired of life and began to say his prayers and to recall what he could of the prayers his mother had once taught him.

But then his heart leapt within him as he saw the shadows of an approaching party. It was a priest of Zarkoona, finely attired, with his entourage of slaves and concubines, none of whom paid the man aught but contemptuous regard.

Only an hour later, another figure came near, that of an ascetic devotee of the three-headed deity Pindol. But neither man was so much as aware of the other's presence, as the wounded man was now past consciousness, and the other was rapt in a mystical ecstasy even as he walked.

Not long after, when the sun had disappeared and his soul made ready to forsake that body for another, the man had a third visitor. Lo, it was one of the very robbers who had so ill-used him hours before! It seems that, as he departed with his companions, his heart smote him, and for shame he could take no part in his fellows' merriment. When they were all besotted with drink, he crept from the camp and found his way back to the place where they had apprehended the man. There his erstwhile victim lay with hardly a sign of life. Lifting up his head, the highwayman opened the man's lips with a gloved finger and poured in the merest trickle of wine.

Looking this way and that, the improbable benefactor gave thought to his position. Of a sudden, he stooped down and wrapped the stiffening form of the man in a cloak and hefted him astride his shoulders as a shepherd carries a lone sheep. Taking a secret path known to none but the Brotherhood of Thieves, he made for a nearby inn.

Entering the smoky tap-room, he cleared space on one of the long tables for the man, whose blood was again warming. The robber took the innkeeper aside, a man long known to him, and whispered, "Here, I have retrieved some of the silver coins we took from him. Take them and provide for his recovery. As for me, I must away before my absence is discovered. Mayhap I shall return in the spring."

The heavy wooden door closed against the bitter mountain night, and the innkeeper stood by the table on which lay the recumbent form. As he looked from the pitiful body to the silver in his hand, his eyes began to glow with more than the reflection of the hearth fire. Summoning one of his hired men, he ordered him to take the man, now returning to consciousness, into the back room, where the innkeeper should tend to him.

Alone with the man, he withdrew an iron knife from his apron and quickly slit the man's throat. Kicking open the back door, he wasted no time in casting the body onto the trash heap. Before many moments went by, a pack of jackals had found the scent and set upon the man. The innkeeper counted it a profitable day and a boon from his gods.

It is a tale they tell in Simrana. True? I know not.

The Devil's Mine

Robert M. Price

Mufastos was a sinner, not in any especially reprehensible way, mind you, no committer of nefarious crimes, no predator among his fellows was he. But the old reprobate paid no heed to the Gods of Simrana. Truth be told, the deities could not be bothered to keep account of such trivia. What mattered it whether a mere mortal worshipped or blasphemed? Either way, they remained sublimely unaffected. The virtues and sins of whole civilizations sometimes caught their notice, though not without some annoyance. But individual men and women? They flattered themselves to think their insect-like concerns were of any interest to Those On High. Such things were left to a bureaucracy of low-level demigods and spirits.

And these took note of how the mortal Mufastos spent little real effort on necessary tasks, whether in his modest home or at his workplace. His longsuffering wife, Gortrulla, to be sure, made up for the indignation which the Gods lacked. His fondness for wine, for instance, far exceeded his love for her, and she knew it, at length abandoning him and returning to her family home. Mufastos noticed her absence only once he had missed regular meals. He only marveled that she had put up with his nonsense for as long as she had. On the other hand, he no longer had to put up with her nagging, and the lack of it nearly compensated for the lack of meals.

With no one to see to his needs, Mufastos' health quickly suffered. His indolent habits took their toll. At length the old wastrel lay abed, abandoned and unattended, dizzy with fever, cognizant of nothing save the climbing of his temperature rung by rung. As he felt himself passing into unconsciousness, his last thought was that at least his comatose slumber would bring relief.

But in this expectation he was badly mistaken, for at once he found himself, with no apparent interval, hard at work, huffing and sweating, his arms aching badly from fatigue as he swung a pick into a vein of rock! For the briefest of moments, he felt as if he belonged wherever he was, and that he was accustomed to the work. But then he recognized the incongruity of it, the shocking unfamiliarity. He was *not* used to this labor—or to *any labor!* How had he come to this awful place of servitude?

Mufastos was not alone. A long chain connected his ankle to that of another man engaged in the same task. The fellow looked to be in no better shape than Mufastos himself. If he had been at the work for long, it had plainly done little to build his muscles. He called over to the new arrival.

"Are you confused, friend? Everyone is at first!"

Mufastos squinted to discern the man's grimy features in the shadows that veiled everything. He was about to reply to the friendly words of his neighbor when a sudden lifting of the gloom startled him. It was a flash of fire from further down the grim tunnel, not bright enough to make him shield his eyes, but suddenly he could see what surrounded him: a cavern, its uneven floor littered with boulders and stone fragments of all sizes. It was a mine, deep in the earth—or under the earth. But this he had already surmised from the pickaxe in his hands. What was a lazy lout such as he *doing here?*

"We work for *him*," the other laborer explained, pointing up higher on the cavern wall. There, in a recessed niche, reposed a statue (in a *mining tunnel?*) depicting a seated creature, roughly manlike in general outline but possessing numerous limbs, seemingly borrowed from a variety of animal species: crab pincers, coiling tentacles, furry forelegs, and human arms, though with too many joints. The troll sported a collection of tusks and fangs crowding a wide maw, above which protruded a blunt proboscis and three bulging eyes, one above the other two. There was a forest of asymmetrical horns and spikes crowning the slope-browed head. These details remained visible only for a moment before misty dimness returned, but poor Mufastos had seen more than enough to frighten the wits out of him!

"That is Druumalgathoth, King of the Dead, is it not?"

"In truth it is, and this place is festooned with his images, to remind us whom we serve—as if we were likely to forget!"

"What is your name, friend?" Mufastos, asked, quickly looking over his shoulder, fearing to be seen slacking.

"My name? I do not recall, it has been so long. Nor will I inquire of yours, as here it matters not."

"I need not ask what this place is, but why do we dig?"

"I know not, but perhaps there are worse sinners than we, and perhaps they are being put to the fire in some deeper circle, and perhaps we are mining the fuel to stoke those flames. But I know not."

Mufastos glanced again, in a renewed bit of fire glow, at the recessed statue of the horrid Master of the Pit and flinched to see, or to think he saw, one of the eyes turn in his direction. Withal he cut short his unenlightening conversation with his fellow slave and got back to his task of breaking rocks.

It was perhaps a mercy that the passage of time here was difficult to mark. Mufastos, a lifelong stranger to any sort of hard work, had expected to collapse quickly into exhaustion, but he never did. Instead, he labored beneath an ever-nagging burden of aching fatigue that never alleviated but also did not hamper his work. The unremitting mine work was punctuated with periodic appearances of shadowy, hoofed figures (at whom he disliked to look too closely) who rolled, very bumpily, iron barrows to collect the dislodged ore to clear the way for further digging and hammering. These intervals provided the workers with rare moments of rest. Mufastos neither knew nor cared if it was the same demon or a series of them who cleared away the stony detritus. He could not have told the difference.

But he could tell that various females would, from time to time, show up to dispense provisions. With their greasy jowls and unwashed, stringy hair, they were harder to look at than the demons as they ladled out bowls of nauseating slop. Was the stuff designed to reinforce the laborers' stamina? Or was it more punishment, like a naughty child forced to down a spoon of cod liver oil?

The real punishment, however, came when one day Mufastos

recognized one of these harridans as his wife Gortrulla. He was by no means surprised to find the disagreeable hag consigned to this place of damnation; if anyone deserved it, it was Gortrulla. Of course her erstwhile husband had no way of knowing of her death or its occasion, nor did he have much of a sense of how long he had abided here. She might have lived a long life making others miserable. But now she could again take up her favorite task of needling him. Oh, it was a devilish cruelty!

"Well lookee here! Fat-ass Mufastos with a tool in his hand! Never seen it! Never *thought* to see it! Maybe if you'd gotten friendlier with hard work in the world above, you wouldn't have ended up here! I—"

By instinctive reaction rather than conscious intent, Mufastos, sizzling with indignation, tightened his calloused grip on his shovel and flung the load of rocks and gravel into his wife's face! Moving faster than he had ever seen her move, Gortrulla somehow managed to dodge the stony spray. Breathing heavily and marveling that even hell could be made worse by her presence, Mufastos waited for her counterattack. But there was none, for Gortrulla's attention had been captivated by something on the cave floor, something from the shovel's fusillade. She stooped down to retrieve a shiny object that had been encrusted by a layer of rock. It had broken apart when it hit the ground.

Their conflict forgotten for the moment, the estranged couple approached close, their wondering faces illumined by the bright but gentle golden radiance that beat like a heart from the newly revealed gem. "What can it be?" said both in unison.

And all at once a third stood with them. At his presence, Mufastos and Gortrulla recoiled, each in the opposite direction. It was the hideous figure of dread Druumalgathoth, in person. His inhuman countenance, for once, did not scowl. In fact, if one could interpret such a face, he seemed as rapt in wonder as the pair of dismal souls who shrank away from his red mist-enshrouded form.

"At last it is restored! All this digging! All this seeking! And you, my children, have rediscovered the prize!"

The lack of sadistic malevolence in his strangely echoing voice took the couple greatly by surprise. Terror gave way to alarmed confusion until Mufastos dared ask, tremblingly, "Uh, what *is* it? What did your servants find, O dread Master of the Pit?"

The monstrous titan for the first time looked away from the shining gem and at the faces of his slaves. It was as if he had completely forgotten them.

"It is my soul!"

The two human faces were blank.

"You see, I am damned to this imprisonment the same as you! Until now, that is! Once I lived in immortal glory atop the Holy Mountain of Simrana's Gods! I reigned alongside them as a God—until that black day when I betrayed them! What I did, no mortal could even understand. But my offense was grave indeed! And for my crime I was cast down, doubly imprisoned in this ugly form and in this ugly place—until that day when I might unearth my soul, buried deeply in this cavernous well of darkness. Becoming thus the Lord and Warden of the Damned, I set my prisoners to work in case it might in this way come to light.

"And now it has! Behold my true likeness, O mortals!"

Withal did Druumalgathoth change in an instant into a glorious man-like shape, so tall that his proud, golden-tressed head just missed bumping against the tunnel's roof. He wore a toga made of shifting rainbow bands of light.

"I shall at once return to my vacant throne on high, my children, but first let me reward you both."

Mufastos found himself in surroundings he had never expected even to behold. In truth, he had never really believed the teachings of childhood that promised such a place to the well-behaved. At first he rejoiced in his new life of empyrean bliss, having been assigned the happy duty of cupbearer to the former Druumalgathoth, who had now reclaimed his ancient name of Euphorion. But old habits die hard, lingering even after their owners depart this life, and once too often was Mufastos discovered imbibing the consecrated nectar of the Gods of Simrana, whereupon his Master caused him to be reassigned. Mufastos dared not complain when he found himself attached to a construction crew refurbishing the ancient palaces of the deities and building new ones.

Well, he mused as he sweated each day, at least it was better than returning to the Pit, where Gortrulla had been rewarded with Druumalgathoth's old job, which seemed to suit her quite nicely.

You ask how any mortal might verify such a tale as this? I confess I know not. But it is what some tell in Simrana.

How Thongor Conquered Zaremm

Robert M. Price

I   The Swooping Skies

In a moment a flock of lizard-hawks darkened the azure skies above golden Patanga. The pterosaurs were rarely seen so thick in flight. The nape hairs of the people in the streets of the City of Flame prickled at the weird sight, signaling that strange danger was imminent. The huge creatures began dropping down among the terrified citizens who fled wildly and in vain. There was no escaping the eager maws of the predators. At once, archers spilled into the streets and broad avenues and loosed feathered fusillades against them. To their astonishment, every shaft splintered against the scaly hides of the monsters. Such was not unknown, given the natural armor of these creatures, but this was extraordinary. Men had long since learned the vulnerable points of the late-lingering saurians of the Lemurian wilderness. But these lizard-hawks were one and all as hard as stone! How could they even fly?

Thongor of Valkarth, Emperor of the West, observing from a palace terrace, lost not a moment ordering his airboat fleet into action. Some were quickly lost, as their anti-gravity *urlium* hulls were necessarily light and readily crushed upon impact with the aerial behemoths. But the monsters proved to be no match for the airships' mounted Sithurls. The beasts of living stone exploded into spraying, jagged fragments once struck by the lightning rays emitted by these power crystals. More Patangans died from the impact of the shrapnel.

Soldiers began to clear away the wreckage, piling up corpses

"

and severed body parts, smashing the larger stone fragments into smaller pieces. Thongor summoned his advisors, the Peers of the Realm, to counsel. Foppish Prince Dru, grizzled Lord Mael, old Barand Thon, and the rest, all veterans of many battles and witnesses of many strange things, confessed bafflement. Some suggested summoning Shahrajsha, but Thongor, always in closer touch with his patron magician, replied, "He is otherwise occupied these days, in vital business, and remains unavailable, else I should have sought his help already."

Thongor, a barbarian from the mountainous north of the continent, disliked the finery of civilization, deeming it effeminate and decadent. Thus he sat at the head of the huge *lotifer*-wood table clad in his accustomed link-mail tunic, voluminous black cloak draped over his massive shoulders. Like many of the men with him, his skin was sun-bronzed. A golden circlet enclosed his broad brow above his haunting golden eyes, prominent cheek bones, and slightly aquiline nose. Before him, his naked broadsword Sarkozan lay across the table in place of a royal sceptre. His advisers, like his subjects, were by no means embarrassed at his rude appearance but instead found comfort in it: here was a man possessing the savage strength and eagerness for battle who would never lapse into the dithering timidity of kings who were too civilized for their own good. Here was a time-displaced creature of a hardier age.

As the hour grew later, shadows deepened, and candles melted away, Thongor ordered that airship crews be refreshed and sent off in widening circles of surveillance lest Patanga be caught by surprise again. Urging his council to get some sleep while they could, Thongor felt a natural fatigue but also a strange instinct that some revelation, possibly telepathically from Shahrajsha, might await him in slumber.

His beloved queen, Sumia, gazed at his immediately snoring form with mixed worry and admiration. She, too, surrendered to slumber, but not for long. She was jolted awake with the spasmodic shuddering of her mighty mate, clearly in the grip of some kind of night terror. Sumia knew that waking someone suffering such trauma might be dangerous, so she paused to consider her best course of action. She decided whatever might happen could certainly be no worse than what her husband was experiencing in dream, so she sought, first, to speak gently and to prod him awake, but without result. Next she tried to shake him back to consciousness, still without success. But then, all at once, Thongor's violent thrashings subsided and he lapsed into a relaxed but comatose state. Sumia took the opportunity to slip on a robe and dash through the halls to find the court physician.

II   An Alien God

Of all this, the dreaming Sark knew nothing. Sumia had departed, that much he knew. He lay abed in a deep darkness unrelieved by candle or lamp light. But all at once, the royal bed chamber was nonetheless filled with sound and brilliance. Thunder crashed, but it seemed to proceed from some source within the room. Before him now stood a statuesque form, that of a black-maned cyclops from whose single orb the strange illumination was projected. The frightful figure gripped a huge battle axe, from which the sounds of thunder and the tearing crack of lightning emerged. The echoing thunder began to sound more and more like intelligible words.

"I am Shadrazur, Lord of Warriors. You are one of my children."

Thongor rolled out of bed, seized the hilt of his sword, whose scabbard hung from his bedpost, and, holding it forth in a gesture of fealty, knelt on the thick rug before the Being who had addressed him.

"I recognize you not, my Lord. You are not of the Nineteen Gods of Lemuria, are you? Nor one of the Lords of Chaos?"

"You have judged rightly, O Thongor, Sark of Patanga. In truth, it is the rare mortal who, having beheld his Gods face to face, knows that a foreign Deity has appeared to him. I and my fellows hold court on the sacred mountains above a realm called Simrana which is known to men of other dimensions only as a land of dreams. It is near you and yet very far. Our world has gone to ruin, its Gods impotent, its heroes long dead and turned to dust. And the shadow which has extinguished us now threatens this world of yours. I have sought you out, O mighty man, to avenge one world and to save another."

"Then tell me more, Great Lord of Steel and Sinew!"

"Centuries agone, my fellow deities met to deliberate the fate of the alabaster city of Neol-Shendis, an ancient metropolis of great achievement and overweening pride. Such pride leads men to neglect their Gods and to dare regard themselves as gods. If we destroyed them for their effrontery, would we not show ourselves inferior to them, lashing out in a tantrum? But if we did not, would we not also be signaling their superiority, that their wonders were a threat to us? Long did we dispute atop the Mountain of Judgment but could come to no decision. Now others have usurped our prerogative, blasting the ancient city to ashes."

Thongor found himself puzzled, never having heard of such a city, especially odd if it were renowned for its high culture.

"I know only the inner sea of Neol-Shendis, upon which the Dragon Isles do float."

"Aye, the men of old named it the Nyranian Sea. The alabaster city stood radiant upon its shore, and, as its fame increased, men named the inner sea for the city itself."

"But the Inner Sea is to be found here in Lemuria. You seem to speak of some other world."

"You know of the islands where the Dragon Kings once ruled. I know it was you who brought about their demise. That is how I know you are the one to do my will. If you can do that deed, you will be able to do this one. These serpent-men were great masters of sorcery. They discovered there a unique portal between adjacent worlds. There it is still possible to pass between the realms. The Dragon Kings once passed over to Simrana and taught their magic to the elders of the city Zaremm. As legends rightly tell, the magicians employed that sorcery to render their city immune from attack. There were many attempts, as Zaremm's renown made it a prize coveted by kings and warlords. But all alike went down to defeat and doom.

"Once content to bide their time in their fortified city, they have of late elected to spread their power across all Simrana and its neighbor worlds. Fair Babdalorna was their second conquest after Neol-Shendis. And there were many more, till all Simrana was despoiled."

Thongor anticipated the next revelation of Shadrazur.

"So it was they who sent the animated gargoyles to Patanga, ignorant of the power and ingenuity of the sciences of this earth. But they, too, are ingenious and will no doubt attack again."

The cyclops nodded silently.

"I shall go to the Dragon Isles where I shall pass over into Simrana and somehow defeat the sorcerers of Zaremm where others have failed. But, if I may, why do not the Gods of Simrana strike down Zaremm's rulers?"

Taking no apparent offense, the War God patiently replied, "My son, the Gods must ever work through mortals because, even in Simrana, their mountain habitation is to Simrana as Simrana is to your earth, and they cannot cross over directly to intervene. You see, the Gods need men as much as men need their Gods!"

III The Dragon Prince

Awakening to the noontide sun in his eyes, Thongor found himself surrounded by most of his advisors and companions. All alike beamed with relief to see him again possessed of his senses. He reached out to Sumia, drawing her slender form to his bosom, gripping her full, red lips in his own.

"How fares Patanga, my friends? Have our enemies struck again?"

The dapper Dru reported. "No, Lord Thongor. Nor have our men discerned anything out of the ordinary for many leagues around. Nor do we yet know the source of the attack."

"Then allow me to satisfy your curiosity, my friend."

Many pairs of eyes widened.

"The Gods have vouchsafed to me the truth of the matter." He recounted the vision and the import of the revelation. None of his listeners registered the smallest sign of skepticism. Ancient Lemuria was a place of wonders, so much so that even marvels had become routine (though no less dangerous betimes).

Thongor declined the offers of his comrades to share the adventure. The foreign God had commissioned him alone to the task. Sumia accompanied him to the stables where Thongor harnessed a lizard-hawk for the journey to the Inner Sea. He dared not take an airboat in case they should be needed to repel a second attack. And observers at Zaremm might not notice his approach atop a familiar-looking beast.

As the pterosaur winged its way across the continent, Thongor thrilled, as he always did, to the godlike perspective of flight. It would be many millennia before man rediscovered the means of flight, but when he did, he would too quickly come to take it for granted. But mainly the Valkarthan was preoccupied with what he might face when he arrived at the Dragon Isles. Had he really eradicated the race of the serpent-men? If any survived, would they interfere in his task? And even if no such fear were justified, what dangers might he face in ruined Simrana with its power-greedy magicians? In the end, he acquiesced to the confidence Lord Shadrazur had placed in him. Usually one thought of a man having faith in his God, but here was a God placing his hopes on a mortal.

Some days later, after several descents for a night's sleep for man as well as beast, the inner sea of Neol-Shendis came into view. As Thongor guided his monstrous mount downward through the atmosphere, he recognized the layout of the miniature archipelago. Closer still, he could make out structures familiar to him from his previous mission there. The only discernible movement appeared to be the normal bush-shaking of small animals. Landing, Thongor tied the pterosaur to a tree branch and set out at random to look for any sign of the dimensional gateway. His senses were the equal of any wild animal's. They had to be, or their owner should never have survived so long in such a world. And those keen senses now alerted him to the approach of a tall figure, concealed behind a screen of primitive vegetation.

"Show yourself, be you friend or foe!" His hand found Sarkozan's hilt without having to think about it.

A tall youth emerged from the bushes. He spoke in a friendly tone, though with an odd-sounding accent. It had a sibilant hiss, a kind of lisp. His handsome face was crowned with a mop of unkempt brown hair. He wore a plain blue shirt and faded, colorless pants. The lad carried a skinning knife, implying he lived on such wildlife as he could catch.

"Are you a hunter, too, good sir?"

"I am hunting for something, that is true. But tell me, my friend: why do I find you in this accursed place, the haunt of the ancient Dragon Kings?"

The fellow laughed, but not derisively. Despite the peculiarity of the man's voice, the laughter somehow conveyed a good-hearted nature.

"Why? Because I am *one* of them!"

The stranger's image flickered and resolved itself into that of one of the serpent-men! The cheek bones rose and expanded, the nose reduced to mere nostril openings, the cranium flattening, the eyes turning yellow, pupils narrowing to vertical slits. The head was a triangular wedge. Fangs protruded over the lipless mouth. Eyes were shaded by a prominent brow ridge. The creature's scaly hide was, of course, emerald green. Thongor automatically assumed a fighting stance, though the other now bore no weapon. Speaking rapidly in a thicker hiss, so as to forestall Thongor's impending attack, the humanoid held out open hands. "Hold! I feared you would attack me if you saw my true form before I could explain. I mean you no harm!"

"Why not? I slew your kings! Don't tell me you care nothing for revenge!"

"Then you are Thongor of Valkarth? I am called Zylac, and the blood of the Dragon Kings gushes through my veins. But I, too, hate the Druids of Zaremm, for they betrayed my people with the very magic my race taught them! I knew you would come. A one-eyed God appeared to me and told me to join you when you appeared. He thought you might find me of some use. You have seen that I possess some knowledge of magic that may come in handy.

"And, I may add, I know the location of the Portal."

In silent reply, Thongor sheathed his sword, then, after a moment, extended his hand to clasp the mottled claw of Zylac.

IV The Sword of Ancient Valor

The portal to Simrana turned out to be nothing remarkable in outward appearance. It was a framed archway inside one of the decaying buildings in the compound. Anyone might suppose it led to a store room or a meeting chamber. But as the two companions stepped through it they could see that they had arrived in a wholly different landscape. They were outside, wedged into the claustrophobic confines of what once had been a mighty forest. Fire had consumed vast areas of it, leaving fertile ash from which a few new saplings had begun to peek out. Zylac seemed fully apprised of which direction to take.

"What is our goal here, friend Zylac? Are we nearing the city of Zaremm? I grow impatient."

"Nay, Lord Thongor. First we must needs visit the dead city of once-towering Babdalorna. A potent weapon awaits us there." Thongor glanced at his sheathed sword Sarkozan and wondered why it was not sufficient. But he would wait and see.

Thongor drew his blade and proceeded to chop their way through the crumbling tree-corpses. So fragile were these that the Valkarthan knew no damage would come to the sword, and he was eager to be on his way. Here and there could be seen copses of intact greenery. One of these was thick enough, as it turned out, to have concealed a small band of attackers. Their weapons were pitiful, fragile and corroded, and of little use, unless perhaps against one another. Thongor found them quite as easy to chop down as the charcoal trees.

Thongor paused, feeling it unfair to offer a real defense against such pitiful foes. Two remained. The forest dwellers, Zylac informed him, were the last specimens of the Athreeb, ancient enemies of the men of Babdalorna. Most had been slain in the Zaremmite attack on the city, which had caused them to make common cause with the city dwellers for the first time. Thongor judged them to occupy a rung or two above the Lemurian Beast Men with whom he had more than once dealt. Zylac was able to understand some of their crude language (presumably having encountered them on previous trips through the Portal). When the Athreeb understood they were no longer in danger, and learned of Thongor's purpose, they enthusiastically begged that they might join them. As Zylac translated their words to Thongor, the latter merely shrugged. "Why not?"

The forest had long since undermined the once stolid walls of Babdalorna. The trees, now their remains, had grown as thickly within the walls as outside them. Bones and dry tree limbs were thickly interspersed underfoot. There was no hope of advancing silently. Zylac led the way unerringly to the city's hall of ancient weapons. It rose, largely intact, above the surrounding piles of masonry, a stone tower still intact, though there were none left to visit it—till now. The party of four felt they had shrunk when measuring their height against the high interior walls and the impressive scale of the remaining exhibits. Many had been looted, but one had remained remarkably unmolested. Some charm protected it, perhaps from within the glass case where reposed the relics and trophies of the heroes of history and epic. The four stood in quiet awe before the holy history in which they were now to take their places.

At length, Zylac pointed to one weapon in particular and whispered, "That is the great sword *Zingazar*. The greatest warriors have borne it: Young Anarbion wielded it against the invading Athreeb. Ionax the Brave whelmed the marauders of the hills with it. In the hands of Diomardanon it slaked its thirst for blood. Thence it passed to Belzimer the Bold. And to Konary the Tall. Now it is yours." Withal did Zylac kick the glass in, causing the other three to flinch. He handed the ancient sword to his royal companion.

Thongor said nothing but gingerly hefted the great blade, admiring the light-reflecting length of it and the razor-sharp edge which seemed almost to slice the ambient air like a thunderbolt. The sturdy hilt, confined by dry, sweat-salted leather, seemed almost a sturdy sword-wielding arm in its own right. The pommel contained an inset emerald, at first dulled like a cataract, but then alive with pulsing sentience. Even Sarkozan did not compare with it. The Valkarthan weighed the two swords in his hands, Sarkozan in the left, Zingazar in his right. He felt a current of occult power passing between them. He even felt hypnotic communication from the rune-engraved blade.

After a few more moments of silence, Thongor turned to Zylac and asked, "How did Babdalorna fall when it possessed such a weapon?"

"There was no man to wield it. In the decadence of the city, no man had an ear tuned to the beckoning voice of Zingazar. The man wields the sword. The sword wields the man. And you are the man."

Thongor considered this. He had the sudden notion that Zylac was but the mouthpiece for Shadrazur, the War God of Simrana. And that he had been all along. He recalled how the deity had said the Gods could work their will only through their mortal agents. And he was sure he was right when, moments later, he beheld his lizard-hawk descending to the ground just outside. He knew neither he nor Zylac had brought it through the Portal. But Someone had.

Zylac made at once to mount the winged beast, while the two Athreeb looked on with open terror. It might have been fear of the monster, or it might have been the prospect of flying far above their arboreal haunts. Thongor grinned. He motioned to Zylac, already strapping himself to the lizard-hawk's harness, to wait a moment. Zylac dropped to the ground and followed Thongor, who had signaled the two forest-dwellers to come with him.

It took but a few minutes to find the royal palace, now deserted. Threading their way through fallen masonry and other detritus, the little company approached the throne room where, in an earlier day, Babdalorna's kings would hear cases and administer justice. Thongor looked the Athreeb over, then took the hairy, matted arm of the taller one, pointing to the vacant throne and nodding at him.

"For centuries, I am told, your people strove to enter the city and take it for your own. Zingazar stopped you. But now your destiny shall be fulfilled by Zingazar."

The poor fellow twitched and fidgeted on the throne, uncertain as to what Thongor had in mind, especially when the Valkarthan outlander drew forth the rune sword. But the apish countenance brightened when Thongor touched the flat of the blade to the crown of the Athreeb's head and to both shoulders.

"Behold: I, the Sark of the West, make you king of Babdalorna!" And, turning to the other gaping forest-man, he added, "And you, my fine fellow, shall be his vizier!"

As the two Athreeb began to hop and strut like children, giddy over their new status, empty as it was, Thongor bowed toward them theatrically, motioning the amused Zylac to join him.

V   Wizards on the Wall

The city wall of Zaremm came into view from the air as two riders clung tightly to the harness of the soaring lizard-hawk. Thongor and his reptilian companion strained to make out a line of unmoving sentinels ranged along the parapets. As they drew closer it became evident that the motionless figures were not armed fighters but actually old men passively watching the plains below. Naturally, if the riders could see them, the watchers on the wall could see them, too, and must be on the very point of raising an alarm. But so far, none made a move. Only their purple-dyed robes, embroidered with silver threads forming zodiacal sigils, fluttered in the wind. Closer still, Thongor saw, through the whipping locks of his unbound black mane, that the gaunt and white-bearded watchmen were but robed corpses bound in place with cords. Their clothing identified them as having once been wizards. Somehow, Thongor surmised, their bodies must retain sufficient sorcerous energies to serve as a line of defense.

But in fact, they offered no obstacle as the pterosaur's vast shadow engulfed them. Thongor saw he was close enough to reach down with Sarkozan and lop off one of the mummified heads. There was no blood, only a puff of dust. The lizard-hawk passed on. Unopposed, Thongor and his companion landed behind the wall, jumped down from their winged steed, keenly watchful for any guards. The absolute silence made Thongor imagine the city was holding its breath in anticipation—but of what?

Continuing to the palace, they entered and heard the sound of echoing but brittle laughter. Galvanized by the awful sound, the companions proceeded with caution toward the origin of the cackling. Suddenly Thongor sensed a slight change in the air currents around him and turned to discover that he was alone! Had Zylac deserted him? Or worse, had the whole thing been a trap, with the serpent-man as the Judas Goat?

Thongor rounded a corner and saw before him a great chamber tapestried with vast cobwebs that must have been many decades in forming. The place was desolate. The statues lining the walls were unrecognizable with caked dust and unrepaired damage. Aesthetics was low on the list here. Thongor himself cared little for such things, but he acknowledged the importance of finery and pomp to communicate the strength and pride of a kingdom. By contrast, this desuetude bespoke an utter indifference. It told Thongor in a single glance that the imperial ambitions here were not those of a vigorous kingdom, whose people should share in the gains of conquest, but rather the self-aggrandizing vanity of one man. Clearly, this one disdained glory in favor of sheer power, two goals that usually went together.

At first Thongor saw no one in the room. At the far end stood a strangely configured statue, towering toward the ceiling. As near as Thongor could tell, it appeared to be a half-size effigy of a crouching lizard-hawk, as if sitting on her nest. On closer inspection, there was a seat where the nest would be, and a man sat upon it.

"Thongor of Patanga! And before that, I believe, Thongor of Valkarth! Welcome! I am Mordrax, priest-king of Zaremm, the City That May not Be Taken in War."

Thongor strode forward and stopped some ten feet before the throne. He now saw that the man on the cushionless seat looked like no mere colleague of the dead scarecrows propped up on the ramparts of Zaremm but a specimen indistinguishable from his species.

"My sympathies for the loss of your brethren. Someone seems to have forgotten to bury them. Would you like my help with the task?"

Mordrax replied with a belly laugh, though he had little in the way of a belly. The man was so wizened, so drawn and shriveled, one could hardly tell any difference between his living form and those of his sawdusty brethren. He coughed and paused to catch his fleeing breath.

"Ah yes, my fellow mages! It was, I admit, tragic, but, I fear, needful. For years mounting to centuries we derived great amusement from watching the foolish efforts of brainless oafs such as your royal self who sought to enhance their renown by overthrowing our sorcerous principality. At length I grew bored with such sport and announced to the others my intent to exchange a defensive posture for an aggressive one. Why not spread our enlightened dominion to all corners of Simrana, and thence to other realms which our ever-advancing occult science had revealed to us? But I found my brethren were not so wise as I had thought, for they rejected my plan. Fools they may have been, but nonetheless powerful ones. So, while pretending to defer to them, I laid plans whereby they might be eliminated one by one. I secretly drained their power, which had so prolonged their ancient lives, absorbing their vitality into myself. By this means I collected enough magical potency to pursue my scheme of conquest. And, very shortly now, King Thongor, you shall become a part of those plans. Are you not honored? You should be!" More phlegmy chuckling followed.

"That seems most unlikely to me, old man. You may have cannibalized your fellows to extend your years, but it seems to have slowed the course of senility not at all. You are mad."

"So you say, stupid barbarian! You are but an ignorant savage, while I am destined for very Godhood! I mean to conquer all known worlds and the Gods they worship. But my time in the flesh is very short. And that is where you come in."

Before Mordrax could pontificate further, both he and Thongor were startled by the last thing either expected to see. The crest of the throne-statue rang with the sudden impact of feet. In a moment, the newcomer stooped over to allow himself to be seen: it was Thongor, Sarkozan in his fist! Or so it seemed.

Thongor, as he faced the throne, looked to his hip only to discover Sarkozan's scabbard was empty! He looked back at his double, who had now climbed down within reach of the seated sorcerer. Mordrax sought to stand up and flee. But the spindle-shanked scarecrow's knee joints failed him, and he plopped back down, panic ruling his vulture-like face. As he saw sharp-edged doom approaching swiftly, he managed to utter a Word whose reverberations shook the building.

"Sargoth! *Rise!*"

If he had hoped to say anything else, it was drowned in a bloody gurgle.

Thongor stared wide-eyed at his twin, who now faced him. He smiled even as his illusory likeness began to melt away.

The Valkarthan and the serpent-man began to speak light-heartedly to one another, thinking they had fulfilled their mission by this assassination, though it seemed almost anticlimactically simple. Thongor clapped Zylac on his squamous shoulder. "You would make a fine cutpurse, my friend! Never has anyone else managed to. . ."

An awful grinding, scraping sound assaulted their ears as a hidden shaft opened in the floor close to them and a marble casket rose to floor level and sprang open. By itself, this was impressive engineering, but what came next was far more. From the casket arose the reanimated form of the ancient emperor Sargoth, last and greatest of those who sought in vain to conquer Zaremm. They knew this because he himself announced it in a dry and dusty voice.

"Behold, you fools, the shell I have abandoned!" His pointing, gold-gilded finger indicated the dead man's throne, where the corpse of Mordrax had collapsed and begun to disintegrate.

The Sargoth-thing was resplendent in golden mail armor, his heroic physique and handsome features somehow unspoiled by long ages. But his face was blank, the only motion that of his lips as he functioned as Mordrax's puppet.

"I will continue on either in this form or in your own body, Sark of Lemuria! Let us find out which of you buffoons is the stronger. Then I shall choose." As he boasted, Zylac turned to Thongor and said, "Would it be honorable for two to fight one?"

Thongor feared that Zylac did not take the challenge seriously enough, but he allowed himself a quip. "I'd say we're evenly matched. There are really two of them as well!"

He who had been Sargoth lunged clumsily at Thongor, who easily dodged him, but as the reanimated champion tried to regain his footing, he lashed out with his blade and impaled the shocked Zylac. Thongor had seen plenty of comrades fall in battle, but this death was somehow worse, doubly infuriating. Perhaps it was the fact of his friend having once been an enemy, or the son of an enemy race. It made him a rare gem.

His foe, delighted at having dispatched one opponent, was gaining a surer command of his movements. Thongor noticed this at once and realized he must finish him quickly. Sargoth, as he understood, had been the greatest warrior of his era, no doubt resourceful and skilled. He regretted having to fight the man, but there was no choice. Besides, it was really Mordrax that he fought.

But the longer the duel lasted, the more truly he would be battling Sargoth.

Mordrax had always made speech his main weapon, and he still relied upon it, wildly blustering. "In this form I shall conquer all lands, all dimensions! In this body I shall gain divine immortality, no longer as conjurer or conqueror—but as Universal God!"

He had apparently discarded any plan of usurping Thongor's mighty form, finding the possession of his one-time antagonist so ecstatic, so full of rich irony, that he decided to settle into Sargoth's body for good. Sargoth was fast becoming less a suit of unwieldy armor and more a new Mordrax.

Thongor reached for the sword Zingazar. Sarkozan had clattered away when Zylac dropped to the floor, and Thongor resolved to retrieve it later. This would be his first time wielding Babdalorna's holy weapon in battle. Free of its sheath, Zingazar began a high-pitched keening, then an electrical throbbing. Thongor momentarily staggered at the thunderous flooding-in of the spirits of the ancient heroes, whose might and skill were palpably augmenting his own!

Thongor versus Mordrax! Zingazar against Sargoth! Lemuria versus Simrana! The Valkarthan wryly hoped the spectacle pleased Shadrazur, Lord of Red War, who must be watching with his single, central eye.

Thongor struck a mighty blow. Anarbion struck another, as did brave Ionax, and Diomardanon, and Belzimer the Bold. And tall Konary. Against this pummeling Sargoth-Mordrax could not stand. A mass of bruises and lacerations, bleeding freely, Sargoth returned to the age-long rest his valiant career had long ago earned him, and from which he had been covetously snatched. And with him went vile Mordrax, albeit to a very different destination. Thongor saluted the fallen form of Sargoth the Great.

He turned to recover Sarkozan and sheathed it. He considered what to do with the bodies that now populated the throne room floor. But at once a familiar, if extraordinary, voice shook him. He looked up and saw what he expected to see: the cycloptic visage of axe-wielding Shadrazur. The rumbling of the thunder produced by his weapon's energy discharge blended with his words so that it took a keen ear to distinguish them.

"Well done, my servant! The greedy tentacles of Mordrax have forever curled and withered away! Verily, you might make a better War God than I! And you, a man, have earned the eternal gratitude of an immortal God. Now it is high time you went home."

Thongor nodded in modesty—then felt himself sinking and endlessly falling. Consciousness slipped away.

VI A Return and a Relic

Thongor stirred and tried to clear his head. He was lying in bed, his loved ones around him, rejoicing in his return to waking life. They embraced one another, and the Sarkoja Sumia hastened into his brawny arms. The sweet scent of her perfume helped quicken his presence of mind. Her husband half-rose and rested on an elbow.

"What has happened? How did I get here? I mean, back to Patanga?"

Sumia's cousin, the mustachioed Dru, answered as best he could, not quite understanding the question.

"You took to bed last evening after our council meeting. The queen found you tossing and struggling. Then you fell into a coma and have slept soundly for many hours."

Thongor's gaze turned from his friend's face and stared past the ranks of his companions. He muttered, to himself: "He said it was a realm of dream... Yet it seemed real..." Withal, his golden eyes rested on Sarkozan in its accustomed scabbard, hanging in its familiar place, his harness slung over the bedpost.

The others watched him carefully until those closest to his bedside were distracted by a sudden pulsation of light visible through the silken bed sheets. Thongor saw it, too, and whipped the sheet away.

What he saw was the incandescent glowing of runes up and down the length of a sword that lay alongside him. He thrust it into the air for all to see. As they gazed at it in awe, Thongor said one Word.

"*Zingazar!*"

The River

Lord Dunsany

There arises a river in Pegāna that is neither a river of water nor yet a river of fire, and it flows through the skies and the Worlds to the Rim of the Worlds, a river of silence. Through all the Worlds are sounds, the noises of moving, and the echoes of voices and song; but upon the River is no sound ever heard, for there all echoes die.

The River arises out of the drumming of Skarl, and flows for ever between banks of thunder, until it comes to the waste beyond the Worlds, behind the farthest star, down to the Sea of Silence.

I lay in the desert beyond all cities and sounds, and above me flowed the River of Silence through the sky; and on the desert's edge night fought against the Sun, and suddenly conquered.

Then on the River I saw the dream-built ship of the god Yoharneth-Lahai, whose great prow lifted grey into the air above the River of Silence.

Her timbers were olden dreams dreamed long ago, and poets' fancies made her tall, straight masts, and her rigging was wrought out of the people's hopes.

Upon her deck were rowers with dream-made oars, and the rowers were the people of men's fancies, and princes of old story and people who had died, and people who had never been.

These swung forward and swung back to row Yoharneth-Lahai through the Worlds with never a sound of rowing. For ever on every wind float up to Pegāna the hopes and the fancies of the people which have no home in the Worlds, and there Yoharneth-Lahai weaves them into dreams, to take them to the people again.

And every night in his dream-built ship Yoharneth-Lahai setteth forth, with all his dreams on board, to take again their old hopes back to the people and all forgotten fancies.

But ere the day comes back to her own again, and all the conquering armies of the dawn hurl their red lances in the face of the night, Yoharneth-Lahai leaves the sleeping Worlds, and rows back up the River of Silence, that flows from Pegāna into the Sea of Silence that lies beyond the Worlds.

And the name of the River is Imrāna the River of Silence. All they that be weary of the sound of cities and very tired of clamour creep down in the night-time to Yoharneth-Lahai's ship, and going aboard it, among the dreams and the fancies of old times, lie down upon the deck, and pass from sleeping to the River, while Mung, behind them, makes the sign of Mung because they would have it so. And, lying there upon the deck among their own remembered fancies, and songs that were never sung, and they drift up Imrāna ere the dawn, where the sound of the cities comes not, nor the voice of the thunder is heard, nor the midnight howl of Pain as he gnaws at the bodies of men, and far away and forgotten bleat the small sorrows that trouble all the Worlds.

But where the River flows through Pegāna's gates, between the great twin constellations Yum and Gothum, where Yum stands sentinel upon the left and Gothum upon the right, there sits Sirāmi, the lord of All Forgetting. And, when the ship draws near, Sirāmi looketh with his sapphire eyes into the faces and beyond them of those that were weary of cities, and as he gazes, as one that looketh before him remembering naught, he gently waves his hands. And amid the waving of Sirāmi's hands there fall from all that behold him all their memories, save certain things that may not be forgot even beyond the Worlds.

It hath been said that when Skarl ceases to drum, and MĀ-NA-YOOD-SUSHĀĪ awakes, and the gods of Pegāna know that it is THE END, that then the gods will enter galleons of gold, and with dream-born rowers glide down Imrāna (who knows whither or why?) till they come where the River enters the Silent Sea, and shall there be gods of nothing, where nothing is, and never a sound shall come. And far away upon the River's banks shall bay their

old hound Time, that shall seek to rend his masters; while MĀ-
NA-YOOD-SUSHĀĪ shall think some other plan concerning
gods and worlds.

The Fortress Unvanquishable, Save For Sacnoth

Lord Dunsany

In a wood older than record, a foster brother of the hills, stood the village of Allathurion; and there was peace between the people of that village and all the folk who walked in the dark ways of the wood, whether they were human or of the tribes of the beasts or of the race of the fairies and the elves and the little sacred spirits of trees and streams. Moreover, the village people had peace among themselves and between them and their lord, Lorendiac. In front of the village was a wide and grassy space, and beyond this the great wood again, but at the back the trees came right up to the houses, which, with their great beams and wooden framework and thatched roofs, green with moss, seemed almost to be a part of the forest.

Now in the time I tell of, there was trouble in Allathurion, for of an evening fell dreams were wont to come slipping through the tree trunks and into the peaceful village; and they assumed dominion of men's minds and led them in watches of the night through the cindery plains of Hell. Then the magician of that village made spells against those fell dreams; yet still the dreams came flitting through the trees as soon as the dark had fallen, and led men's minds by night into terrible places and caused them to praise Satan openly with their lips.

And men grew afraid of sleep in Allathurion. And they grew worn and pale, some through the want of rest, and others from fear of the things they saw on the cindery plains of Hell.

Then the magician of the village went up into the tower of his house, and all night long those whom fear kept awake could see his window high up in the night glowing softly alone. The next day, when the twilight was far gone and night was gathering fast, the magician went away to the forest's edge, and uttered there the spell that he had made. And the spell was a compulsive, terrible thing, having a power over evil dreams and over spirits of ill; for it was a verse of forty lines in many languages, both living and dead, and had in it the word wherewith the people of the plains are wont to curse their camels, and the shout wherewith the whalers of the north lure the whales shoreward to be killed, and a word that causes elephants to trumpet; and every one of the forty lines closed with a rhyme for "wasp."

And still the dreams came flitting through the forest, and led men's souls into the plains of Hell. Then the magician knew that the dreams were from Gaznak. Therefore he gathered the people of the village, and told them that he had uttered his mightiest spell—a spell having power over all that were human or of the tribes of the beasts; and that since it had not availed the dreams must come from Gaznak, the greatest magician among the spaces of the stars. And he read to the people out of the Book of Magicians, which tells the comings of the comet and foretells his coming again. And he told them how Gaznak rides upon the comet, and how he visits Earth once in every two hundred and thirty years, and makes for himself a vast, invincible fortress and sends out dreams to feed on the minds of men, and may never be vanquished but by the sword Sacnoth.

And a cold fear fell on the hearts of the villagers when they found that their magician had failed them.

Then spake Leothric, son of the Lord Lorendiac, and twenty years old was he: "Good Master, what of the sword Sacnoth?"

And the village magician answered: "Fair Lord, no such sword as yet is wrought, for it lies as yet in the hide of Tharagavverug, protecting his spine."

Then said Leothric: "Who is Tharagavverug, and where may he be encountered?"

And the magician of Allathurion answered: "He is the dragon-crocodile who haunts the Northern marshes and ravages the homesteads by their marge. And the hide of his back is of steel, and his under parts are of iron; but along the midst of his back, over his spine, there lies a narrow strip of unearthly steel. This strip of steel is Sacnoth, and it may be neither cleft nor molten, and there is nothing in the world that may avail to break it, nor even leave a scratch upon its surface. It is of the length of a good sword, and of the breadth thereof. Shouldst thou prevail against Tharagavverug, his hide may be melted away from Sacnoth in a furnace; but there is only one thing that may sharpen Sacnoth's edge, and this is one of Tharagavverug's own steel eyes; and the other eye thou must fasten to Sacnoth's hilt, and it will watch for thee. But it is a hard task to vanquish Tharagavverug, for no sword can pierce his hide; his back cannot be broken, and he can neither burn nor drown. In one way only can Tharagavverug die, and that is by starving."

Then sorrow fell upon Leothric, but the magician spoke on:

"If a man drive Tharagavverug away from his food with a stick for three days, he will starve on the third day at sunset. And though he is not vulnerable, yet in one spot he may take hurt, for his nose is only of lead. A sword would merely lay bare the uncleavable bronze beneath, but if his nose be smitten constantly with a stick he will always recoil from the pain, and thus may Tharagavverug, to left and right, be driven away from his food."

Then Leothric said: "What is Tharagavverug's food?"

And the magician of Allathurion said: "His food is men."

But Leothric went straightway thence, and cut a great staff from a hazel tree, and slept early that evening. But the next morning, awaking from troubled dreams, he arose before the dawn, and, taking with him provisions for five days, set out through the forest northwards towards the marshes. For some hours he moved through the gloom of the forest, and when he emerged from it the sun was above the horizon shining on pools of water in the waste land. Presently he saw the claw-marks of Tharagavverug deep in the soil, and the track of his tail between them like a furrow in a field. Then Leothric followed the tracks till he heard the bronze heart of Tharagavverug before him, booming like a bell.

And Tharagavverug, it being the hour when he took the first meal of the day, was moving towards a village with his heart tolling. And all the people of the village were come out to meet him, as it was their wont to do; for they abode not the suspense of awaiting Tharagavverug and of hearing him sniffing brazenly as he went from door to door, pondering slowly in his metal mind what habitant he should choose. And none dared to flee, for in the days when the villagers fled from Tharagavverug, he, having chosen his victim, would track him tirelessly, like a doom. Nothing availed them against Tharagavverug. Once they climbed the trees when he came, but Tharagavverug went up to one, arching his back and leaning over slightly, and rasped against the trunk until it fell. And when Leothric came near, Tharagavverug saw him out of one of his small steel eyes and came towards him leisurely, and the echoes of his heart swirled up through his open mouth. And Leothric stepped sideways from his onset, and came between him and the village and smote him on the nose, and the blow of the stick made a dint in the soft lead. And Tharagavverug swung clumsily away, uttering one fearful cry like the sound of a great church bell that had become possessed of a soul that fluttered upward from the tombs at night—an evil soul, giving the bell a voice. Then he attacked Leothric, snarling, and again Leothric leapt aside, and smote him on the nose with his stick. Tharagavverug uttered like a bell howling. And whenever the dragon-crocodile attacked him, or turned towards the village, Leothric smote him again.

So all day long Leothric drove the monster with a stick, and he drove him farther and farther from his prey, with his heart tolling angrily and his voice crying out for pain.

Towards evening Tharagavverug ceased to snap at Leothric, but ran before him to avoid the stick, for his nose was sore and shining; and in the gloaming the villagers came out and danced to cymbal and psaltery. When Tharagavverug heard the cymbal and psaltery, hunger and anger came upon him, and he felt as some lord might feel who was held by force from the banquet in his own castle and heard the creaking spit go round and round and the good meat crackling on it. And all that night he attacked Leothric fiercely, and ofttimes nearly caught him in the darkness; for his gleaming eyes of steel could see as well by night as by day. And Leothric gave ground slowly till the dawn, and when the light came they were near the village again; yet not so near to it as they had been when they encountered, for Leothric drove Tharagavverug farther in the day than Tharaga-vverug had forced him back in the night. Then Leothric drove him again with his stick till the hour came when it was the custom of the dragon-crocodile to find his man. One third of his man he would eat at the time he found him, and the rest at noon and evening. But when the hour came for finding his man a great fierceness came on Tharagavverug, and he grabbed rapidly at Leothric, but could not seize him, and for a long while neither of them would retire. But at last the pain of the stick on his leaden nose overcame the hunger of the dragon-crocodile, and he turned from it howling. From that moment Tharagavverug weakened. All that day Leothric drove him with his stick, and at night both held their ground; and when the dawn of the third day was come the heart of Tharagavverug beat slower and fainter. It was as though a tired man was ringing a bell. Once Tharagavverug nearly seized a frog, but Leothric snatched it away just in time. Towards noon the dragon-crocodile lay still for a long while, and Leothric stood near him and leaned on his trusty stick. He was very tired and sleepless, but had more leisure now for eating his provisions. With Tharagavverug the end was coming fast, and in the afternoon his breath came hoarsely, rasping in his throat. It was as the sound of many huntsmen blowing blasts on horns, and towards evening his breath came faster but fainter, like the sound of a hunt going furious to the distance and dying away, and he made desperate rushes towards the village; but Leothric still leapt about him, battering his leaden nose. Scarce audible now at all was the sound of his heart: it was like a church bell tolling beyond hills for the death of some one unknown and far away. Then the sun set and flamed in the village windows, and a chill went over the world, and in some small garden a woman sang; and Tharagavverug lifted up his head and starved, and his life went from his invulnerable body, and Leothric lay down beside him and slept. And later in the starlight the villagers came out and carried Leothric, sleeping, to the village, all praising him in whispers as they went. They laid him down upon a couch in a house, and danced outside in silence, without psaltery or cymbal. And the next day, rejoicing, to Allathurion they hauled the dragon-crocodile. And Leothric went with them, holding his battered staff; and a tall, broad man, who was smith of Allathurion, made a great furnace, and melted Tharagavverug away till only Sacnoth was left, gleaming among the ashes. Then he took one of the small eyes that had been chiselled out, and filed an edge on Sacnoth, and gradually the steel eye wore away facet by facet, but ere it was quite gone it had sharpened redoubtably Sacnoth. But the other eye they set in the butt of the hilt, and it gleamed there bluely.

And that night Leothric arose in the dark and took the sword, and went westwards to find Gaznak; and he went through the dark forest till the dawn, and all the morning and till the afternoon. But in the afternoon he came into the open and saw in the midst of The Land Where No Man Goeth the fortress of Gaznak, mountainous before him, little more than a mile away.

And Leothric saw that the land was marsh and desolate. And the fortress went up all white out of it, with many buttresses, and was broad below but narrowed higher up, and was full of gleaming windows with the light upon them. And near the top of it a few white clouds were floating, but above them some of its pinnacles reappeared. Then Leothric advanced into the marshes, and the eye of Tharagavverug looked out warily from the hilt of Sacnoth; for Tharagavverug had known the marshes well, and the sword nudged Leothric to the right or pulled him to the left away from the dangerous places, and so brought him safely to the fortress walls.

And in the wall stood doors like precipices of steel, all studded with boulders of iron, and above every window were terrible gargoyles of stone; and the name of the fortress shone on the wall, writ large in letters of brass: "The Fortress Unvanquishable, Save For Sacnoth."

Then Leothric drew and revealed Sacnoth, and all the gargoyles grinned, and the grin went flickering from face to face right up into the cloud-abiding gables.

And when Sacnoth was revealed and all the gargoyles grinned, it was like the moonlight emerging from a cloud to look for the first time upon a field of blood, and passing swiftly over the wet faces of the slain that lie together in the horrible night. Then Leothric advanced towards a door, and it was mightier than the marble quarry, Sacremona, from which of old men cut enormous slabs to build the Abbey of the Holy Tears. Day after day they wrenched out the very ribs of the hill until the Abbey was builded, and it was more beautiful than anything in stone. Then the priests blessed Sacremona, and it had rest, and no more stone was ever taken from it to build the houses of men. And the hill stood looking southwards lonely in the sunlight, defaced by that mighty scar. So vast was the door of steel. And the name of the door was The Porte Resonant, the Way of Egress for War.

Then Leothric smote upon the Porte Resonant with Sacnoth, and the echo of Sacnoth went ringing through the halls, and all the dragons in the fortress barked. And when the baying of the remotest dragon had faintly joined in the tumult, a window opened far up among the clouds below the twilit gables, and a woman screamed, and far away in Hell her father heard her and knew that her doom was come.

And Leothric went on smiting terribly with Sacnoth, and the grey steel of the Porte Resonant, the Way of Egress for War, that was tempered to resist the swords of the world, came away in ringing slices.

Then Leothric, holding Sacnoth in his hand, went in through the hole that he had hewn in the door, and came into the unlit, cavernous hall.

An elephant fled trumpeting. And Leothric stood still, holding Sacnoth. When the sound of the feet of the elephant had died away in the remoter corridors, nothing more stirred, and the cavernous hall was still.

Presently the darkness of the distant halls became musical with the sound of bells, all coming nearer and nearer.

Still Leothric waited in the dark, and the bells rang louder and louder, echoing through the halls, and there appeared a procession of men on camels riding two by two from the interior of the fortress, and they were armed with scimitars of Assyrian make and were all clad with mail, and chain-mail hung from their helmets about their faces, and flapped as the camels moved. And they all halted before Leothric in the cavernous hall, and the camel bells clanged and stopped. And the leader said to Leothric:

"The Lord Gaznak has desired to see you die before him. Be pleased to come with us, and we can discourse by the way of the manner in which the Lord Gaznak has desired to see you die."

And as he said this he unwound a chain of iron that was coiled upon his saddle, and Leothric answered:

"I would fain go with you, for I am come to slay Gaznak."

Then all the camel-guard of Gaznak laughed hideously, disturbing the vampires that were asleep in the measureless vault of the roof. And the leader said:

"The Lord Gaznak is immortal, save for Sacnoth, and weareth armour that is proof even against Sacnoth himself, and hath a sword the second most terrible in the world."

Then Leothric said: "I am the Lord of the sword Sacnoth."

And he advanced towards the camel-guard of Gaznak, and Sacnoth lifted up and down in his hand as though stirred by an exultant pulse. Then the camel-guard of Gaznak fled, and the riders leaned forward and smote their camels with whips, and they went away with a great clamour of bells through colonnades and corridors and vaulted halls, and scattered into the inner darknesses of the fortress. When the last sound of them had died away, Leothric was in doubt which way to go, for the camel-guard was dispersed in many directions, so he went straight on till he came to a great stairway in the midst of the hall. Then Leothric set his foot in the middle of a wide step, and climbed steadily up the stairway for five minutes. Little light was there in the great hall through which Leothric ascended, for it only entered through arrow slits here and there, and in the world outside evening was waning fast. The stairway led up to two folding doors, and they stood a little ajar, and through the crack Leothric entered and tried to continue straight on, but could get no farther, for the whole room seemed to be full of festoons of ropes which swung from wall to wall and were looped and draped from the ceiling. The whole chamber was thick and black with them. They were soft and light to the touch, like fine silk, but Leothric was unable to break any one of them, and though they swung away from him as he pressed forward, yet by the time he had gone three yards they were all about him like a heavy cloak. Then Leothric stepped back and drew Sacnoth, and Sacnoth divided the ropes without a sound, and without a sound the severed pieces fell to the floor. Leothric went forward slowly, moving Sacnoth in front of him up and down as he went. When he was come into the middle of the chamber, suddenly, as he parted with

Sacnoth a great hammock of strands, he saw a spider before him that was larger than a ram, and the spider looked at him with eyes that were little, but in which there was much sin, and said:

"Who are you that spoil the labour of years all done to the honour of Satan?"

And Leothric answered: "I am Leothric, son of Lorendiac."

And the spider said: "I will make a rope at once to hang you with."

Then Leothric parted another bunch of strands, and came nearer to the spider as he sat making his rope, and the spider, looking up from his work, said: "What is that sword which is able to sever my ropes?"

And Leothric said: "It is Sacnoth."

Thereat the black hair that hung over the face of the spider parted to left and right, and the spider frowned; then the hair fell back into its place, and hid everything except the sin of the little eyes which went on gleaming lustfully in the dark. But before Leothric could reach him, he climbed away with his hands, going up by one of his ropes to a lofty rafter, and there sat, growling. But clearing his way with Sacnoth, Leothric passed through the chamber, and came to the farther door; and the door being shut, and the handle far up out of his reach, he hewed his way through it with Sacnoth in the same way as he had through the Porte Resonant, the Way of Egress for War. And so Leothric came into a well-lit chamber, where Queens and Princes were banqueting together, all at a great table; and thousands of candles were glowing all about, and their light shone in the wine that the Princes drank and on the huge gold candelabra, and the royal faces were irradiant with the glow, and the white table-cloth and the silver plates and the jewels in the hair of the Queens, each jewel having a historian all to itself, who wrote no other chronicles all his days. Between the table and the door there stood two hundred footmen in two rows of one hundred facing one another. Nobody looked at Leothric as he entered through the hole in the door, but one of the Princes asked a question of a footman, and the question was passed from mouth to mouth by all the hundred footmen till it came to the last one nearest Leothric; and he said to Leothric, without looking at him:

"What do you seek here?"

And Leothric answered: "I seek to slay Gaznak."

And footman to footman repeated all the way to the table: "He seeks to slay Gaznak."

And another question came down the line of footmen: "What is your name?"

And the line that stood opposite took his answer back.

Then one of the Princes said: "Take him away where we shall not hear his screams."

And footman repeated it to footman till it came to the last two, and they advanced to seize Leothric.

Then Leothric showed to them his sword, saying, "This is Sacnoth," and both of them said to the man nearest: "It is Sacnoth;" then screamed and fled away.

And two by two, all up the double line, footman to footman repeated, "It is Sacnoth," then screamed and fled, till the last two gave the message to the table, and all the rest had gone. Hurriedly then arose the Queens and Princes, and fled out of the chamber. And the goodly table, when they were all gone, looked small and disorderly and awry. And to Leothric, pondering in the desolate chamber by what door he should pass onwards, there came from far away the sounds of music, and he knew that it was the magical musicians playing to Gaznak while he slept.

Then Leothric, walking towards the distant music, passed out by the door opposite to the one through which he had cloven his entrance, and so passed into a chamber vast as the other, in which were many women, weirdly beautiful. And they all asked him of his quest, and when they heard that it was to slay Gaznak, they all besought him to tarry among them, saying that Gaznak was immortal, save for Sacnoth, and also that they had need of a knight to protect them from the wolves that rushed round and round the wainscot all the night and sometimes broke in upon them through the mouldering oak. Perhaps Leothric had been tempted to tarry had they been human women, for theirs was a strange beauty, but he perceived that instead of eyes they had little flames that flickered in their sockets, and knew them to be the fevered dreams of Gaznak. Therefore he said:

"I have a business with Gaznak and with Sacnoth," and passed on through the chamber.

And at the name of Sacnoth those women screamed, and the flames of their eyes sank low and dwindled to sparks.

And Leothric left them, and, hewing with Sacnoth, passed through the farther door.

Outside he felt the night air on his face, and found that he stood upon a narrow way between two abysses. To left and right of him, as far as he could see, the walls of the fortress ended in a profound precipice, though the roof still stretched above him; and before him lay the two abysses full of stars, for they cut their way through the whole Earth and revealed the under sky; and threading its course between them went the way, and it sloped upward and its sides were sheer. And beyond the abysses, where the way led up to the farther chambers of the fortress, Leothric heard the musicians playing their magical tune. So he stepped on to the way, which was scarcely a stride in width, and moved along it holding Sacnoth naked. And to and fro beneath him in each abyss whirred the wings of vampires passing up and down, all giving praise to Satan as they flew. Presently he perceived the dragon Thok lying upon the way, pretending to sleep, and his tail hung down into one of the abysses.

And Leothric went towards him, and when he was quite close Thok rushed at Leothric.

And he smote deep with Sacnoth, and Thok tumbled into the abyss, screaming, and his limbs made a whirring in the darkness as he fell, and he fell till his scream sounded no louder than a whistle and then could be heard no more. Once or twice Leothric saw a star blink for an instant and reappear again, and this momentary eclipse of a few stars was all that remained in the world of the body of Thok. And Lunk, the brother of Thok, who had lain a little behind him, saw that this must be Sacnoth and fled lumbering away. And all the while that he walked between the abysses, the mighty vault of the roof of the fortress still stretched over Leothric's head, all filled with gloom. Now, when the farther side of the abyss came into view, Leothric saw a chamber that opened with innumerable arches upon the twin abysses, and the pillars of the arches went away into the distance and vanished in the gloom to left and right.

Far down the dim precipice on which the pillars stood he could see windows small and closely barred, and between the bars there showed at moments, and disappeared again, things that I shall not speak of.

There was no light here except for the great Southern stars that shone below the abysses, and here and there in the chamber through the arches lights that moved furtively without the sound of footfall.

Then Leothric stepped from the way, and entered the great chamber.

Even to himself he seemed but a tiny dwarf as he walked under one of those colossal arches.

The last faint light of evening flickered through a window painted in sombre colours commemorating the achievements of Satan upon Earth. High up in the wall the window stood, and the streaming lights of candles lower down moved stealthily away.

Other light there was none, save for a faint blue glow from the steel eye of Tharagavverug that peered restlessly about it from the hilt of Sacnoth. Heavily in the chamber hung the clammy odour of a large and deadly beast.

Leothric moved forward slowly with the blade of Sacnoth in front of him feeling for a foe, and the eye in the hilt of it looking out behind.

Nothing stirred.

If anything lurked behind the pillars of the colonnade that held aloft the roof, it neither breathed nor moved.

The music of the magical musicians sounded from very near.

Suddenly the great doors on the far side of the chamber opened to left and right. For some moments Leothric saw nothing move, and waited clutching Sacnoth. Then Wong Bongerok came towards him, breathing.

This was the last and faithfullest guard of Gaznak, and came from slobbering just now his master's hand.

More as a child than a dragon was Gaznak wont to treat him, giving him often in his fingers tender pieces of man all smoking from his table.

Long and low was Wong Bongerok, and subtle about the eyes, and he came breathing malice against Leothric out of his faithful breast, and behind him roared the armoury of his tail, as when sailors drag the cable of the anchor all rattling down the deck.

And well Wong Bongerok knew that he now faced Sacnoth, for it had been his wont to prophesy quietly to himself for many years as he lay curled at the feet of Gaznak.

And Leothric stepped forward into the blast of his breath, and lifted Sacnoth to strike.

But when Sacnoth was lifted up, the eye of Tharagavverug in the butt of the hilt beheld the dragon and perceived his subtlety.

For he opened his mouth wide, and revealed to Leothric the ranks of his sabre teeth, and his leather gums flapped upwards. But while Leothric made to smite at his head, he shot forward scorpion-wise over his head the length of his armoured tail. All this the eye perceived in the hilt of Sacnoth, who smote suddenly sideways. Not with the edge smote Sacnoth, for, had he done so, the severed end of the tail had still come hurtling on, as some pine tree that the avalanche has hurled point foremost from the cliff right through the broad breast of some mountaineer. So had Leothric been transfixed; but Sacnoth smote sideways with the flat of his blade, and sent the tail whizzing over Leothric's left shoulder; and it rasped upon his armour as it went, and left a groove upon it. Sideways then at Leothric smote the foiled tail of Wong Bongerok, and Sacnoth parried, and the tail went shrieking up the blade and over Leothric's head. Then Leothric and Wong Bongerok fought sword to tooth, and the sword smote as only Sacnoth can, and the evil faithful life of Wong Bongerok the dragon went out through the wide wound.

Then Leothric walked on past that dead monster, and the armoured body still quivered a little. And for a while it was like all the ploughshares in a county working together in one field behind tired and struggling horses; then the quivering ceased, and Wong Bongerok lay still to rust.

And Leothric went on to the open gates, and Sacnoth dripped quietly along the floor.

By the open gates through which Wong Bongerok had entered, Leothric came into a corridor echoing with music. This was the first place from which Leothric could see anything above his head, for hitherto the roof had ascended to mountainous heights and had stretched indistinct in the gloom. But along the narrow corridor hung huge bells low and near to his head, and the width of each brazen bell was from wall to wall, and they were one behind the other. And as he passed under each the bell uttered, and its voice was mournful and deep, like to the voice of a bell speaking to a man for the last time when he is newly dead. Each bell uttered once as Leothric came under it, and their voices sounded solemnly and wide apart at ceremonious intervals. For if he walked slow, these bells came closer together, and when he walked swiftly they moved farther apart. And the echoes of each bell tolling above his head went on before him whispering to the others. Once when he stopped they all jangled angrily till he went on again.

Between these slow and boding notes came the sound of the magical musicians. They were playing a dirge now very mournfully.

And at last Leothric came to the end of the Corridor of the Bells, and beheld there a small black door. And all the corridor behind him was full of the echoes of the tolling, and they all muttered to one another about the ceremony; and the dirge of the musicians came floating slowly through them like a procession of foreign elaborate guests, and all of them boded ill to Leothric.

The black door opened at once to the hand of Leothric, and he found himself in the open air in a wide court paved with marble. High over it shone the moon, summoned there by the hand of Gaznak.

There Gaznak slept, and around him sat his magical musicians, all playing upon strings. And, even sleeping, Gaznak was clad in armour, and only his wrists and face and neck were bare.

But the marvel of that place was the dreams of Gaznak; for beyond the wide court slept a dark abyss, and into the abyss there poured a white cascade of marble stairways, and widened out below into terraces and balconies with fair white statues on them, and descended again in a wide stairway, and came to lower terraces in the dark, where swart uncertain shapes went to and fro. All these were the dreams of Gaznak, and issued from his mind, and, becoming gleaming marble, passed over the edge of the abyss as the musicians played. And all the while out of the mind of Gaznak, lulled by that strange music, went spires and pinnacles beautiful and slender, ever ascending skywards. And the marble dreams moved slow in time to the music. When the bells tolled and the musicians played their dirge, ugly gargoyles came out suddenly all over the spires and pinnacles, and great shadows passed swiftly down the steps and terraces, and there was hurried whispering in the abyss.

When Leothric stepped from the black door, Gaznak opened his eyes. He looked neither to left nor right, but stood up at once facing Leothric.

Then the magicians played a deathspell on their strings, and there arose a humming along the blade of Sacnoth as he turned the spell aside. When Leothric dropped not down, and they heard the humming of Sacnoth, the magicians arose and fled, all wailing, as they went, upon their strings.

Then Gaznak drew out screaming from its sheath the sword that was the mightiest in the world except for Sacnoth, and slowly walked towards Leothric; and he smiled as he walked, although his own dreams had foretold his doom. And when Leothric and Gaznak came together, each looked at each, and neither spoke a word; but they smote both at once, and their swords met, and each sword knew the other and from whence he came. And whenever the sword of Gaznak smote on the blade of Sacnoth it rebounded gleaming, as hail from off slated roofs; but whenever it fell upon the armour of Leothric, it stripped it off in sheets. And upon Gaznak's armour Sacnoth fell oft and furiously, but ever he came back snarling, leaving no mark behind, and as Gaznak fought he held his left hand hovering close over his head. Presently Leothric smote fair and fiercely at his enemy's neck, but Gaznak, clutching his own head by the hair, lifted it high aloft, and Sacnoth went cleaving through an empty space. Then Gaznak replaced his head upon his neck, and all the while fought nimbly with his sword; and again and again Leothric swept with Sacnoth at Gaznak's bearded neck, and ever the left hand of Gaznak was quicker than the stroke, and the head went up and the sword rushed vainly under it.

And the ringing fight went on till Leothric's armour lay all round him on the floor and the marble was splashed with his blood, and the sword of Gaznak was notched like a saw from meeting the blade of Sacnoth. Still Gaznak stood unwounded and smiling still.

At last Leothric looked at the throat of Gaznak and aimed with

Sacnoth, and again Gaznak lifted his head by the hair; but not at his throat flew Sacnoth, for Leothric struck instead at the lifted hand, and through the wrist of it went Sacnoth whirring, as a scythe goes through the stem of a single flower.

And bleeding, the severed hand fell to the floor; and at once blood spurted from the shoulders of Gaznak and dripped from the fallen head, and the tall pinnacles went down into the earth, and the wide fair terraces all rolled away, and the court was gone like the dew, and a wind came and the colonnades drifted thence, and all the colossal halls of Gaznak fell. And the abysses closed up suddenly as the mouth of a man who, having told a tale, will for ever speak no more.

Then Leothric looked around him in the marshes where the night mist was passing away, and there was no fortress nor sound of dragon or mortal, only beside him lay an old man, wizened and evil and dead, whose head and hand were severed from his body.

And gradually over the wide lands the dawn was coming up, and ever growing in beauty as it came, like to the peal of an organ played by a master's hand, growing louder and lovelier as the soul of the master warms, and at last giving praise with all its mighty voice.

Then the birds sang, and Leothric went homeward, and left the marshes and came to the dark wood, and the light of the dawn ascending lit him upon his way. And into Allathurion he came ere noon, and with him brought the evil wizened head, and the people rejoiced, and their nights of trouble ceased.

This is the tale of the vanquishing of The Fortress Unvanquishable, Save For Sacnoth, and of its passing away, as it is told and believed by those who love the mystic days of old.

Others have said, and vainly claim to prove, that a fever came to Allathurion, and went away; and that this same fever drove Leothric into the marshes by night, and made him dream there and act violently with a sword.

And others again say that there hath been no town of Allathurion, and that Leothric never lived.

Peace to them. The gardener hath gathered up this autumn's leaves. Who shall see them again, or who wot of them? And who shall say what hath befallen in the days of long ago?

The Sword of Welleran

Lord Dunsany

Where the great plain of Tarphet runs up, as the sea in estuaries, among the Cyresian mountains, there stood long since the city of Merimna well-nigh among the shadows of the crags. I have never seen a city in the world so beautiful as Merimna seemed to me when first I dreamed of it. It was a marvel of spires and figures of bronze, and marble fountains, and trophies of fabulous wars, and broad streets given over wholly to the Beautiful. Right through the centre of the city there went an avenue fifty strides in width, and along each side of it stood likenesses in bronze of the Kings of all the countries that the people of Merimna had ever known. At the end of that avenue was a colossal chariot with three bronze horses driven by the winged figure of Fame, and behind her in the chariot the huge form of Welleran, Merimna's ancient hero, standing with extended sword. So urgent was the mien and attitude of Fame, and so swift the pose of the horses, that you had sworn that the chariot was instantly upon you, and that its dust already veiled the faces of the Kings. And in the city was a mighty hall wherein were stored the trophies of Merimna's heroes. Sculptured it was and domed, the glory of the art of masons a long while dead, and on the summit of the dome the image of Rollory sat gazing across the Cyresian mountains towards the wide lands beyond, the lands that knew his sword. And beside Rollory, like an old nurse, the figure of Victory sat, hammering into a golden wreath of laurels for his head the crowns of fallen Kings.

Such was Merimna, a city of sculptured Victories and warriors of bronze. Yet in the time of which I write the art of war had been forgotten in Merimna, and the people almost slept. To and fro and up and down they would walk through the marble streets, gazing at memorials of the things achieved by their country's swords in the hands of those that long ago had loved Merimna well. Almost they slept, and dreamed of Welleran, Soorenard, Mommolek, Rollory, Akanax, and young Iraine. Of the lands beyond the mountains that lay all round about them they knew nothing, save that they were the theatre of the terrible deeds of Welleran, that he had done with his sword. Long since these lands had fallen back into the possession of the nations that had been scourged by Merimna's armies. Nothing now remained to Merimna's men save their inviolate city and the glory of the remembrance of their ancient fame. At night they would place sentinels far out in the desert, but these always slept at their posts dreaming of Rollory, and three times every night a guard would march around the city clad in purple, bearing lights and singing songs of Welleran. Always the guard went unarmed, but as the sound of their song went echoing across the plain towards the looming mountains, the desert robbers would hear the name of Welleran and steal away to their haunts. Often dawn would come across the plain, shimmering marvellously upon Merimna's spires, abashing all the stars, and find the guard still singing songs of Welleran, and would change the colour of their purple robes and pale the lights they bore. But the guard would go back leaving the ramparts safe, and one by one the sentinels in the plain would awake from dreaming of Rollory and shuffle back into the city quite cold. Then something of the menace would pass away from the faces of the Cyresian mountains, that from the north and the west and the south lowered upon Merimna, and clear in the morning the statues and the pillars would arise in the old inviolate city. You would wonder that an unarmed guard and sentinels that slept could defend a city that was stored with all the glories of art, that was rich in gold and bronze, a haughty city that had erst oppressed its neighbours, whose people had forgotten the art of war. Now this is the reason that, though all her other lands had long been taken from her, Merimna's city was safe. A strange thing was believed or feared by the fierce tribes beyond the mountains, and it was credited among them that at certain stations round Merimna's ramparts there still rode Welleran,

Soorenard, Mommolek, Rollory, Akanax, and young Iraine. Yet it was close on a hundred years since Iraine, the youngest of Merimna's heroes, fought his last battle with the tribes.

Sometimes indeed there arose among the tribes young men who doubted and said: "How may a man for ever escape death?"

But graver men answered them: "Hear us, ye whose wisdom has discerned so much, and discern for us how a man may escape death when two score horsemen assail him with their swords, all of them sworn to kill him, and all of them sworn upon their country's gods; as often Welleran hath. Or discern for us how two men alone may enter a walled city by night, and bring away from it that city's king, as did Soorenard and Mommolek. Surely men that have escaped so many swords and so many sleety arrows shall escape the years and Time."

And the young men were humbled and became silent. Still, the suspicion grew. And often when the sun set on the Cyresian mountains, men in Merimna discerned the forms of savage tribesmen black against the light, peering towards the city.

All knew in Merimna that the figures round the ramparts were only statues of stone, yet even there a hope lingered among a few that some day their old heroes would come again, for certainly none had ever seen them die. Now it had been the wont of these six warriors of old, as each received his last wound and knew it to be mortal, to ride away to a certain deep ravine and cast his body in, as somewhere I have read great elephants do, hiding their bones away from lesser beasts. It was a ravine steep and narrow even at the ends, a great cleft into which no man could come by any path. There rode Welleran alone, panting hard; and there later rode Soorenard and Mommolek, Mommolek with a mortal wound upon him not to return, but Soorenard was unwounded and rode back alone from leaving his dear friend resting among the mighty bones of Welleran. And there rode Soorenard, when his day was come, with Rollory and Akanax, and Rollory rode in the middle and Soorenard and Akanax on either side. And the long ride was a hard and weary thing for Soorenard and Akanax, for they both had mortal wounds; but the long ride was easy for Rollory, for he was dead. So the bones of these five heroes whitened in an enemy's land, and very still they were, though they had troubled cities, and none knew where they lay saving only Iraine, the young captain, who was but twenty-five when Mommolek, Rollory, and Akanax rode away. And among them were strewn their saddles and their bridles, and all the accoutrements of their horses, lest any man should ever find them afterwards and say in some foreign city: "Lo! the bridles or the saddles of Merimna's captains, taken in war," but their beloved trusty horses they turned free.

Forty years afterwards, in the hour of a great victory, his last wound came upon Iraine, and the wound was terrible and would not close. And Iraine was the last of the captains, and rode away alone. It was a long way to the dark ravine, and Iraine feared that he would never come to the resting-place of the old heroes, and he urged his horse on swiftly, and clung to the saddle with his hands. And often as he rode he fell asleep, and dreamed of earlier days, and of the times when he first rode forth to the great wars of Welleran, and of the time when Welleran first spake to him, and of the faces of Welleran's comrades when they led charges in the battle. And ever as he awoke a great longing arose in his soul as it hovered on his body's brink, a longing to lie among the bones of the old heroes. At last when he saw the dark ravine making a scar across the plain, the soul of Iraine slipped out through his great wound and spread its wings, and pain departed from the poor hacked body and, still urging his horse forward, Iraine died. But the old true horse cantered on till suddenly he saw before him the dark ravine and put his forefeet out on the very edge of it and stopped. Then the body of Iraine came toppling forward over the right shoulder of the horse, and his bones mingle and rest as the years go by with the bones of Merimna's heroes.

Now there was a little boy in Merimna named Rold. I saw him first, I, the dreamer, that sit before my fire asleep, I saw him first as his mother led him through the great hall where stand the trophies of Merimna's heroes. He was five years old, and they stood before the great glass casket wherein lay the sword of Welleran, and his mother said: "The sword of Welleran." And Rold said: "What should a man do with the sword of Welleran?" And his mother answered: "Men look at the sword and remember Welleran." And they went on and stood before the great red cloak of Welleran, and the child said: "Why did Welleran wear this great red cloak?" And his mother answered: "It was the way of Welleran."

When Rold was a little older he stole out of his mother's house quite in the middle of the night when all the world was still, and Merimna asleep dreaming of Welleran, Soorenard, Mommolek, Rollory, Akanax, and young Iraine. And he went down to the ramparts to hear the purple guard go by singing of Welleran. And the purple guard came by with lights, all singing in the stillness, and dark shapes out in the desert turned and fled. And Rold went back again to his mother's house with a great yearning towards the name of Welleran, such as men feel for very holy things.

And in time Rold grew to know the pathway all round the ramparts, and the six equestrian statues that were there guarding Merimna still. These statues were not like other statues, they were so cunningly wrought of many-coloured marbles that none might be quite sure until very close that they were not living men. There was a horse of dappled marble, the horse of Akanax. The horse of Rollory was of alabaster, pure white, his armour was wrought out of a stone that shone, and his horseman's cloak was made of a blue stone, very precious. He looked northwards.

But the marble horse of Welleran was pure black, and there sat Welleran upon him looking solemnly westwards. His horse it was whose cold neck Rold most loved to stroke, and it was Welleran whom the watchers at sunset on the mountains the most clearly saw as they peered towards the city. And Rold loved the red nostrils of the great black horse and his rider's jasper cloak.

Now beyond the Cyresians the suspicion grew that Merimna's heroes were dead, and a plan was devised that a man should go by night and come close to the figures upon the ramparts and see whether they were Welleran, Soorenard, Mommolek, Rollory, Akanax, and young Iraine. And all were agreed upon the plan, and many names were mentioned of those who should go, and the plan matured for many years. It was during these years that watchers clustered often at sunset upon the mountains but came no nearer. Finally, a better plan was made, and it was decided that two men who had been by chance condemned to death should be given a pardon if they went down into the plain by night and discovered whether or not Merimna's heroes lived. At first the two prisoners dared not go, but after a while one of them, Seejar, said to his companion, Sajar-Ho: "See now, when the King's axeman smites a man upon the neck that man dies."

And the other said that this was so. Then said Seejar: "And even though Welleran smite a man with his sword no more befalleth him than death."

Then Sajar-Ho thought for a while. Presently he said: "Yet the eye of the King's axeman might err at the moment of his stroke or his arm fail him, and the eye of Welleran hath never erred nor his arm failed. It were better to bide here."

Then said Seejar: "Maybe that Welleran is dead and that some other holds his place upon the ramparts, or even a statue of stone."

But Sajar-Ho made answer: "How can Welleran be dead when he even escaped from two score horsemen with swords that were sworn to slay him, and all sworn upon our country's gods?"

And Seejar said: "This story his father told my grandfather concerning Welleran. On the day that the fight was lost on the plains of Kurlistan he saw a dying horse near to the river, and the horse looked piteously towards the water but could not reach it. And the father of my grandfather saw Welleran go down to the river's brink and bring water from it with his own hand and give it to the horse. Now we are in as sore a plight as was that horse, and as near to death; it may be that Welleran will pity us, while the King's axeman cannot because of the commands of the King."

Then said Sajar-Ho: "Thou wast ever a cunning arguer. Thou broughtest us into this trouble with thy cunning and thy devices, we will see if thou canst bring us out of it. We will go."

So news was brought to the King that the two prisoners would go down to Merimna.

That evening the watchers led them to the mountain's edge, and Seejar and Sajar-Ho went down towards the plain by the way of a deep ravine, and the watchers watched them go. Presently their figures were wholly hid in the dusk. Then night came up, huge and holy, out of waste marshes to the eastwards and low lands and the sea; and the angels that watched over all men through the day closed their great eyes and slept, and the angels that watched over all men through the night awoke and ruffled their deep blue feathers and stood up and watched. But the plain became a thing of mystery filled with fears. So the two spies went down the deep ravine, and coming to the plain sped stealthily across it. Soon they came to the line of sentinels asleep upon the sand, and one stirred in his sleep calling on Rollory, and a great dread seized upon the spies and they whispered "Rollory lives," but they remembered the King's axeman and went on. And next they came to the great bronze statue of Fear, carved by some sculptor of the old glorious years in the attitude of flight towards the mountains, calling to her children as she fled. And the children of Fear were carved in the likeness of the armies of all the trans-Cyresian tribes with their backs towards Merimna, flocking after Fear. And from where he sat on his horse behind the ramparts the sword of Welleran was stretched out over their heads as ever it was wont. And the two spies kneeled down in the sand and kissed the huge bronze foot of the statue of Fear, saying: "O Fear, Fear." And as they knelt they saw lights far off along the ramparts coming nearer and nearer, and heard men singing of Welleran. And the purple guard came nearer and went by with their lights, and passed on into the distance round the ramparts still singing of Welleran. And all the while the two spies clung to the foot of the statue, muttering: "O Fear, Fear." But when they could hear the name of Welleran no more they arose and came to the ramparts and climbed over them and came at once upon the figure of Welleran, and they bowed low to the ground, and Seejar said: "O Welleran, we came to see whether thou didst yet live." And for a long while they waited with their faces to the earth. At last Seejar looked up towards Welleran's terrible sword, and it was still stretched out pointing to the carved armies that followed after Fear. And Seejar bowed to the ground again and touched the horse's hoof, and it seemed cold to him. And he moved his hand higher and touched the leg of the horse, and it seemed quite cold. At last he touched Welleran's foot, and the armour on it seemed hard and stiff. Then as Welleran moved not and spake not, Seejar climbed up at last and touched his hand, the terrible hand of Welleran, and it was marble. Then Seejar laughed aloud, and he and Sajar-Ho sped down the empty pathway and found Rollory, and he was marble too. Then they climbed down over the ramparts and went back across the plain, walking contemptuously past the figure of Fear, and heard the guard returning round the ramparts for the third time, singing of Welleran; and Seejar said: "Ay, you may sing of Welleran, but Welleran is dead and a doom is on your city."

And they passed on and found the sentinel still restless in the night and calling on Rollory. And Sajar-Ho muttered: "Ay, you may call on Rollory, but Rollory is dead and naught can save your city."

And the two spies went back alive to their mountains again, and as they reached them the first ray of the sun came up red over the desert behind Merimna and lit Merimna's spires. It was the hour when the purple guard were wont to go back into the city with their tapers pale and their robes a brighter colour, when the cold sentinels came shuffling in from dreaming in the desert; it was the hour when the desert robbers hid themselves away, going back to their mountain caves; it was the hour when gauze-winged insects are born that only live for a day; it was the hour when men die that are condemned to death; and in this hour a great peril, new and terrible, arose for Merimna and Merimna knew it not.

Then Seejar turning said: 'See how red the dawn is and how red the spires of Merimna. They are angry with Merimna in Paradise and they bode its doom."

So the two spies went back and brought the news to their King, and for a few days the Kings of those countries were gathering their armies together; and one evening the armies of four Kings were massed together at the top of the deep ravine, all crouching below the summit waiting for the sun to set. All wore resolute and fearless faces, yet inwardly every man was praying to his gods, unto each one in turn.

Then the sun set, and it was the hour when the bats and the dark creatures are abroad and the lions come down from their lairs, and the desert robbers go into the plains again, and fevers rise up winged and hot out of chill marshes, and it was the hour when safety leaves the thrones of Kings, the hour when dynasties change. But in the desert the purple guard came swinging out of Merimna with their lights to sing of Welleran, and the sentinels lay down to sleep.

Now into Paradise no sorrow may ever come, but may only beat like rain against its crystal walls, yet the souls of Merimna's heroes were half aware of some sorrow far away as some sleeper feels that some one is chilled and cold yet knows not in his sleep that it is he. And they fretted a little in their starry home. Then unseen there drifted earthward across the setting sun the souls of Welleran, Soorenard, Mommolek, Rollory, Akanax, and young Iraine. Already when they reached Merimna's ramparts it was just dark, already the armies of the four Kings had begun to move, jingling, down the deep ravine. But when the six warriors saw their city again, so little changed after so many years, they looked towards her with a longing that was nearer to tears than any that their souls had known before, crying to her:

"O Merimna, our city: Merimna, our walled city.

"How beautiful thou art with all thy spires, Merimna. For thee we left the earth, its kingdoms and little flowers, for thee we have come away for awhile from Paradise.

"It is very difficult to draw away from the face of God—it is like a warm fire, it is like dear sleep, it is like a great anthem, yet there is a stillness all about it, a stillness full of lights.

"We have left Paradise for awhile for thee, Merimna.

"Many women have we loved, Merimna, but only one city.

"Behold now all the people dream, all our loved people. How beautiful are dreams! In dreams the dead may live, even the long dead and the very silent. Thy lights are all sunk low, they have all gone out, no sound is in thy streets. Hush! Thou art like a maiden that shutteth up her eyes and is asleep, that draweth her breath softly and is quite still, being at ease and untroubled.

"Behold now the battlements, the old battlements. Do men defend them still as we defended them? They are worn a little, the battlements," and drifting nearer they peered anxiously. "It is not by the hand of man that they are worn, our battlements. Only the years have done it and indomitable Time. Thy battlements are like the girdle of a maiden, a girdle that is round about her. See now the dew upon them, they are like a jewelled girdle.

"Thou art in great danger, Merimna, because thou art so beautiful. Must thou perish tonight because we no more defend thee, because we cry out and none hear us, as the bruised lilies cry out and none have known their voices?"

Thus spake those strong-voiced, battle-ordering captains, calling to their dear city, and their voices came no louder than the whispers of little bats that drift across the twilight in the evening. Then the purple guard came near, going round the ramparts for the first time in the night, and the old warriors called to them, "Merimna is in danger! Already her enemies gather in the darkness." But their voices were never heard because they were only wandering ghosts. And the guard went by and passed unheeding away, still singing of Welleran.

Then said Welleran to his comrades: "Our hands can hold swords no more, our voices cannot be heard, we are stalwart men no longer. We are but dreams, let us go among dreams. Go all of you, and thou too, young Iraine, and trouble the dreams of all the men that sleep, and urge them to take the old swords of their grandsires that hang upon the walls, and to gather at the mouth of the ravine; and I will find a leader and make him take my sword."

Then they passed up over the ramparts and into their dear city. And the wind blew about, this way and that, as he went, the soul of Welleran who had upon his day withstood the charges of tempestuous armies. And the souls of his comrades, and with them young Iraine, passed up into the city and troubled the dreams of every man who slept, and to every man the souls said in their dreams: "It is hot and still in the city. Go out now into the desert, into the cool under the mountains, but take with thee the old sword that hangs upon the wall for fear of the desert robbers."

And the god of that city sent up a fever over it, and the fever brooded over it and the streets were hot; and all that slept awoke from dreaming that it would be cool and pleasant where the breezes came down the ravine out of the mountains; and they took the old swords that their grandsires had, according to their dreams, for fear of the desert robbers. And in and out of dreams passed the souls of Welleran's comrades, and with them young Iraine, in great haste as the night wore on; and one by one they troubled the dreams of all Merimna's men and caused them to arise and go out armed, all save the purple guard who, heedless of danger, sang of Welleran still, for waking men cannot hear the souls of the dead.

But Welleran drifted over the roofs of the city till he came to the form of Rold lying fast asleep. Now Rold was grown strong and was eighteen years of age, and he was fair of hair and tall like Welleran, and the soul of Welleran hovered over him and went into his dreams as a butterfly flits through trellis-work into a garden of flowers, and the soul of Welleran said to Rold in his dreams: "Thou wouldst go and see again the sword of Welleran, the great curved sword of Welleran. Thou wouldst go and look at it in the night with the moonlight shining upon it."

And the longing of Rold in his dreams to see the sword caused him to walk still sleeping from his mother's house to the hall wherein were the trophies of the heroes. And the soul of Welleran urging the dreams of Rold caused him to pause before the great red cloak, and there the soul said among the dreams: "Thou art cold in the night; fling now a cloak around thee."

And Rold drew round about him the huge red cloak of Welleran. Then Rold's dreams took him to the sword, and the soul said to the dreams: "Thou hast a longing to hold the sword of Welleran: take up the sword in thy hand."

But Rold said: "What should a man do with the sword of Welleran?"

And the soul of the old captain said to the dreams: "It is a good sword to hold: take up the sword of Welleran."

And Rold, still sleeping and speaking aloud, said: "It is not lawful; none may touch the sword."

And Rold turned to go. Then a great and terrible cry arose in the soul of Welleran, all the more bitter for that he could not utter it, and it went round and round his soul finding no utterance, like a cry evoked long since by some murderous deed in some old haunted chamber that whispers through the ages heard by none.

And the soul of Welleran cried out to the dreams of Rold: "Thy knees are tied! Thou art fallen in a marsh! Thou canst not move."

And the dreams of Rold said to him: "Thy knees are tied, thou art fallen in a marsh," and Rold stood still before the sword. Then the soul of the warrior wailed among Rold's dreams, as Rold stood before the sword.

"Welleran is crying for his sword, his wonderful curved sword. Poor Welleran, that once fought for Merimna, is crying for his sword in the night. Thou wouldst not keep Welleran without his beautiful sword when he is dead and cannot come for it, poor Welleran who fought for Merimna."

And Rold broke the glass casket with his hand and took the sword, the great curved sword of Welleran; and the soul of the warrior said among Rold's dreams: "Welleran is waiting in the deep ravine that runs into the mountains, crying for his sword."

And Rold went down through the city and climbed over the ramparts, and walked with his eyes wide open but still sleeping over the desert to the mountains.

Already a great multitude of Merimna's citizens were gathered in the desert before the deep ravine with old swords in their hands, and Rold passed through them as he slept holding the sword of Welleran, and the people cried in amaze to one another as he passed: "Rold hath the sword of Welleran!"

And Rold came to the mouth of the ravine, and there the voices of the people woke him. And Rold knew nothing that he had done in his sleep, and looked in amazement at the sword in his hand and said: "What art thou, thou beautiful thing? Lights shimmer in thee, thou art restless. It is the sword of Welleran, the curved sword of Welleran!"

And Rold kissed the hilt of it, and it was salt upon his lips with the battle-sweat of Welleran. And Rold said: "What should a man do with the sword of Welleran?"

And all the people wondered at Rold as he sat there with the sword in his hand muttering, "What should a man do with the sword of Welleran?"

Presently there came to the ears of Rold the noise of a jingling up in the ravine, and all the people, the people that knew naught of war, heard the jingling coming nearer in the night; for the four armies were moving on Merimna and not yet expecting an enemy. And Rold gripped upon the hilt of the great curved sword, and the sword seemed to lift a little. And a new thought came into the hearts of Merimna's people as they gripped their grandsires' swords. Nearer and nearer came the heedless armies of the four Kings, and old ancestral memories began to arise in the minds of Merimna's people in the desert with their swords in their hands sitting behind Rold.

And all the sentinels were awake holding their spears, for Rollory had put their dreams to flight, Rollory that once could put to flight armies and now was but a dream struggling with other dreams.

And now the armies had come very near. Suddenly Rold leaped up, crying: "Welleran! And the sword of Welleran!" And the savage, lusting sword that had thirsted for a hundred years went up with the hand of Rold and swept through a tribesman's ribs. And with the warm blood all about it there came a joy into the curved soul of that mighty sword, like to the joy of a swimmer coming up dripping out of warm seas after living for long in a dry land. When they saw the red cloak and that terrible sword a cry ran through the tribal armies, "Welleran lives!" And there arose the sounds of the exulting of victorious men, and the panting of those that fled, and the sword singing softly to itself as it whirled dripping through the air. And the last that I saw of the battle as it poured into the depth and darkness of the ravine was the sword of Welleran sweeping up and falling, gleaming blue in the moonlight whenever it arose and afterwards gleaming red, and so disappearing into the darkness.

But in the dawn Merimna's men came back, and the sun arising to give new life to the world, shone instead upon the hideous things that the sword of Welleran had done. And Rold said: "O sword, sword! How horrible thou art! Thou art a terrible thing to have come among men. How many eyes shall look upon gardens no more because of thee? How many fields must go empty that might have been fair with cottages, white cottages with children all about them? How many valleys must go desolate that might have nursed warm hamlets, because thou hast slain long since the men that might have built them? I hear the wind crying against thee, thou sword! It comes from the empty valleys. It comes over the bare fields. There are children's voices in it. They were never born. Death brings an end to crying for those that had life once, but these must cry for ever. O sword! sword! why did the gods send thee among men?" And the tears of Rold fell down upon the proud sword but could not wash it clean.

And now that the ardour of battle had passed away, the spirits of Merimna's people began to gloom a little, like their leader's, with their fatigue and with the cold of the morning; and they looked at the sword of Welleran in Rold's hand and said: "Not any more, not any more for ever will Welleran now return, for his sword is in the hand of another. Now we know indeed that he is dead. O Welleran, thou wast our sun and moon and all our stars. Now is the sun fallen down and the moon broken, and all the stars are scattered as the diamonds of a necklace that is snapped off one who is slain by violence."

Thus wept the people of Merimna in the hour of their great victory, for men have strange moods, while beside them their old inviolate city slumbered safe. But back from the ramparts and beyond the mountains and over the lands that they had conquered of old, beyond the world and back again to Paradise, went the souls of Welleran, Soorenard, Mommolek, Rollory, Akanax, and young Iraine.

Carcassonne

Lord Dunsany

[In a letter from a friend whom I have never seen, one of those that read my books, this line was quoted—"But he, he never came to Carcassonne." I do not know the origin of the line, but I made this tale about it.]

When Camorak reigned at Arn, and the world was fairer, he gave a festival to all the weald to commemorate the splendour of his youth.

They say that his house at Arn was huge and high, and its ceiling painted blue; and when evening fell men would climb up by ladders and light the scores of candles hanging from slender chains. And they say, too, that sometimes a cloud would come, and pour in through the top of one of the oriel windows, and it would come over the edge of the stonework as the sea-mist comes over a sheer cliff's shaven lip where an old wind has blown for ever and ever (he has swept away thousands of leaves and thousands of centuries, they are all one to him, he owes no allegiance to Time). And the cloud would re-shape itself in the hall's lofty vault and drift on through it slowly, and out to the sky again through another window. And from its shape the knights in Camorak's hall would prophesy the battles and sieges of the next season of war. They say of the hall of Camorak at Arn that there hath been none like it in any land, and foretell that there will be never.

Hither had come in the folk of the Weald from sheepfold and from forest, revolving slow thoughts of food, and shelter, and love, and they sat down wondering in that famous hall; and therein also were seated the men of Arn, the town that clustered round the King's high house, and was all roofed with red, maternal earth.

If old songs may be trusted, it was a marvellous hall.

Many who sat there could only have seen it distantly before, a clear shape in the landscape, but smaller than a hill. Now they beheld along the wall the weapons of Camorak's men, of which already the lute-players made songs, and tales were told at evening in the byres. There they described the shield of Camorak that had gone to and fro across so many battles, and the sharp but dinted edges of his sword; there were the weapons of Gadriol the Leal, and Norn, and Athoric of the Sleety Sword, Heriel the Wild, Yarold, and Thanga of Esk, their arms hung evenly all round the hall, low where a man could reach them; and in the place of honour in the midst, between the arms of Camorak and of Gadriol the Leal, hung the harp of Arleon. And of all the weapons hanging on those walls none were more calamitous to Camorak's foes than was the harp of Arleon. For to a man that goes up against a strong place on foot, pleasant indeed is the twang and jolt of some fearful engine of war that his fellow-warriors are working behind him, from which huge rocks go sighing over his head and plunge among his foes; and pleasant to a warrior in the wavering light are the swift commands of his King, and a joy to him are his comrades' distant cheers exulting suddenly at a turn of the war. All this and more was the harp to Camorak's men; for not only would it cheer his warriors on, but many a time would Arleon of the Harp strike wild amazement into opposing hosts by some rapturous prophecy suddenly shouted out while his hand swept over the roaring strings. Moreover, no war was ever declared till Camorak and his men had listened long to the harp, and were elate with the music and mad against peace. Once Arleon, for the sake of a rhyme, had made war upon Estabonn; and an evil king was overthrown, and honour and glory won; from such queer motives does good sometimes accrue.

Above the shields and the harps all round the hall were the painted figures of heroes of fabulous famous songs. Too trivial, because too easily surpassed by Camorak's men, seemed all the victories that the earth had known; neither was any trophy displayed of

Camorak's seventy battles, for these were as nothing to his warriors or him compared with those things that their youth had dreamed and which they mightily purposed yet to do.

Above the painted pictures there was darkness, for evening was closing in, and the candles swinging on their slender chain were not yet lit in the roof; it was as though a piece of the night had been builded in to the edifice like a huge natural rock that juts into a house. And there sat all the warriors of Arn and the Weald-folk wondering at them; and none were more than thirty, and all were skilled in war. And Camorak sat at the head of all, exulting in his youth.

We must wrestle with Time for some seven decades, and he is a weak and puny antagonist in the first three bouts.

Now there was present at this feast a diviner, one who knew the schemes of Fate, and he sat among the people of the Weald and had no place of honour, for Camorak and his men had no fear of Fate. And when the meat was eaten and the bones cast aside, the king rose up from his chair, and having drunken wine, and being in the glory of his youth and with all his knights about him, called to the diviner, saying, "Prophesy."

And the diviner rose up, stroking his grey beard, and spake guardedly—"There are certain events," he said, "upon the ways of Fate that are veiled even from a diviner's eyes, and many more are clear to us that were better veiled from all; much I know that is better unforetold, and some things that I may not foretell on pain of centuries of punishment. But this I know and foretell—that you will never come to Carcassonne."

Instantly there was a buzz of talk telling of Carcassonne—some had heard of it in speech or song, some had read of it, and some had dreamed of it. And the king sent Arleon of the Harp down from his right hand to mingle with the Weald-folk to hear aught that any told of Carcassonne. But the warriors told of the places they had won to—many a hard-held fortress, many a far-off land, and swore that they would come to Carcassonne.

And in a while came Arleon back to the king's right hand, and raised his harp and chanted and told of Carcassonne. Far away it was, and far and far away, a city of gleaming ramparts rising one over other, and marble terraces behind the ramparts, and fountains shimmering on the terraces. To Carcassonne the elf-kings with their fairies had first retreated from men, and had built it on an evening late in May by blowing their elfin horns. Carcassonne! Carcassonne!

Travellers had seen it sometimes like a clear dream, with the sun glittering on its citadel upon a far-off hilltop, and then the clouds had come or a sudden mist; no one had seen it long or come quite close to it; though once there were some men that came very near, and the smoke from the houses blew into their faces, a sudden gust— no more, and these declared that some one was burning cedarwood there. Men had dreamed that there is a witch there, walking alone through the cold courts and corridors of marmorean palaces, fearfully beautiful and still for all her four-score centuries, singing the second oldest song, which was taught her by the sea, shedding tears for loneliness from eyes that would madden armies, yet will she not call her dragons home—Carcassonne is terribly guarded. Sometimes she swims in a marble bath through whose deeps a river tumbles, or lies all morning on the edge of it to dry slowly in the sun, and watches the heaving river trouble the deeps of the bath. It flows through the caverns of earth for further than she knows, and coming to light in the witch's bath goes down through the earth again to its own peculiar sea.

In autumn sometimes it comes down black with snow that spring has molten in unimagined mountains, or withered blooms of mountain shrubs go beautifully by.

When there is blood in the bath she knows there is war in the mountains; and yet she knows not where those mountains are.

When she sings the fountains dance up from the dark earth, when she combs her hair they say there are storms at sea, when she is angry the wolves grow brave and all come down to the byres, when she is sad the sea is sad, and both are sad for ever. Carcassonne! Carcassonne!

This city is the fairest of the wonders of Morning; the sun shouts when he beholdeth it; for Carcassonne Evening weepeth when Evening passeth away.

And Arleon told how many goodly perils were round about the city, and how the way was unknown, and it was a knightly venture. Then all the warriors stood up and sang of the splendour of the venture. And Camorak swore by the gods that had builded Arn, and by the honour of his warriors that, alive or dead, he would come to Carcassonne.

But the diviner rose and passed out of the hall, brushing the crumbs from him with his hands and smoothing his robe as he went.

Then Camorak said, "There are many things to be planned, and counsels to be taken, and provender to be gathered. Upon what day shall we start?" And all the warriors answering shouted, "Now." And Camorak smiled thereat, for he had but tried them. Down then from the walls they took their weapons, Sikorix, Kelleron, Aslof, Wole of the Axe; Huhenoth, Peace-breaker; Wolwuf, Father of War; Tarion, Lurth of the War-cry, and many another. Little then dreamed the spiders that sat in that ringing hall of the unmolested leisure they were soon to enjoy.

When they were armed they all formed up and marched out of the hall, and Arleon strode before them singing of Carcassonne.

But the folk of the Weald arose and went back well-fed to their byres. They had no need of wars or of rare perils. They were ever at war with hunger. A long drought or hard winter were to them pitched battles; if the wolves entered a sheep-fold it was like the loss of a fortress, a thunder-storm on the harvest was like an ambuscade. Well-fed, they went back slowly to their byres, being at truce with hunger: and the night filled with stars.

And black against the starry sky appeared the round helms of the warriors as they passed the tops of the ridges, but in the valleys they sparkled now and then as the starlight flashed on steel.

They followed behind Arleon going south, whence rumours had always come of Carcassonne: so they marched in the starlight, and he before them singing.

When they had marched so far that they heard no sound from Arn, and even inaudible were her swinging bells, when candles burning late far up in towers no longer sent them their disconsolate welcome; in the midst of the pleasant night that lulls the rural spaces, weariness came upon Arleon and his inspiration failed. It failed slowly. Gradually he grew less sure of the way to Carcassonne. Awhile he stopped to think, and remembered the way again; but his clear certainty was gone, and in its place were efforts in his mind to recall old prophecies and shepherd's songs that told of the marvellous city. Then as he said over carefully to himself a song that a wanderer had learnt from a goatherd's boy far up the lower slope of ultimate southern mountains, fatigue came down upon his toiling mind like snow on the winding ways of a city noisy by night, stilling all.

He stood, and the warriors closed up to him. For long they had passed by great oaks standing solitary here and there, like giants taking huge breaths of the night air before doing some furious deed; now they had come to the verge of a black forest; the tree-trunks stood like those great columns in an Egyptian hall whence God in an older mood received the praise of men; the top of it sloped the way of an ancient wind. Here they all halted and lighted a fire of branches, striking sparks from flint into a heap of bracken. They eased them of their armour, and sat round the fire, and Camorak stood up there and addressed them, and Camorak said: "We go to war with Fate, who has doomed that I shall not come to Carcassonne. And if we turn aside but one of the dooms of Fate, then the whole future of the world is ours, and the future that Fate has ordered is like the dry course of an averted river. But if such men as we, such resolute conquerors, cannot prevent one doom that Fate has planned, then is the race of man enslaved for ever to do its petty and allotted task."

Then they all drew their swords, and waved them high in the firelight, and declared war on Fate.

Nothing in the sombre forest stirred or made any sound.

Tired men do not dream of war. When morning came over the gleaming fields a company that had set out from Arn discovered the camping-place of the warriors, and brought pavilions and provender. And the warriors feasted, and the birds in the forest sang, and the inspiration of Arleon awoke.

Then they rose, and following Arleon, entered the forest, and marched away to the South. And many a woman of Arn sent her thoughts with them as they played alone some old monotonous tune, but their own thoughts were far before them, skimming over the bath through whose deeps the river tumbles in marble Carcassonne.

When butterflies were dancing on the air, and the sun neared the zenith, pavilions were pitched, and all the warriors rested; and then they feasted again, and then played knightly games, and late in the afternoon marched on once more, singing of Carcassonne.

And night came down with its mystery on the forest, and gave their demoniac look again to the trees, and rolled up out of misty hollows a huge and yellow moon.

And the men of Arn lit fires, and sudden shadows arose and leaped fantastically away. And the night-wind blew, arising like a ghost, and passed between the tree-trunks, and slipped down shimmering glades, and waked the prowling beasts still dreaming of day, and drifted nocturnal birds afield to menace timorous things, and beat the roses against cottagers' panes, and whispered news of the befriending night, and wafted to the ears of wandering men the sound of a maiden's song, and gave a glamour to the lutanist's tune played in his loneliness on distant hills; and the deep eyes of moths glowed like a galleon's lamps, and they spread their wings and sailed their familiar sea. Upon this night-wind also the dreams of Camorak's men floated to Carcassonne.

All the next morning they marched, and all the evening, and knew they were nearing now the deeps of the forest. And the citizens of Arn kept close together and close behind the warriors. For the deeps of the forest were all unknown to travellers, but not unknown to those tales of fear that men tell at evening to their friends, in the comfort and the safety of their hearths. Then night appeared, and an enormous moon. And the men of Camorak slept. Sometimes they woke, and went to sleep again; and those that stayed awake for long and listened heard heavy two-footed creatures pad through the night on paws.

As soon as it was light the unarmed men of Arn began to slip away, and went back by bands through the forest. When darkness came they did not stop to sleep, but continued their flight straight on until they came to Arn, and added there by the tales they told to the terror of the forest.

But the warriors feasted, and afterwards Arleon rose, and played his harp, and led them on again; and a few faithful servants stayed with them still. And they marched all day through a gloom that was as old as night, but Arleon's inspiration burned in his mind like a star. And he led them till the birds began to drop into the treetops, and it was evening and they all encamped. They had only one pavilion left to them now, and near it they lit a fire, and Camorak posted a sentry with drawn sword just beyond the glow of the fire-light. Some of the warriors slept in the pavilion and others round about it.

When dawn came something terrible had killed and eaten the sentry. But the splendour of the rumours of Carcassonne and Fate's decree that they should never come there, and the inspiration of Arleon and his harp, all urged the warriors on; and they marched deeper and deeper all day into the forest.

Once they saw a dragon that had caught a bear and was playing with it, letting it run a little way and overtaking it with a paw.

They came at last to a clear space in the forest just before nightfall. An odour of flowers arose from it like a mist, and every drop of dew interpreted heaven unto itself.

It was the hour when twilight kisses Earth.

It was the hour when a meaning comes into senseless things, and trees out-majesty the pomp of monarchs, and the timid creatures steal abroad to feed, and as yet the beasts of prey harmlessly dream, and Earth utters a sigh, and it is night.

In the midst of the wide clearing Camorak's warriors camped, and rejoiced to see the stars again appearing one by one.

That night they ate the last of their provisions, and slept unmolested by the prowling things that haunt the gloom of the forest.

On the next day some of the warriors hunted stags, and others lay in rushes by a neighbouring lake and shot arrows at water-fowl. One stag was killed, and some geese, and several teal.

Here the adventurers stayed, breathing the pure wild air that cities know not; by day they hunted, and lit fires by night, and sang and feasted, and forgot Carcassonne. The terrible denizens of the gloom never molested them, venison was plentiful, and all manner of water-fowl: they loved the chase by day, and by night their favourite songs. Thus day after day went by, thus week after week. Time flung over this encampment a handful of moons, the gold and silver moons that waste the year away; Autumn and Winter passed, and Spring appeared; and still the warriors hunted and feasted there.

One night of the springtide they were feasting about a fire and telling tales of the chase, and the soft moths came out of the dark and flaunted their colours in the firelight, and went out grey into the dark again; and the night wind was cool upon the warriors' necks, and the camp-fire was warm in their faces, and a silence had settled among them after some song, and Arleon all at once rose suddenly up, remembering Carcassonne. And his hand swept over the strings of his harp, awaking the deeper chords, like the sound of a nimble people dancing their steps on bronze, and the music rolled away into the night's own silence, and the voice of Arleon rose:

"When there is blood in the bath she knows there is war in the mountains, and longs for the battle-shout of kingly men."

And suddenly all shouted, "Carcassonne!" And at that word their idleness was gone as a dream is gone from a dreamer waked with a shout. And soon the great march began that faltered no more nor wavered. Unchecked by battles, undaunted in lonesome spaces, ever unwearied by the vulturous years, the warriors of Camorak held on; and Arleon's inspiration led them still. They cleft with the music of Arleon's harp the gloom of ancient silences; they went singing into battles with terrible wild men, and came out singing, but with fewer voices; they came to villages in valleys full of the music of bells, or saw the lights at dusk of cottages sheltering others.

They became a proverb for wandering, and a legend arose of strange, disconsolate men. Folks spoke of them at nightfall when the fire was warm and rain slipped down the eaves; and when the wind was high small children feared the Men Who Would Not Rest were going clattering past. Strange tales were told of men in old grey armour moving at twilight along the tops of the hills and never asking shelter; and mothers told their boys who grew impatient of home that the grey wanderers were once so impatient and were now hopeless of rest, and were driven along with the rain whenever the wind was angry.

But the wanderers were cheered in their wandering by the hope of coming to Carcassonne, and later on by anger against Fate, and at last they marched on still because it seemed better to march on than to think.

For many years they had wandered and had fought with many tribes; often they gathered legends in villages and listened to idle singers singing songs; and all the rumours of Carcassonne still came from the South.

And then one day they came to a hilly land with a legend in it that only three valleys away a man might see, on clear days, Carcassonne. Tired though they were and few, and worn with the years which had all brought them wars, they pushed on instantly, led still by Arleon's inspiration which dwindled in his age, though he made music with his old harp still.

All day they climbed down into the first valley and for two days ascended, and came to the Town That May Not Be Taken In War below the top of the mountain, and its gates were shut against them, and there was no way round. To left and right steep precipices stood for as far as eye could see or legend tell of, and the pass lay through the city. Therefore Camorak drew up his remaining warriors in line of battle to wage their last war, and they stepped forward over the crisp bones of old, unburied armies.

No sentinel defied them in the gate, no arrow flew from any tower of war. One citizen climbed alone to the mountain's top, and the rest hid themselves in sheltered places.

Now, in the top of the mountain was a deep, bowl-like cavern in the rock, in which fires bubbled softly. But if any cast a boulder into the fires, as it was the custom for one of those citizens to do when enemies approached them, the mountain hurled up intermittent rocks for three days, and the rocks fell flaming all over the town and all round about it. And just as Camorak's men began to batter the gate they heard a crash on the mountain, and a great rock fell beyond them and rolled into the valley. The next two fell in front of them on the iron roofs of the town. Just as they entered the town a rock found them crowded in a narrow street, and shattered two of them. The mountain smoked and panted; with every pant a rock plunged into the streets or bounced along the heavy iron roofs, and the smoke went slowly up, and up, and up.

When they had come through the long town's empty streets to the locked gate at the end, only fifteen were left. When they had broken down the gate there were only ten alive. Three more were killed as they went up the slope, and two as they passed near the terrible cavern. Fate let the rest go some way down the mountain upon the other side, and then took three of them. Camorak and Arleon alone were left alive. And night came down on the valley to which they had come, and was lit by flashes from the fatal mountain; and the two mourned for their comrades all night long.

But when the morning came they remembered their war with Fate, and their old resolve to come to Carcassonne, and the voice of Arleon rose in a quavering song, and snatches of music from his old harp, and he stood up and marched with his face southwards as he had done for years, and behind him Camorak went. And when at last they climbed from the third valley, and stood on the hill's summit in the golden sunlight of evening, their aged eyes saw only miles of forest and the birds going to roost.

Their beards were white, and they had travelled very far and hard; it was the time with them when a man rests from labours and dreams in light sleep of the years that were and not of the years to come.

Long they looked southwards; and the sun set over remoter forests, and glow-worms lit their lamps, and the inspiration of Arleon rose and flew away for ever, to gladden, perhaps, the dreams of younger men.

And Arleon said: "My King, I know no longer the way to Carcassonne."

And Camorak smiled, as the aged smile, with little cause for mirth, and said: "The years are going by us like huge birds, whom Doom and Destiny and the schemes of God have frightened up out of some old grey marsh. And it may well be that against these no warrior may avail, and that Fate has conquered us, and that our quest has failed."

And after this they were silent.

Then they drew their swords, and side by side went down into the forest, still seeking Carcassonne.

I think they got not far; for there were deadly marshes in that forest, and gloom that outlasted the nights, and fearful beasts accustomed to its ways. Neither is there any legend, either in verse or among the songs of the people of the fields, of any having come to Carcassonne.

How Nuth Would Have Practised
His Art upon the Gnoles

Lord Dunsany

Despite the advertisements of rival firms, it is probable that every tradesman knows that nobody in business at the present time has a position equal to that of Mr. Nuth. To those outside the magic circle of business, his name is scarcely known; he does not need to advertise, he is consummate. He is superior even to modern competition, and, whatever claims they boast, his rivals know it. His terms are moderate, so much cash down when the goods are delivered, so much in blackmail afterwards. He consults your convenience. His skill may be counted upon; I have seen a shadow on a windy night move more noisily than Nuth, for Nuth is a burglar by trade. Men have been known to stay in country houses and to send a dealer afterwards to bargain for a piece of tapestry that they saw there—some article of furniture, some picture. This is bad taste: but those whose culture is more elegant invariably send Nuth a night or two after their visit. He has a way with tapestry; you would scarcely notice that the edges had been cut. And often when I see some huge, new house full of old furniture and portraits from other ages, I say to myself, "These mouldering chairs, these full-length ancestors and carved mahogany are the produce of the incomparable Nuth."

It may be urged against my use of the word incomparable that in the burglary business the name of Slith stands paramount and alone; and of this I am not ignorant; but Slith is a classic, and lived long ago, and knew nothing at all of modern competition; besides which the surprising nature of his doom has possibly cast a glamour upon Slith that exaggerates in our eyes his undoubted merits.

It must not be thought that I am a friend of Nuth's, on the contrary such politics as I have are on the side of Property; and he needs no words from me, for his position is almost unique in trade, being among the very few that do not need to advertise.

At the time that my story begins Nuth lived in a roomy house in Belgrave Square: in his inimitable way he had made friends with the caretaker. The place suited Nuth, and, whenever anyone came to inspect it before purchase, the caretaker used to praise the house in the words that Nuth had suggested. "If it wasn't for the drains," she would say, "it's the finest house in London," and when they pounced on this remark and asked questions about the drains, she would answer them that the drains also were good, but not so good as the house. They did not see Nuth when they went over the rooms, but Nuth was there.

Here in a neat black dress on one spring morning came an old woman whose bonnet was lined with red, asking for Mr. Nuth; and with her came her large and awkward son. Mrs. Eggins, the caretaker, glanced up the street, and then she let them in, and left them to wait in the drawing-room amongst furniture all mysterious with sheets. For a long while they waited, and then there was a smell of pipe-tobacco, and there was Nuth standing quite close to them.

"Lord," said the old woman whose bonnet was lined with red, "you did make me start." And then she saw by his eyes that that was not the way to speak to Mr. Nuth.

And at last Nuth spoke, and very nervously the old woman explained that her son was a likely lad, and had been in business already but wanted to better himself, and she wanted Mr. Nuth to teach him a livelihood.

First of all Nuth wanted to see a business reference, and when he was shown one from a jeweller with whom he happened to be hand-in-glove the upshot of it was that he agreed to take young Tonker (for this was the surname of the likely lad) and to make him his apprentice. And the old woman whose bonnet was lined with red went back to her little cottage in the country, and every evening said to her old man, "Tonker, we must fasten the shutters of a night-time, for Tommy's a burglar now."

The details of the likely lad's apprenticeship I do not propose to give; for those that are in the business know those details already, and those that are in other businesses care only for their own, while men of leisure who have no trade at all would fail to appreciate the gradual degrees by which Tommy Tonker came first to cross bare boards, covered with little obstacles in the dark, without making any sound, and then to go silently up creaky stairs, and then to open doors, and lastly to climb.

Let it suffice that the business prospered greatly, while glowing reports of Tommy Tonker's progress were sent from time to time to the old woman whose bonnet was lined with red in the laborious handwriting of Nuth. Nuth had given up lessons in writing very early, for he seemed to have some prejudice against forgery, and therefore considered writing a waste of time. And then there came the transaction with Lord Castlenorman at his Surrey residence. Nuth selected a Saturday night, for it chanced that Saturday was observed as Sabbath in the family of Lord Castlenorman, and by eleven o'clock the whole house was quiet. Five minutes before midnight Tommy Tonker, instructed by Mr. Nuth, who waited outside, came away with one pocketful of rings and shirt-studs. It was quite a light pocketful, but the jewellers in Paris could not match it without sending specially to Africa, so that Lord Castlenorman had to borrow bone shirt-studs.

Not even rumour whispered the name of Nuth. Were I to say that this turned his head, there are those to whom the assertion would give pain, for his associates hold that his astute judgment was unaffected by circumstance. I will say, therefore, that it spurred his genius to plan what no burglar had ever planned before. It was nothing less than to burgle the house of the gnoles. And this that abstemious man unfolded to Tonker over a cup of tea. Had Tonker not been nearly insane with pride over their recent transaction, and had he not been blinded by a veneration for Nuth, he would have—but I cry over spilt milk. He expostulated respectfully: he said he would rather not go; he said it was not fair; he allowed himself to argue; and in the end, one windy October morning with a menace in the air found him and Nuth drawing near to the dreadful wood.

Nuth, by weighing little emeralds against pieces of common

rock, had ascertained the probable weight of those house-ornaments that the gnoles are believed to possess in the narrow, lofty house wherein they have dwelt from of old. They decided to steal two emeralds and to carry them between them on a cloak; but if they should be too heavy one must be dropped at once. Nuth warned young Tonker against greed, and explained that the emeralds were worth less than cheese until they were safe away from the dreadful wood.

Everything had been planned, and they walked now in silence.

No track led up to the sinister gloom of the trees, either of men or cattle; not even a poacher had been there snaring elves for over a hundred years. You did not trespass twice in the dells of the gnoles. And, apart from the things that were done there, the trees themselves were a warning, and did not wear the wholesome look of those that we plant ourselves.

The nearest village was some miles away with the backs of all its houses turned to the wood, and without one window at all facing in that direction. They did not speak of it there, and elsewhere it is unheard of.

Into this wood stepped Nuth and Tommy Tonker. They had no firearms. Tonker had asked for a pistol, but Nuth replied that the sound of a shot "would bring everything down on us," and no more was said about it.

Into the wood they went all day, deeper and deeper. They saw the skeleton of some early Georgian poacher nailed to a door in an oak tree; sometimes they saw a fairy scuttle away from them; once Tonker stepped heavily on a hard, dry stick, after which they both lay still for twenty minutes. And the sunset flared full of omens through the tree trunks, and night fell, and they came by fitful starlight, as Nuth had foreseen, to that lean, high house where the gnoles so secretly dwelt.

All was so silent by that unvalued house that the faded courage of Tonker flickered up, but to Nuth's experienced sense it seemed too silent; and all the while there was that look in the sky that was worse than a spoken doom, so that Nuth, as is often the case when men are in doubt, had leisure to fear the worst. Nevertheless he did not abandon the business, but sent the likely lad with the instruments of his trade by means of the ladder to the old green casement. And the moment that Tonker touched the withered boards, the silence that, though ominous, was earthly, became unearthly like the touch of a ghoul. And Tonker heard his breath offending against that silence, and his heart was like mad drums in a night attack, and a string of one of his sandals went tap on a rung of a ladder, and the leaves of the forest were mute, and the breeze of the night was still; and Tonker prayed that a mouse or a mole might make any noise at all, but not a creature stirred, even Nuth was still. And then and there, while yet he was undiscovered, the likely lad made up his mind, as he should have done long before, to leave those colossal emeralds where they were and have nothing further to do with the lean, high house of the gnoles, but to quit this sinister wood in the nick of time and retire from business at once and buy a place in the country. Then he descended softly and beckoned to Nuth. But the gnoles had watched him though knavish holes that they bore in trunks of the trees, and the unearthly silence gave way, as it were with a grace, to the rapid screams of Tonker as they picked him up from behind—screams that came faster and faster until they were incoherent. And where they took him it is not good to ask, and what they did with him I shall not say.

Nuth looked on for a while from the corner of the house with a mild surprise on his face as he rubbed his chin, for the trick of the holes in the trees was new to him; then he stole nimbly away through the dreadful wood.

"And did they catch Nuth?" you ask me, gentle reader.

"Oh, no, my child" (for such a question is childish). "Nobody ever catches Nuth."

The Distressing Tale of Thangobrind the Jeweller, and of the Doom That Befel Him

Lord Dunsany

When Thangobrind the jeweller heard the ominous cough, he turned at once upon that narrow way. A thief was he, of very high repute, being patronised by the lofty and elect, for he stole nothing smaller than the Moo-moo's egg, and in all his life stole only four kinds of stone—the ruby, the diamond, the emerald, and the sapphire; and, as jewellers go, his honesty was great. Now there was a Merchant Prince who had come to Thangobrind and had offered his daughter's soul for the diamond that is larger than the human head and was to be found on the lap of the spider-idol, Hlo-hlo, in his temple of Moung-ga-ling; for he had heard that Thangobrind was a thief to be trusted.

Thangobrind oiled his body and slipped out of his shop, and went secretly through byways, and got as far as Snarp, before anybody knew that he was out on business again or missed his sword from its place under the counter. Thence he moved only by night, hiding by day and rubbing the edges of his sword, which he called Mouse because it was swift and nimble. The jeweller had subtle methods of travelling; nobody saw him cross the plains of Zid; nobody saw him come to Mursk or Tlun. O, but he loved shadows! Once the moon peeping out unexpectedly from a tempest had betrayed an ordinary jeweller; not so did it undo Thangobrind: the watchmen only saw a crouching shape that snarled and laughed: "'Tis but a hyena," they said. Once in the city of Ag one of the guardians seized him, but Thangobrind was oiled and slipped from his hand; you scarcely heard his bare feet patter away. He knew that the Merchant Prince awaited his return, his little eyes open all night and glittering with greed; he knew how his daughter lay chained up and screaming night and day. Ah, Thangobrind knew. And had he not been out on business he had almost allowed himself one or two little laughs. But business was business, and the diamond that he sought still lay on the lap of Hlo-hlo, where it had been for the last two million years since Hlo-hlo created the world and gave unto it all things except that precious stone called Dead Man's Diamond. The jewel was often stolen, but it had a knack of coming back again to the lap of Hlo-hlo. Thangobrind knew this, but he was no common jeweller and hoped to outwit Hlo-hlo, perceiving not the trend of ambition and lust and that they are vanity.

How nimbly he threaded his way through the pits of Snood!— now like a botanist, scrutinising the ground; now like a dancer, leaping from crumbling edges. It was quite dark when he went by the towers of Tor, where archers shoot ivory arrows at strangers lest any foreigner should alter their laws, which are bad, but not to be altered by mere aliens. At night they shoot by the sound of the strangers' feet. O, Thangobrind, Thangobrind, was ever a jeweller like you! He dragged two stones behind him by long cords, and at these the archers shot. Tempting indeed was the snare that they set in Woth, the emeralds loose-set in the city's gate; but Thangobrind discerned the golden cord that climbed the wall from each and the weights that would topple upon him if he touched one, and so he left them, though he left them weeping, and at last came to Theth. There all men worship Hlo-hlo; though they are willing to believe in other gods, as missionaries attest, but only as creatures of the chase for the hunting of Hlo-hlo, who wears Their halos, so these people say, on golden hooks along his hunting-belt. And from Theth he came to the city of Moung and the temple of Moung-ga-ling, and entered and saw the spider-idol, Hlo-hlo, sitting there with Dead Man's Diamond glittering on his lap, and looking for all the world like a full moon, but a full moon seen by a lunatic who had slept too long in its rays, for there was in Dead Man's Diamond a certain sinister look and a boding of things to happen that are better not mentioned here. The face of the spider-idol was lit by that fatal gem; there was no other light. In spite of his shocking limbs and that demoniac body his face was serene and apparently unconscious.

A little fear came into the mind of Thangobrind the jeweller, a passing tremor—no more; business was business and he hoped for the best. Thangobrind offered honey to Hlo-hlo and prostrated himself before him. Oh, he was cunning! When the priests stole out of the darkness to lap up the honey they were stretched senseless on the temple floor, for there was a drug in the honey that was offered to Hlo-hlo. And Thangobrind the jeweller picked Dead Man's Diamond up and put it on his shoulder and trudged away from the shrine; and Hlo-hlo the spider-idol said nothing at all, but he laughed softly as the jeweller shut the door. When the priests awoke out of the grip of the drug that was offered with the honey to Hlo-hlo, they rushed to a little secret room with an outlet on the stars and cast a horoscope of the thief. Something that they saw in the horoscope seemed to satisfy the priests.

It was not like Thangobrind to go back by the road by which he had come. No, he went by another road, even though it led to the narrow way, night-house and spider-forest.

The city of Moung went towering up behind him, balcony above balcony, eclipsing half the stars, as he trudged away with his diamond. He was not easy as he trudged away. Though when a soft pittering as of velvet feet arose behind him he refused to acknowledge that it might be what he feared, yet the instincts of his trade told him that it is not well when any noise whatever follows a diamond by night, and this was one of the largest that had ever come to him in the way of business. When he came to the narrow way that leads to spider-forest, Dead Man's Diamond feeling cold and heavy, and the velvety footfall seeming fearfully close, the jeweller stopped and almost hesitated. He looked behind him; there was nothing there. He listened attentively; there was no sound now. Then he thought of the screams of the Merchant Prince's daughter, whose soul was the diamond's price, and smiled and went stoutly on. There watched him, apathetically, over the narrow way, that grim and dubious woman whose house is the Night. Thangobrind, hearing no longer the sound of suspicious feet, felt easier now. He was all but come to the end of the narrow way, when the woman listlessly uttered that ominous cough.

The cough was too full of meaning to be disregarded. Thango-brind turned round and saw at once what he feared. The spider-idol had not stayed at home. The jeweller put his diamond gently upon the ground and drew his sword called Mouse. And then began that famous fight upon the narrow way, in which the grim old woman whose house was Night seemed to take so little interest. To the spi-der-idol you saw at once it was all a horrible joke. To the jeweller it was grim earnest. He fought and panted and was pushed back slow-ly along the narrow way, but he wounded Hlo-hlo all the while with terrible long gashes all over his deep, soft body till Mouse was slimy with blood. But at last the persistent laughter of Hlo-hlo was too much for the jeweller's nerves, and, once more wounding his demoni-ac foe, he sank aghast and exhausted by the door of the house called Night at the feet of the grim old woman, who having uttered once that ominous cough interfered no further with the course of events. And there carried Thangobrind the jeweller away those whose duty it was, to the house where the two men hang, and taking down from his hook the left-hand of the two, they put that venturous jeweller in his place; so that there fell on him the doom that he feared, as all men know though it is so long since, and there abated somewhat the ire of the envious gods.

And the only daughter of the Merchant Prince felt so little gratitude for this great deliverance that she took to respectability of a militant kind, and became aggressively dull, and called her home the English Riviera, and had platitudes worked in worsted upon her tea-cosy, and in the end never died, but passed away at her residence.

In Zaccarath

Lord Dunsany

"Come," said the King in sacred Zaccarath, "and let our prophets prophesy before us."

A far-seen jewel of light was the holy palace, a wonder to the nomads on the plains.

There was the King with all his underlords, and the lesser kings that did him vassalage, and there were all his queens with all their jewels upon them.

Who shall tell of the splendour in which they sat; of the thousand lights and the answering emeralds; of the dangerous beauty of that hoard of queens, or the flash of their laden necks?

There was a necklace there of rose-pink pearls beyond the art of the dreamer to imagine. Who shall tell of the amethyst chandeliers, where torches, soaked in rare Bhyrinian oils, burned and gave off a scent of blethany? *

Enough to say that when the dawn came up it appeared by contrast pallid and unlovely and stripped all bare of its glory, so that it hid itself with rolling clouds.

"Come," said the King, "let our prophets prophesy."

Then the heralds stepped through the ranks of the King's silk-clad warriors who lay oiled and scented upon velvet cloaks, with a pleasant breeze among them caused by the fans of slaves; even their casting-spears were set with jewels; through their ranks the heralds

---

* This herb marvellous, which, growing near the summit of Mount Zaumnos, scents all the Zaumnian range, and is smelt far out on the Kepuscran plains, and even, when the wind is from the mountains, in the streets of the city of Ognoth. At night it closes its petals and is heard to breathe, and its breath is a swift poison. This it does even by day if the snows are disturbed about it. No plant of this has ever been captured alive by a hunter.

went with mincing steps, and came to the prophets, clad in brown and black, and one of them they brought and set him before the King. And the King looked at him and said, "Prophesy unto us."

And the prophet lifted his head, so that his beard came clear from his brown cloak, and the fans of the slaves that fanned the warriors wafted the tip of it a little awry. And he spake to the King, and spake thus:

"Woe unto thee, King, and woe unto Zaccarath. Woe unto thee, and woe unto thy women, for your fall shall be sore and soon. Already in Heaven the gods shun thy god: they know his doom and what is written of him: he sees oblivion before him like a mist. Thou hast aroused the hate of the mountaineers. They hate thee all along the crags of Droom. The evilness of thy days shall bring down the Zeedians on thee as the suns of springtide bring the avalanche down. They shall do unto Zaccarath as the avalanche doth unto the hamlets of the valley." When the queens chattered or tittered among themselves, he merely raised his voice and still spake on: "Woe to these walls and the carven things upon them. The hunter shall know the camping-places of the nomads by the marks of the camp-fires on the plain, but he shall not know the place of Zaccarath."

A few of the recumbent warriors turned their heads to glance at the prophet when he ceased. Far overhead the echoes of his voice hummed on awhile among the cedarn rafters.

"Is he not splendid?" said the King. And many of that assembly beat with their palms upon the polished floor in token of applause. Then the prophet was conducted back to his place at the far end of that mighty hall, and for a while musicians played on marvellous curved horns, while drums throbbed behind them hidden in a recess. The musicians were sitting cross-legged on the floor, all blowing their huge horns in the brilliant torchlight, but as the drums throbbed louder in the dark they arose and moved slowly nearer to the King. Louder and louder drummed the drums in the dark, and nearer and nearer moved the men with the horns, so that their music should not be drowned by the drums before it reached the King.

A marvellous scene it was when the tempestuous horns were halted before the King, and the drums in the dark were like the thunder of God; and the queens were nodding their heads in time to the music, with their diadems flashing like heavens of falling stars; and the warriors lifted their heads and shook, as they lifted them, the plumes of those golden birds which hunters wait for by the Liddian lakes, in a whole lifetime killing scarcely six, to make the crests that the warriors wore when they feasted in Zaccarath. Then the King shouted and the warriors sang—almost they remembered then old battle-chants. And, as they sang, the sound of the drums dwindled, and the musicians walked away backwards, and the drumming became fainter and fainter as they walked, and altogether ceased, and they blew no more on their fantastic horns. Then the assemblage beat on the floor with their palms. And afterwards the queens besought the King to send for another prophet. And the heralds brought a singer, and placed him before the King; and the singer was a young man with a harp. And he swept the strings of it, and when there was silence he sang of the iniquity of the King. And he foretold the onrush of the Zeedians, and the fall and the forgetting of Zaccarath, and the coming again of the desert to its own, and the playing about of little lion cubs where the courts of the palace had stood.

"Of what is he singing?" said a queen to a queen.

"He is singing of everlasting Zaccarath."

As the singer ceased the assemblage beat listlessly on the floor, and the King nodded to him, and he departed.

When all the prophets had prophesied to them and all the singers sung, that royal company arose and went to other chambers, leaving the hall of festival to the pale and lonely dawn. And alone were left the lion-headed gods that were carven out of the walls; silent they stood, and their rocky arms were folded. And shadows over their faces moved like curious thoughts as the torches flickered and the dull dawn crossed the fields. And the colours began to change in the chandeliers.

When the last lutanist fell asleep the birds began to sing.

Never was greater splendour or a more famous hall. When the queens went away through the curtained door with all their diadems, it was as though the stars should arise in their stations and troop together to the West at sunrise.

And only the other day I found a stone that had undoubtedly been a part of Zaccarath; it was three inches long and an inch broad; I saw the edge of it uncovered by the sand. I believe that only three other pieces have been found like it.

How the Enemy Came to Thlūnrāna

Lord Dunsany

It had been prophesied of old and foreseen from the ancient days that its enemy would come upon Thlūnrāna. And the date of its doom was known and the gate by which it would enter, yet none had prophesied of the enemy who he was save that he was of the gods though he dwelt with men. Meanwhile Thlūnrāna, that secret lamaserai, that chief cathedral of wizardry, was the terror of the valley in which it stood and of all lands round about it. So narrow and high were the windows and so strange when lighted at night that they seemed to regard men with the demoniac leer of something that had a secret in the dark. Who were the magicians and the deputy-magicians and the great arch-wizard of that furtive place nobody knew, for they went veiled and hooded and cloaked completely in black.

Though her doom was close upon her and the enemy of prophecy should come that very night through the open, southward door that was named the Gate of the Doom, yet that rocky edifice Thlūnrāna remained mysterious still, venerable, terrible, dark, and dreadfully crowned with her doom. It was not often that anyone dared wander near to Thlūnrāna by night when the moan of the magicians invoking we know not Whom rose faintly from inner chambers, scaring the drifting bats: but on the last night of all the man from the black-thatched cottage by the five pine-trees came, because he would see Thlūnrāna once again before the enemy that was divine, but that dwelt with man, should come against it and it should be no more. Up the dark valley he went like a bold man, but his fears were thick upon him; his bravery bore their weight but stooped a little beneath them. He went in at the southward gate that is named the Gate of the Doom. He came into a dark hall, and up a marble stairway passed to see the last of Thlūnrāna. At the top a curtain of black velvet hung and he passed into a chamber heavily hung with curtains, with a gloom in it that was blacker than anything they could account for. In a sombre chamber beyond, seen through a vacant archway, magicians with lighted tapers plied their wizardry and whispered incantations. All the rats in the place were passing away, going whimpering down the stairway. The man from the black-thatched cottage passed through that second chamber: the magicians did not look at him and did not cease to whisper. He passed from them through heavy curtains still of black velvet and came into a chamber of black marble where nothing stirred. Only one taper burned in the third chamber; there were no windows. On the smooth floor and under the smooth wall a silk pavilion stood with its curtains drawn close together: this was the holy of holies of that ominous place, its inner mystery. One on each side of it dark figures crouched, either of men or women or cloaked stone, or of beasts trained to be silent. When the awful stillness of the mystery was more than he could bear the man from the black-thatched cottage by the five pine-trees went up to the silk pavilion, and with a bold and nervous clutch of the hand drew one of the curtains aside, and saw the inner mystery, and laughed. And the prophecy was fulfilled, and Thlūnrāna was never more a terror to the valley, but the magicians passed away from their terrific halls and fled through the open fields wailing and beating their breasts, for laughter was the enemy that was doomed to come against Thlūnrāna through her southward gate (that was named the Gate of the Doom), and it is of the gods but dwells with man.

The Jest of Droom-Avista

Henry Kuttner

There is a tale they tell of voices that called eerily by night in the marble streets of long-fallen Bel Yarnak, saying: "Evil is come to the land; doom falls on the fair city where our children's children walk. Woe, woe unto Bel Yarnak." Then did the dwellers in the city gather affrightedly in huddled groups, casting furtive glances at the Black Minaret that spears up gigantically from the temple gardens; for, as all men know, when doom comes to Bel Yarnak, the Black Minaret will play its part in that dreadful Ragnarok.

Woe, woe unto Bel Yarnak! Fallen forever are the shining silver towers, lost the magic, soiled the glamor. For stealthily and by night, under the triple moons that hurtle swiftly across the velvet sky, doom crept out inexorably from the Black Minaret.

Mighty magicians were the priests of the Black Minaret. Mighty were they, alchemists and sorcerers, and always they sought the Stone of the Philosophers, that strange power which would enable them to transmute all things into the rarest of metals. And in a vault far below the temple gardens, toiling endlessly at glittering alembics and shining crucibles, lit by the violet glow of *ocuru*-lamps, stood Thorazor, mightiest of priests, wisest of all who dwelt in Bel Yarnak. Days and weeks and years he had toiled, while strange moons reeled down to the horizons, seeking the Elixir. Gold and silver paved the streets; blazing diamonds, moon-glowing opals, purple gems of strange fire, meteor-fallen, made of Bel Yarnak a splendid vision, shining by night to guide the weary traveler across the sandy wastes. But a rarer element Thorazor sought. Other worlds possessed it, for the intricate telescopes of the astronomers revealed its presence in the flaming suns that fill the chaotic sky, making night over Bel Yarnak a mirror reflecting the blazing scintillance of the city, a star-carpeted purple tapestry where the triple moons weave their arabesque patterns. So toiled Thorazor under the Black Minaret all of glistening jet onyx.

He failed, and again he failed, and at length he knew that only with the gods' aid could he find the Elixir he sought. Not the little gods, nor the gods of good and evil, but Droom-avista, the Dweller Beyond, the Dark Shining One, Thorazor called up blasphemously from the abyss. For Thorazor's brain was warped; he had toiled endlessly, and failed as often; in his mind was but one thought. So he did that which is forbidden: he traced the Seven Circles and spoke the Name which wakens Droom-avista from his brooding sleep.

A shadow swept down, darkening over the Black Minaret. Yet Bel Yarnak was untroubled; glorious and beautiful the shining city glowed while thin voices called weirdly in the streets.

Woe, woe unto Bel Yarnak! For the shadow darkened and encompassed the Black Minaret, and midnight black closed ominously about the sorcerer Thorazor. All alone he stood in his chamber, no gleam of light relieving the awful darkness that heralded the coming of the Dark Shining One, and slowly, ponderously, there rose up before him a Shape. But Thorazor cried out and hid his eyes, for none may look upon the Dweller Beyond lest his soul be blasted forever.

Like the groaning tocsin of a Cyclopean bell came the voice of the Dweller, rumbling terribly under the Black Minaret. Yet only Thorazor heard it, for he alone had called up Droom-avista.

"Now my sleep is troubled," the god cried. "Now my dreams are shattered and I must weave new visions. Many worlds, a mightier cosmos, have you ruined; yet there are other worlds and other dreams, and perchance I shall find amusement in this little planet. For is not one of my names the Jester?"

Shuddering and fearful, still hiding his eyes, Thorazor spoke.

"Great Droom-avista, I know your name; I have said it. By the doom even upon you, you must obey one command of him who calls you up."

The darkness throbbed and pulsed. Ironically Droom-avista

assented. "Command, then. O little fool, command your god! For always have men sought to enslave gods, and ever have they succeeded too well."

Yet Thorazor heeded not the warning. One thought only had he: the Elixir, the mighty magic that would transmute all things into the rarest of elements, and to Droom-avista he spoke fearlessly. He said his desire.

"But is that all?" the god said slowly. "Now this is but a small thing for which to disturb my slumber. So shall I grant your desire—for am I not named the Jester? Do thus and thus." And Droom-avista spoke of that which would transmute all things into the rarest of metals on Bel Yarnak.

Then the god withdrew, and the shadow lifted. Again Droom-avista sank into his dreaming sleep, weaving intricate cosmogonies; and speedily he forgot Thorazor. But the sorcerer stood in his chamber, trembling with exultation, for at his feet lay a jewel. This had the god left behind.

Flaming, blazing, streaming with weird fire the gem illuminated the dark chamber, driving the shadows back into the distant corners. Yet Thorazor had no eyes for its beauty; this was the Philosopher's Stone, this the Elixir! A glory was in the wizard's eyes as he prepared a brew as Droom-avista had commanded.

Then the mixture seethed and bubbled in the golden crucible, and over it Thorazor held the shining jewel. The culmination of a lifetime's hopes was reached as he dropped the gem into the frothing brew.

For a heartbeat nothing happened. Then, slowly at first, but with increasing swiftness, the golden crucible changed in color, slowly darkening. Thorazor cried out, blessing Droom-avista, for the crucible was no longer golden. It had been transmuted, by the power of the jewel, into the rarest of metals.

The gem, as though lighter than the bubbling mixture, lay lightly on the liquid surface. But the metamorphosis was not yet complete. The darkness crept down the pedestal that supported the crucible; it spread out like a fungoid stain across the onyx floor. It reached the feet of Thorazor, and the sorcerer stood frozen, glaring down at the frightful transmutation that was changing his body from flesh and blood into solid metal. And in a flash of blinding realization Thorazor knew Droom-avista's jest, and knew that by the power of the Elixir all things are changed to the rarest of elements.

He shrieked once, and then his throat was no longer flesh. And slowly, slowly, the stain spread across the floor and up the stone walls of the chamber. The shining onyx dulled and lost its sheen. And the hungry stain crept out through the Black Minaret, out upon Bel Yarnak, while the thin voices cried sadly in the marble streets.

Woe, woe unto Bel Yarnak! Fallen is the glory, dulled and tarnished the gold and silver splendor, cold and lifeless the beauty of the magic citadel. For outward and ever outward crept the stain, and in its path all was changed. The people of Bel Yarnak no longer move light-heartedly about their houses; lifeless images throng the streets and palaces. Immovable and silent sits the Sindara on a tarnished throne; dark and grim looms the city under the hurtling moons. It is Dis; it is the damned city, and sad voices in the silent metropolis mourn for lost glory.

Fallen is Bel Yarnak! Changed by the magic of Thorazor and by Droom-avista's jest, changed to the rarest of all elements in the planet of gold and silver and shining gems.

No longer Bel Yarnak—it is Dis, the City of Iron!

Outroduction

Robert M. Price

I believe the reader should encounter a story first with fresh eyes, knowing and needing to know as little as possible to allow the tale to make its own impact. You watch *Star Wars* before watching *The Making of Star Wars*, don't you? Otherwise, the myth is already demythologized. You might want to know how the stage magician pulls off his illusion, but not before you see him do it. That would pop the balloon before you try to inflate it, wouldn't it? Right, then. Now that you've read Lin Carter's Simrana tales, let's look beneath the surface.

Like H.P. Lovecraft, Lin Carter was heavily influenced by Lord Dunsany from the start. This is most evident in the Simrana stories.

> The most Dunsanian of my fiction is the Simrana series – and I rather imagine I coined the name Simrana half remembering such Dunsanian names as Imbaun or Izbahn or Ildaun or Imrāna (the River of Silence in *The Gods of Pegāna*). I cannot be certain of its exact origin, because the name was coined many years ago and lay in my notebooks awaiting the right kind of story to occur to me. Readers who may recall such of my Simrana cycle as the story "The Whelming of Oom" in *The Young Magicians* and "The Gods of Neol-Shendis" in L. Sprague de Camp's anthology *Warlock[s] and Warriors* and "Zingazar" in *New Worlds for Old* are well aware they are deliberate and loving pastiches on Dunsany. (Lin Carter, "Afterword: The Naming of Names, Lord Dunsany's Influence on Modern Fantasy Writers," in Dunsany, *Beyond the Fields We Know*. Adult Fantasy Series (New York: Ballantine Books, 1972), p. 298)

I think he must have cobbled the name, probably subconsciously, from two names in Dunsany's "The River" (to which he here refers), "Imrāna the River of Silence" and "Sirāmi the Lord of all Forgetting," just as Lovecraft no doubt got the blasphemous name of Nyarlathotep from Dunsany's prophet "Mynarthitep" and deity "Alhireth-Hotep."

And, speaking of names, Carter picked up some of the Simrana names from Islam and the Koran. "Zaqqoum" is the terrible tree that grows in hell, whose bitter fruit the damned are force-fed. "Yathrib" was the pre-Islamic name for Medina, the city that welcomed Muhammad as its theocratic ruler. "Aad" and "Thamooud" were two cities who had spurned the admonitions of the ancient prophets Hud and Salih (possibly to be identified with the apostolic figures Jude and Silas). "Babdoul" is obviously derived from the name "Abdoul" (as in Abdul Alhazred), while "Athreeb" and "Hathrib" are based on "Yathrib."

In the passage quoted above, Lin speaks of "The Gods of Neol Shendis" when he means "The Gods of Niom Parma." It is an easy, almost inevitable, mistake to make because "Niom Parma" was a revised version of "Neol-Shendis," a story belonging to his earlier cycle of tales set in another Dunsanian realm of dream, Ikranos. It appeared in *Amra*, volume 2, whole number 43, 1966. I'm speculating that "Neol" was a tribute to his wife Noel. And could "Parma" be a wink, for some reason, to Parma, Ohio? After all, he named his later character Prince Paramis for Paramus, New Jersey, where he was often a guest at Philip de Pardo's science fiction club. Who knows? (And if you *do*, please tell me!) So you can compare, or as just an excuse for pretty much reading a good story again, I have appended "The Gods of Neol Shendis," too.

Occasionally, Lin may be judged to have stuck a bit too close to his Dunsanian prototypes. Darrell Schweitzer, himself a talented fantasist, observed that "How Her Doom Came Down at Last on Adrazoon"

> is a textbook case of how *not* to write a pastiche. A pastiche should be an original story in the manner of someone else, not an inferior retelling of a specific story. "How Her Doom, etc." reads like

a discarded draft of "In Zaccarath" . . . save that Dunsany always got things right on the first try and didn't *have* discarded drafts. . . . Once you've read "In Zaccarath," "How Her Doom, etc." has nothing going for it. (Letter to *Crypt of Cthulhu* # 50, p. 70).

Compare the end of "Adrazoon" with that of " In Zaccarath": Only the other day I found a stone that had undoubtedly been a part of Zaccarath, it was three inches long and an inch broad; I saw the edge of it uncovered by the sand. I believe that only three other pieces have been found like it." Lin was by no means oblivious of the similarity, as he had quoted the very passage in his nonfiction book *Imaginary Worlds* (p. 32). He was certainly not trying to steal Dunsany's work to claim as his own, since he himself drew attention to the parallels (if you want to call them that). So what was he doing? It is an example of what we would call *hypertext*. He knows you know about Dunsany's original; after all, he went out of his way to make sure you did. He wants to bounce his version off Dunsany's. Nor is this completely speculative on my part, for I once asked him about a similar case: his reproducing of a climactic scene from Lovecraft's "Under the Pyramids" in his own "The Thing in the Pit." Far from trying to weasel out of it, Lin explained that he was, so to speak, attempting to sound the same note like a theme repeating in a musical composition. This reminds me of what Michael Riffaterre (*Fictional Truth*) says about the function of a narrative's subtext that accumulates, piece by piece, as certain descriptions occur again and again throughout a story or a novel. They gradually create a kind of soundboard against which further allusions come to have the ring of truth for the reader. What Lin is doing is to regard the whole Dunsanian (or Lovecraftian) megatext (including his own stories, and Henry Kuttner's – see below) as a single narrative complex in which parallels or borrowings serve as a subtext in Riffaterre's sense. I can't say I think it works very well for him, but at least that seems to have been Lin's intent.

On the other hand, it is barely possible he had simply *forgotten* the source he was inadvertently drawing from. Once Lin was bragging to S.T. Joshi and myself about a new Anton Zarnak tale he had written, "Dead of Night," in which the fall of darkness unleashes a Lovecraftian devil. S.T. pointed out the use of the same idea in Lovecraft's "The Haunter of the Dark" and Henry Kuttner's "Bells of Horror," but Lin was unfazed; it seemed not to have occurred to him, though of course he well knew both tales. He was a heavy drinker, and it may have been taking its toll on his memory. (He was a chain smoker, too. His manuscripts still reek of cigarette smoke more than thirty years later!)

But all this is nothing compared with "Zingazar," which is in its entirety a virtual rewrite of Dunsany's classic "The Sword of Welleran," extending even to most of the details. There is a pinch of Dunsany's "The Fortress Unvanquishable, Save for Sacnoth" in it, too, in that the "hero" of both tales is a magic sword. And, apparently, Lin expected you to *know* that he was rewriting Dunsany, as he had reprinted "The Sword of Welleran" in his anthology *The Young Magicians* only two years prior. Make of it what thou wilt.

"How Sargoth Laid Siege to Zaremm" is not quite so close to Dunsany's "Carcassonne," but you can't miss the resemblance. Both depict the hubris of a mighty warrior king overreaching himself by setting out to conquer a "Town That May Not Be Taken In War." ("The Laughter of Han" has a similar theme.) This story is the mirror opposite of Lin Carter's heroic tales of Sword-&-Sorcery. In "How Sargoth Laid Siege to Zaremm" sorcery wins out over swords, while in the Thongor stories, the swords prevail. And as for "The Laughter of Han," it must have been inspired by Dunsany's story "How the Enemy Came to Thlūnrāna." One might expect some connection to the early Lovecraft pastiches of Robert Bloch in which we read of an entity called "Dark Han" along with "Serpent-bearded Byatis," but there is none beyond the use of the Chinese name Han, as in the Han Dynasty.

"How Ghuth Would Have Hunted the Silth" and "The Thievery of Yish" owe an obvious debt to Lord Dunsany's "The Distressing Tale of Thangobrind the Jeweller, and of the Doom That Befel Him" and "How Nuth Would Have Practised His Art Upon the Gnoles." Both Carter tales (as well as the fragment "Caolin the Conjurer") end with practically identical lines, both in turn deriving from Dunsany: "And the tale is one of those that have not a happy ending."

Lin loved both Dunsany's and Dunsanian tales. He particularly preferred Henry Kuttner's "The Jest of Droom-Avista" and "The Eater of Souls," yarns set in the fantasy realm of Bel Yarnak. It must have been the opening of the former ("They tell it in Bel Yarnak...") that gave Lin the idea of introducing his own stories with similar formulae: "They say in Simrana...," "In Simrana they speak of...," "As they tell the tale in Simrana...," etc.

I have included in this collection a hitherto-unpublished text to which I have given the title "How Jal Set Forth Upon His Journeying." It appears to date from the early 1960s, earlier than any of the published Simrana tales, though various draft pages show he had made several revisions before abandoning it, and these were likely made once he began publishing Simrana stories, hoping to add this one to the list. "How Jal Set Forth Upon His Journeying" started out as "How Jal Became King of Thieves," but Lin struck out the name Jal and hand-wrote "Shand" instead, deciding to use "Jal" somewhere else. What I am calling "How Jal Set Forth Upon His Journeying" comes to an abrupt conclusion with the revelation that Jal is the bastard son of the minor divinity he has stumbled upon in his wandering. A set of dashed-off notes continues the story, but the notes stem from the "King of Thieves" version, which he would decide to develop separately. Originally, it was his newly-discovered divine connections that enabled young Jal to become Chief Thief, so the revelation of his true parentage was originally contributory to a greater climax. The seven-armed Entity would have served as a "donor" figure enabling the hero to win his quest. But by itself it might be judged a satisfactory ending to a short tale. Thus I am not sure whether "How Jal Set Forth Upon His Journeying" should be considered a mere fragment or a story in its own right. As it can be understood as a self-contained tale of self-discovery, I prefer to think of it as a story.

But what happened to Shand? We don't know. From the extant text, consisting of disparate draft pages surviving from various false starts, we can see that the young Shand must end up winning the thievish throne out from under his more experienced mentors, but whether Lin intended to have Shand employ newly-discovered magical connections and advantages, we don't know.

With both of these stories, "Shand" seeming especially promising, I have produced eclectic texts, combining what seemed to me the best readings from different drafts.

A third fragment, titled "Caolin the Conjurer" in handwritten notes and "Dzimadazoul" in a typescript, is frustratingly brief, but it is a nice little nugget of what might have been. The close of the story is found in that hand-written set of notes.

Lin Carter (often collaborating with L. Sprague de Camp) wrote several "posthumous collaborations" with Robert E. Howard, filling out abortive drafts and fragments of Conan and Kull stories left by Howard. Thus it seems quite fitting to give Lin the same treatment. So I have endeavored here to finish "How Shand Became King of Thieves" and "Caolin the Conjurer." The Carter original of "Shand" ends with the words "there befell a silence long and deep and ominous." Lin's fragment of "Caolin the Conjurer" stops after "showing what sights it would." His conclusion begins with "And he looked and saw the thing."